A Particular
Circumstance

A Particular Circumstance

Shirley Smith

ROBERT HALE · LONDON

ISBN 978-0-7090-8279-8

Robert Hale Limited
Clerkenwell House
Clerkenwell Green
London EC1R 0HT

2 4 6 8 10 9 7 5 3

Dedicated with love and best wishes
to
my daughters, Helen and Lucy

Typeset in 11½/14pt Palatino
by Derek Doyle & Associates, Shaw Heath
Printed and bound in Great Britain
by Biddles Limited, King's Lynn

CHAPTER ONE

Charlotte Grayson looked across the room at her mother, who was nodding with satisfaction and pleasure at the two gentlemen from the law firm, Messrs Brown and King.

Charlotte knew this was a tremendously important day in Jane Grayson's life and she also knew that it would herald a significant change in her own life and that of her sister, Kitty.

'This is indeed wonderful news, Mr Brown,' her mother was saying as she accepted the deeds. 'Felbrook Manor, mine at last.'

Jane Grayson was a small, slim woman, dressed soberly as befitted her widowed state and with her greying hair tucked neatly under a pretty lace cap. Eagerly she took up the legal documents, written on heavy parchment and tied with official-looking legal tape. She almost stroked them, so intense was her pride of ownership.

Adam Brown smiled over his steel spectacles. 'Yes, my dear ma'am, you are now sole owner of the house you have longed to possess ever since your dear husband passed away. Felbrook Manor, your childhood home, ma'am. I hope that you and your charming daughters will be very happy there.'

'I am sure we will be, Mr Brown. I have told my girls of the happy years I spent there as a child and my fervent wish is for the three of us to be settled at Felbrook Manor as soon as may be.'

Carefully, she placed the legal documents on a small

polished bureau with hands that trembled slightly and then she turned to smile at him.

'I trust that you and Mr King will stay and take some tea with us, sir?'

Adam Brown, a tall, spare man in his fiftieth year, looked quizzically at his young partner, Matthew King, and then he bowed.

'It would be a pleasure, ma'am, especially for an elderly gentleman like myself, to take tea with such charming ladies.'

'Pooh,' laughed Jane Grayson. 'Why, down in Felbrook village, they would call you "no' but a lad", my dear sir. And as for Matthew, now that he and Charlotte are almost betrothed, why, I count him as one of the family. Charlotte, my love, ring for some tea, if you please and Kitty, I can smell the lardy cake that Mrs Palmer has made for us. Do go to the kitchen, my dear, and see if it is cooled enough to eat.'

Both girls rose obediently to do their mother's bidding. Charlotte, at twenty the elder of the two, was tall and graceful, with the sort of vivid dark good looks which always commanded attention. Kitty was two years younger than her sister and was smaller with brown hair and her mama's steady grey eyes and pleasant charm.

They smiled at each other and Charlotte pressed her mother's shoulder affectionately as she passed her chair. In the last eighteen years, they had never been apart, and once childhood was over, had rarely quarrelled.

Adam Brown went to the window and looked out over the garden. 'That cloud is looking very threatening,' he said. 'Judging by its direction, I think there must be a bad thunderstorm over Grimston way.'

As the maid entered the room, Mrs Grayson said, 'Will you bring in the tea, please, Phoebe? I had hoped we might sit in the garden, but Mr Brown is quite right, yonder black cloud means we are going to have a downpour. We would indeed be foolish to risk sitting out.'

6

The girl curtsied and went for the tea tray and Kitty bounced in smiling, to say that Mrs Palmer had declared the lardy cake well and truly ready and was bringing it in personally.

Straight on Kitty's heels came Mrs Palmer herself, a stout body in a large starched pinafore and old-fashioned mob cap, who carried the cake with some ceremony, on its silver cake stand.

'The cake, ma'am,' she declared importantly.

Just as if she were announcing the arrival of the prime minister, thought Charlotte Grayson, and smiled to herself.

The housekeeper placed it on the little side table, bobbed her head at Jane and nodded to the two gentlemen. 'I hope as it's adequate, ma'am,' she sniffed. 'Seein' as no one told me nohow as we was havin' company.'

'Oh, did they not?' Jane Grayson said serenely. 'But we always count on you to know everything, Mary. Come now. Who is always in touch with the village gossips? Who do we go to when we wish to know who's born, who's married, who's died. . . ? Mary Palmer, of course. You are the fount of all our knowledge and wisdom, my dear Mary, but it was very remiss of me if I forgot to mention the visit of Mr Brown and dear Matthew.'

'S'all right, ma'am,' Mary said cheerfully. 'I heard it said in Felbrook market yesterday, as they were coming here this afternoon.'

She waited expectantly, looking at the bureau where the deeds to Felbrook Manor still rested. No one spoke.

Jane Grayson knew that news of the purchase of her old childhood home would get out soon enough and so she said, gently dismissive, 'Thank you, Mary. I am sure the cake will be delicious as always. That will be all for now.'

Her mother seemed to have forgotten about pouring tea and Kitty tactfully filled Matthew's cup and smiled at him. 'It will be so exciting to move house again and we find this is such a gloomy place, do we not, Mama?'

Jane Grayson looked round the dismal high-ceilinged room with its dark furniture and faded curtains and nodded.

'But we have been so grateful to Sir Benjamin Westbury for allowing us to lease his family home,' she said gently. 'And now, we shall soon be leaving.'

As the cake was handed round, Jane Grayson continued to talk enthusiastically about her plans for Felbrook Manor.

She and her husband had brought up their daughters in a Lincolnshire vicarage and when he died, she'd been determined to return to her Norfolk roots and make a new home for them in the house where she herself had spent her youth. She'd been obliged to rent Westbury Hall from Sir Benjamin Westbury who was in India, but now that the lease was almost up, she was pleased and relieved to be moving to her old home.

'It was where I had the honour to be born,' she said. 'And now, think of my delight at being able to take you to live in my childhood home. It is such a wonderful old house and before I married your dear papa, I passed some of my happiest years there.'

Jane Grayson now put down her tea cup and looked round at the assembled company before she said slowly, 'It is quite true that Mary knows everything in the village. She has heard that Sir Benjamin is returning from India with a vast fortune and with his great-nephew in tow.'

Both Kitty and Charlotte looked at her very attentively. Then they automatically turned to gaze just as intently at Adam Brown.

He smiled at their eagerness to have the village gossip confirmed and said, 'Why, as to that, I believe Sir Benjamin and his young relative are already in this country, so it is fortuitous that you will be able to move to your own Felbrook Manor before he comes to claim back his home.'

There was no pretence now of eating or drinking. Both girls began to ply him with questions, while Matthew smiled and listened quietly to Adam Brown's answers.

'And do you think they will make good neighbours?' Charlotte asked.

'I cannot say. My only dealings with Sir Benjamin have been as his man of business. He was more than a client to my late father, he was a friend, but he has lived abroad for so many years. . . .

'All I know is that he is elderly and seemingly rather frail now, but a very wealthy nabob indeed. My friend and partner, young Matthew here, reckons he remembers the greatnephew, Hugo, from Oxford. Is that not so, Matthew?'

Matthew King inclined his golden head and Charlotte took a moment to admire his fine profile and pleasant smile. She knew that his unassuming modesty belied his sharp brain and clever mind and that he was determined to work hard.

He was a tall young man, good-looking and well mannered, but with ambition. An orphan, he lived with his equally handsome Aunt Lavinia on the edge of the village and this lady had nurtured and supported him throughout his childhood until he was now able to make his way in the world.

She saw that Adam was listening to their excited conversation and looking very affectionately at Matthew.

Adam had been Lavinia King's friend for years and had encouraged her young nephew's talents since he was a little boy. Now Matthew was a confident young man of twentyfour, competent and well trained in the complexities of the law.

Yes, thought Charlotte. It was Adam himself who'd recognized his ability and persuaded Lavinia to encourage him. He'd finally rewarded Matthew's persistence by first taking him into the law firm and recently making him a junior partner.

Now, she could see the amusement in Adam Brown's eyes as she and Kitty hung on Matthew's every word and the young man tried to answer all their questions.

'And what is Hugo Westbury like?' Kitty asked eagerly.

9

Matthew smiled at her and Charlotte noticed the kindness in his eyes while he took in every detail of her sister's rather homely appearance. With her slight body, softly curling dark hair and honest grey eyes, Kitty would never be a beauty, but her expressive face was sparkling with interest.

'Well. . . .' he said slowly. 'It is all of five years since I last saw Hugo Westbury. We were never close friends and both of us took our studies seriously. Neither of us had the luxury of a Grand Tour, as I remember. Hugo sailed for India as soon as he left Oxford. He went into Sir Benjamin's business, but I do not know what business it was. Perhaps he was a merchant or importer of goods. I know not.'

'And what does he look like?' Charlotte asked. 'Is he tall? Dark? Fair ? I expect he must be quite burnt by the sun if he has been in India.'

His eyes softened as he looked at her. She'd only lived in the village for just over a year and yet already they somehow had an understanding. Tall, almost too tall for a woman and with a beautiful flawless face dominated by dramatic grey eyes, fringed with coal-black lashes, Charlotte Grayson would stand out in any company. A vivid personality, an arresting beauty all her own and a remarkably strong will. This was Charlotte Grayson as Matthew had come to know her and he was sure she would never alter.

He looked at her for so long that both Charlotte and Kitty became impatient for his answer. 'Well?' Charlotte demanded. 'Are you going to tell us what the nabob's heir is like?'

'He is dark as I remember him,' Matthew said slowly, as though trying to recall a distant face to mind. 'I do not remember his eye colour. Dark skinned with the sun? I know not. We shall no doubt see him and his great-uncle soon enough when they return home.'

Even Adam Brown, who had lived in Norfolk all his life, could tell them no more. 'Suffice it to say,' he said. 'Sir Benjamin has indicated to me that he has vowed to go travelling no more. He has sold out his concerns abroad and is desirous of settling back in his family home.

'This house is not in the very best of condition, but it is his country seat. With lavish care and plenty of money, he intends to restore it to its former glory, to repair and replenish the stables and, in short, to retire and live in the style befitting a wealthy landowner.'

Jane Grayson now thought of a question for the first time. 'And is there a *Lady* Westbury?' she asked quietly.

'No,' Adam Brown said. 'Sir Benjamin never married. His youngest brother had one son and one grandson, Hugo Westbury. His other brother I believe had the same, but I do not know that one's name.'

With that, they had to be content and as soon as Phoebe had cleared away the tea things, Jane Grayson whisked Mr Brown into the library to talk about her plans for the refurbishing of Felbrook Manor.

'Sir Benjamin is not the only one with pretensions to style,' she laughed. 'I too have ideas for my family home, now that it is mine at last.'

Kitty tactfully remembered some sewing that she was very keen to finish and disappeared up to her room, leaving Matthew and Charlotte alone with each other.

After a moment Matthew rose and went to stand by the window, looking out at the darkly threatening sky. 'Your mama seems to be expecting an announcement of our betrothal any time now,' he said quietly.

Charlotte stared at his back, frowning a little. 'What do you mean, Matthew?'

'Well. . . .' There was a pause and he turned away from the window and strode over to her. 'Do your mama and Kitty really believe that we are already engaged to be married?'

Charlotte shook her head. 'No,' she said firmly. 'I have never led anyone to believe such a thing.' She was deliberately flippant as she said, 'After all, a lady usually waits to be asked before making such an announcement.'

Even so, she wondered why Matthew had not so far made a formal declaration for her hand. They'd known each other for a year. He was a frequent visitor to their home and Charlotte was sure he was in love with her.

'I am pleased that you have not led anyone to believe we are as good as engaged, Charlotte. You see, I feel I am not quite ready for such a step. Not yet. I have only just been made a partner. I have my way to make in the world. . . . I want to be able to keep a wife in style. . . . You do understand . . . don't you?'

Charlotte was angry and hurt and spoke more sharply than she intended. 'Yes, I do understand, Matthew. It was merely an ideal dream of romance on the part of my lovely mama,' she snapped. 'I have never hinted at it by word or deed. I am not sure if I want to be betrothed to you either.'

'Hell! What a pig's ear I am making of this,' he said. 'That is not at all as I imagined I was going to say it.'

'And why does it matter?' Charlotte asked coldly. 'I am sure I have no wish to lure you into a parson's mouse-trap if you are so unwilling.'

Matthew took her hand and his eyes were tender. She knew that he was very fond of her, in spite of his rather clumsy remarks, but she still felt angry.

He looked uncomfortable and said diffidently, 'It is just that Adam has been making very pointed remarks recently and then your mama saying. . . .'

'I quite understand. You will just have to disregard it as I do myself. Pointed remarks always abound when my mother is about. I can assure you, I have no intentions of thinking about matrimony yet.'

It was now Charlotte's turn to walk to the window and gaze out over the garden. There was the faintest moaning of the wind in the trees and large drops of rain began to fall heavily on to the terrace under the window. She fully understood Matthew's reluctance to be leg shackled before he was ready, but she felt a slight sense of hurt still. Charlotte was not sure about 'in love', but the fondness and affection which existed between herself and Matthew seemed an excellent basis for a married life together. If he needed more time to be sure of his feelings, well, that was perfectly acceptable to Charlotte Grayson. He could have all the time he wanted.

She continued to look out of the window, silent now and still somewhat puzzled by the behaviour of the young man she thought she knew very well. The rain turned gradually from slow, heavy drops into a torrential downpour, as the storm cloud settled immediately over Westbury Hall and the whole landscape looked drenched and soddened with rain.

When Adam Brown came back into the darkened room with Jane Grayson, he rubbed his hands as though feeling the sudden chill and said, 'Here comes the storm, Matthew. I shall not yet be able to ride back to King's Lynn, although I suppose, you may make a dash for it to Primrose Cottage. No doubt your aunt will be anxious about you.'

'No. Please do not go out in this storm,' Jane Grayson said. 'The thunder seems so much nearer to home now. I am sure there is a lot more rain to come. You will be utterly soaked if you attempt a dash for it now. And what will your dear Aunt Lavinia think of me then? I cannot allow you to risk it, dear Matthew.

'Oh, here is Kitty. Let us ring for more tea and try to finish Mrs Palmer's excellent cake. The weather is so dismal, it is more like November than August. I shall get Phoebe to put a light to the sticks and we may soon have a cheerful fire.'

Kitty came in with her sewing and Matthew went back to his chair. Soon they were all settled down again, but the crashing of the thunder and the jagged flashes of lightning illuminating the angry sky did nothing to make the conversation easy.

Westbury Hall was not a comfortable residence. It had been utterly neglected for years and no amount of cleaning, dusting and flower arranging seemed to dispel the dark musty atmosphere. It was a house which had grown gradually over more than three centuries and had been lived in by generations of the Westbury family and their successors. The south front had been built in the 1620s on the foundations of a Tudor house which had been acquired by Thomas Westbury in the fifteenth century. He had died childless and left the estate to his cousin, Sir John Westbury, whose coat of arms and that of his wife could still be seen above the front door along with the words 'GLORIA DEO IN EXCELSIS' prominently acknowledging God's help in their enterprise. Successive Westburys had added a new west wing, a service wing and stables, with an orangery and a gate house which had been added in 1700. Each new addition had made the hall more substantial and the different architectural styles served as an interesting contrast to the original Jacobean front.

One notable feature had been the old staircase, dating from the 1680s and which had been much criticized by a prominent neighbour of the Westburys, because of its alarming steepness. It had since been replaced by a much more shallow flight, protected by a balustrade of beautiful wrought iron, custom made by a London blacksmith, which added a graceful touch to the old stair hall.

Like all old houses, it had its share of secret hidey holes and it was rumoured that there was an underground tunnel leading from Felbrook woods to the library, which had once been the great chamber of the Jacobean house. So far, though, no one had discovered the underground passage or learned the secret of opening the panelled wall.

As for Jane Grayson, when she'd heard of the so-called secret tunnel from the all-knowing Mrs Palmer, she'd declared herself to be not interested in such tomfoolery and expressed the hope that her darlings would not listen to such idle tales of priests' holes and such. Mrs Palmer had taken umbrage at this and had expressed the hope that Mrs Grayson would not live to regret her scepticism.

The storm, which gave no sign of abating, had caused the

dusk to arrive prematurely and once the candles were lit, Jane Grayson was already planning in her mind to invite the two guests to stay for dinner, rather than send them out to brave the elements on horseback. Having finished the second lot of tea and cake, conversation seemed to have petered out and they were all, it seemed, wrapped up in their own thoughts.

Kitty was still busy sewing and Adam Brown was glancing idly at an out-of-date copy of *The Times*, while Charlotte and Matthew chatted quietly about a riding party they were both going to attend the following week. Aurelia Casterton and her bosom friend, Ann West, were together hosting a picnic in the grounds of the Castertons' country home for various of their young friends and it promised to be an interesting excursion. Except for the spectacular noise of the storm, it was just another pleasant family evening.

Quite suddenly, there was an exceptionally deafening thunderclap and a flash of lightning, which lit up the whole of the countryside for several miles and made the candles flicker and go pale.

This was followed by a terrific crash and then an ominous silence.

There was a muffled shriek and a distant scream and Mrs Palmer burst into the room without knocking, so great was her panic. She was followed closely by a distraught Phoebe, who held her apron over her head and promptly gave way to a bout of hysterics.

Jane Grayson found this irritating. 'Oh dear! What a tiresome girl. Stop that at once, Phoebe. Mrs Palmer, *sal volatile*, if you please. I have no time to spend cosseting silly girls. Come now, let us see what has happened. The noise seemed to come from the library.'

They all trooped out of the drawing-room along the stone corridor and through the stair hall to the library. Mrs Palmer, afraid of missing something, set off in hot pursuit and Phoebe, finding herself alone and her hysterics ignored, threw down the *sal volatile* in disgust and hurried after them.

There was another mighty crack and a rumble of falling masonry as a sizeable piece of the south front collapsed and slid noisily to the ground, destroying part of the fireplace wall in the library and leaving a heap of rubble in the stair hall, just outside the door. The dust rose up like a grey fog and obscured the extent of the damage for several minutes.

Both the men had to put their shoulders to the library door, it being jammed by fallen bricks and splintered panelling, and held their handkerchiefs to their mouths because of the choking dust. When Adam and Matthew had opened it, the ladies lifted their skirts and held them close to their legs as they picked their way into the room.

Adam Brown was the first to reach the old stone fireplace, which appeared to have caved in when the chimney collapsed. This also appeared to have unsettled the wall to the side of the fireplace and more than four feet of the beautifully carved oak panelling had been displaced.

What was revealed behind the panelling was almost too gruesome to be looked on. As Adam bent over the gap in the wall, he exclaimed, 'By all that's holy! A skeleton, Matthew. A skeleton in a cupboard, no less!'

Removing his immaculate handkerchief from his mouth, Matthew could only echo what his guide and mentor, Mr Brown, had said. 'Yes. Good God! A skeleton, Mr Brown, sir. What . . . what on earth can have happened?'

The three ladies were now also in the room and able to view what was revealed by the cracking open of the priest hole. Jane Grayson spoke first. 'Mrs Palmer, please take Phoebe back to the kitchen and make her some tea. I shall come to see her directly, but this is not a sight for Phoebe's young eyes. Charlotte, Kitty, I am persuaded that this is not something either of you would want to look at. Should you wish to return to the drawing-room you may do so now.'

Both Charlotte and Kitty professed themselves desirous of staying where they were. Neither of them was willing to miss any of the excitement of finding an actual skeleton in the proverbial family cupboard.

'Whoever he is, poor soul. He has obviously been here a long time,' Adam Brown said at last.

'He?' Kitty questioned. 'How do we know it is *he*?'

'Well, he has silver buttons on his coat and the remains of leather boots,' Adam said gently. 'Although, to be sure, the boots are crumbled almost into dust. I expect the rats have done their work over the years.

'Perhaps he was a traveller, then,' Charlotte surmised. 'But where could he have been going and how did he meet his end?'

'The answer to your last question is very violently,' Adam said, still speaking quietly in the presence of what was, after all, a deceased person. 'See, this large black stain which has spread all over the floor. That must be a blood stain, unless I am very much mistaken.'

All the ladies shuddered, but Charlotte, steelier than the other two, said, 'What manner of man do you think he was, then, Mr Brown? There are no papers, no jewels, no money; nothing to identify him.'

'Only this,' Adam said. Bending down, he picked up an old signet ring, the gold still gleaming brightly. 'Likewise, this.' He also retrieved a silver fob watch, with a fine chased case, tarnished and slightly dented, but still attached to its handsome silver chain. 'Whoever he was, he seems to have been a gentleman. Any of his other possessions could easily have been removed after his death.'

'Are you suggesting murder, Mr Brown?'

Jane Grayson was obviously surprised and alarmed at the idea of a murder victim on the premises that she'd been renting for a year.

'It seems highly probable, ma'am.'

'But . . . but, surely it could have been an accident or . . . or . . . even suicide, Mr Brown?'

'I think not,' he said quietly. 'There is no weapon, you see. The deceased could not have killed himself with either his ring or this watch. What accident could have caused such a copious amount of blood in so small a space? Of course, we shall have to report this to the proper authorities, but it is my opinion the unfortunate man was murdered.'

'Oh, how dreadful!' Jane Grayson exclaimed. 'Poor man and to think this body has been here all this time and none of us was even aware of it.'

'Quite so,' Adam Brown said. 'I think, Matthew, that there is no point in any more fruitless speculation. And with your permission, ma'am, perhaps we could have the loan of a blanket or sheet, until the body can be removed.'

'Of course,' Jane agreed. 'Come, girls, we shall return to the drawing-room and get Robert to cover the body decently.'

Jane's household was very informal. Although she used the formal system of ringing a bell to summon the maid when they had company, she was just as likely to go to the kitchen herself and even do the baking if she was so inclined. She employed the young footman, Robert, as a cross between a butler and general factotum, a young man of many skills who was in her opinion 'worth his weight in gold'.

They all went back to the drawing-room where Adam Brown asked diffidently if he could have the use of some of Robert's silver polish and a soft cloth. While they all watched with interest, he polished up the silver watch and turned it over so that the engraving on the back of the case was revealed clearly. The owner's initials were hand-engraved and clearly marked: C.W.

'It seems he was one of the Westburys then. "C.W" – that could be Christopher or Charles. . . .'

'Yes, it could be either of those, Matthew, but the favoured family names are Benjamin, Hugo, Charles. This ring is also interesting,' he went on. 'See, a cunning little hinge just here. A locket ring, no less.'

Very carefully, he pulled up the little hinged fastening on the ring and opened it to reveal an exquisite miniature of a mother and child. It showed a beautiful young woman, with dark hair and deep blue eyes. The child was an adorable little cherub, fairer than his mother but with identical blue eyes. Below the portrait in very tiny writing, but easy to read, was the date 1760. There was a profound silence as the ring was carefully and reverently passed from hand to hand.

'Who can they be?' Jane Grayson asked. 'If that pretty little baby has survived, he must be all of fifty-six years. Where can he be? What can have become of him?'

'I do not rightly know,' Adam said. 'And after this lapse of time, it will be nigh on impossible to find out.'

'But if the skeleton and the mother and baby were members of the Westbury family, would not Sir Benjamin know who they were?'

Charlotte spoke with some excitement. She'd always been interested in history and this corpse had excited her curiosity rather than horror or aversion. Adam looked at her with gentle approval.

'Yes, undoubtedly, Miss Grayson, and back at the office in King's Lynn there is a deed box relating to the whole family, complete with names and dates of birth. It may take time, but it should be possible to find out who the unfortunate young man was.

Outside, the storm had run its course and the sky had cleared, just ready for sunset. It promised to be a pleasant and tranquil evening, perfectly calm now, and he should be able to ride home comfortably.

Jane Grayson pressed the two lawyers to stay for dinner. 'We have a good mutton pie, made with Mrs Palmer's delectable pastry,' she said. 'And a nice big ham shank boiled with baby onions and she always makes a good fruit pudding when she knows gentlemen are staying for dinner.'

Adam Brown refused politely. 'Another time, perhaps, Mrs Grayson, ma'am, but I must travel to King's Lynn. I shall inform Sir Benjamin of this unhappy discovery and then I wish to get out my strong boxes and look up the Westbury family history. I shall send word to my housekeeper to delay my supper for a couple of hours. But, thank you. It was a kind thought.'

Matthew was more apologetic. 'I am conscious that Aunt Lavinia will wonder what has become of me,' he said. 'She herself might have been somewhat unnerved by the storm and it would be upsetting for her were I to be unexpectedly late home.'

Jane had no answer to this. After all, how many times had she advised the girls to observe closely how a prospective bridegroom treated his mother? In this case, it was of course his Aunt Lavinia, but still, the sort of loyalty and consideration shown to his aunt would definitely be lavished on his bride, she thought.

No, she could not argue against either of their decisions, but instead said gracefully, 'I do understand. Another time then. Give my kind regards to your aunt, Matthew. You will have much to talk about when you tell her of our dreadful discovery.'

In spite of the warmth of the fire, Kitty shivered as though with a sudden chill and glanced fearfully over her shoulder. 'I feel as though someone has just stepped over my grave,' she whispered. 'Oh, poor thing, dying alone like that and with only the portrait of his dear wife and child to comfort him. And that sweet-looking wife and the dear little baby. What on earth became of them, I wonder?'

'Who knows?' Matthew said. 'Perhaps no one ever will.'

Kitty's gentle grey eyes were still shining with unshed tears when the two men bowed to the ladies and Matthew kissed Charlotte's hand.

Robert brought round the horses and they set off, Adam to his lonely house and Matthew to his lovely Aunt Lavinia and supper.

CHAPTER TWO

Matthew King always felt a deep sense of peace and security as he rounded the final bend of the road and came at last in sight of home. He'd been out early that morning and must now have been away for twelve hours, so that it was doubly pleasant to see Primrose Cottage again. In spite of his familiarity with his surroundings, he often felt as though he'd come across it suddenly and was always struck anew by its beauty and tranquillity. Today was no exception.

It had been known as Primrose Cottage as long as anyone could remember because of the obvious spring beauty of a bank of primroses near the garden gate. There was a gurgling fast-moving stream nearby and Matthew paused for a moment to listen to the water, rushing and chuckling over the smooth pebbles on its bed. After the recent rain, the stream was swollen and everything shone and sparkled. The birds which had been silent during the thunderstorm now hopped about and pulled out worms from ground softened by the downpour. There were a few bright butterflies hovering over the flowers in the garden and his aunt was at the gate, shading her eyes with her hand as she waited for him.

He dismounted and handed the reins to Joshua, Aunt Lavinia's elderly servant, who led the horse to the stables to be fed and watered. Then Matthew and his aunt went into Primrose Cottage arm in arm. Once more, he felt the sense of calm and safety, all the more remarkable after that violent thunderstorm and the startlingly gruesome revelations at Westbury Hall. The feel of his aunt's graceful hand on his arm was both comfortable and comforting and did much to drive away the horror of the day's events. Half an hour later, as they sat together in the comfortable dining-room, he was even more relaxed. As he looked at her calm and tranquil face, Matthew reflected that his beautiful aunt really suited this house.

It was a large cottage, but not big enough to be a farm-house, so it was spacious and cosy, both at the same time. The church clock in the village had already struck six and Matthew waited with ill-concealed impatience as Annie served supper and poured out wine for them. He was in a fever for her to leave the room so that he could speak freely to his aunt of the discovery up at the Hall.

Aunt Lavinia was suitably impatient to hear his tale and flatteringly swift in her dismissal of the maid. Tall and stately, she was young for an aunt, barely five and forty, and although her golden hair had some strands of silver, she still had a handsome bloom.

Matthew, sitting opposite to her, was once more struck by his aunt's calm beauty. With her clear brow and glossy hair, she looked no more than thirty. For the thousandth time, he wondered why she had never married. He knew she was very comfortably off and, being his godmother, had chosen to devote herself to his own upbringing after his parents had died. But still. . . . She must have had opportunities to find happiness herself. . . .

As though aware of her nephew's gaze, Aunt Lavinia raised her eyes to his and said gently, 'Now tell me every-thing, Matthew. I can see that it is something momentously important.' Her full lips parted in a smile. 'Has Adam suddenly sacked you? Has dear Charlotte consented to marry you? Have you become executor to a famous Norwich millionaire? Tell me, I beg you. I am agog with speculation. Annie will not disturb us again until we are ready to move into the drawing-room.'

How did she know that he had so much on his mind, he wondered? But then, she had been able to read him since he was a small child. He smiled to himself and needed no second bidding to describe the finding of the skeleton in such vivid detail that his aunt quite forgot to eat and could only exclaim, 'How dreadful! What a terrible story and fancy that miniature in his signet ring. Poor young man. I hope his wife and child were saved!'

There was a silence and then she said, 'It seems that Sir Benjamin intends to take up residence again very soon. It is a very splendid house, but what a gloomy place, especially the old part. It must be a nightmare for the servants, so many dark corners and long passages. I wonder Mrs Grayson could stand it for a whole year. Of course, those two lovely girls must bring so much light and laughter to the place, I daresay she does not even notice. By the way, Annie has heard from Mrs Palmer that the purchase of Felbrook Manor is now complete and they will be moving shortly.'

'Yes, but they will still not be so very far away, no more than a couple of miles, Aunt.'

She looked at him more keenly. 'And you will still be able to visit just as often, eh, Matthew?'

'Yes, just as often, Aunt.'

'And now you have achieved your advancement with Adam – Mr Brown, that is – you will be thinking of wedding bells, perhaps?'

Matthew coloured slightly and said, 'Aunt Lavinia, you are incorrigible. No wedding bells just yet. I need to make my way in the world first and be able to earn enough to keep a wife in some style and comfort.'

'Of course,' said his aunt and continued to smile as they made their way to the drawing-room.

As his Aunt Lavinia rang for tea, Matthew set up the card table. He knew that his aunt would return to the grisly subject of the dead body while the game was in progress and he wondered how the Grayson family had taken the appalling discovery at Westbury Hall and what they were doing at that moment.

The Grayson family, in fact, were remarkably cheerful, despite the macabre circumstances of the skeleton. Although the drawing-room at Westbury Hall was rather a dismal environment, the red gold of the setting sun, now that the storm clouds had rolled away, cast a more benign light, which even the massive oak doorcases and the heavy old-fashioned curtains hanging in the south bay were unable to dispel. The discovery of the skeleton had at first lowered everyone's spirits, but with her usual positive outlook on life, Jane Grayson had said bracingly, 'Poor young man, he must have died so lonely and bereft, but still, my dears, he is now hopefully reunited with his loved ones in heaven, as we all hope to be one day.'

Charlotte and Kitty knew that she was not just referring to the unfortunate body in the cupboard, but to the death of their own dear papa, a gentle erudite clergyman, who had died just over a year before and had left a gap in their lives out of all proportion to his unassuming personality and habitual goodness.

They sat on chatting in the drawing-room, gradually relaxing, at ease with each other and coming to terms with the implications of their terrible discovery until Mrs Palmer entered unannounced and informed them that dinner would be served in twenty minutes.

She obviously expected more reaction from the young ladies and their mama, but Jane Grayson merely said, 'Thank you, Mrs Palmer. That gives us a little time to tidy up,' and she calmly folded up her sewing and left the room.

As she did so, there was a commotion outside the front door and when Robert opened it, Jane heard the distinctive huffing and puffing of her brother-in-law, Bertram Grayson, who was petulantly berating his coachman for not handling the luggage, letting down the steps and seeing to the horses all at the same time. Uncle Bertram himself merely concentrated on easing himself down the steps of the coach and walking up to the front door.

'Jane! How are you?' he exclaimed heartily at the sight of his sister-in-law. 'And what is that wonderful smell? One of Mrs Palmer's delicious dinners, no doubt. I seem to be just in time, thank goodness. Drat that stupid Robert. Why cannot he send for the stable lad to see to the horses?'

As the smell of Mrs Palmer's delicious dinner wafted ever closer towards his nostrils, he called impatiently to Robert. 'Good Lord! Stop dithering like this, you stupid fellow. I tell you, Jane, he deserves to be dismissed for his tardiness.'

Jane Grayson stepped forward and offered her hand to her brother-in-law, saying comfortably, 'How are you, Bertram? You are indeed in time for one of Mrs Palmer's delicious dinners and you are most welcome. Leave Robert alone to see to everything. Come in. Come in. How was your journey?'

'Tolerable, my dear Jane. The journey from Lincoln was tedious in the extreme. So many country carts and loaded hay wains clogging up the road. I am glad to be able to stop for the evening here and not have to put up with bad food and sour wine at some costly inn. I disapprove of extravagance, as you know, and am impatient of any excess.' He broke off to yell, 'Get a move on, man! The housekeeper is about to serve my supper.'

Jane smiled at this. Uncle Bertram was on his way to stay with friends in King's Lynn and had predictably arrived in time to be invited for dinner, which pleased him greatly. He might disapprove of her extravagance, but she knew that he was delighted to be receiving a good meal and refreshment for his horses, at no cost to himself.

As for Jane, she had a soft spot for her late husband's younger brother, maddening though he was. There was twenty years' difference in the ages of the two men and while Jane's husband was alive, Bertram visited rarely, and had been something of a Jack-the-lad, frequenting gaming houses and constantly at the races. He had often referred to the Reverend Grayson as a 'dull stick', while he himself was a bit of a gay dog, being handsome, reckless and an accomplished flirt. Now that his only brother was dead, Jane knew that Bertram often found himself alone. He had never quite managed to grow up and establish a long-term relationship with any of the young women he had charmed, and they had of course gone on to make worthwhile marriages, leaving him to his fate. He seemed destined to be a lonely bachelor.

She sighed and signalled to Phoebe to take his coat and driving gloves and then she ushered him into the drawing-room, where Charlotte and Kitty greeted him politely.

He seemed to have forgotten his earlier bad temper and said jovially, 'And how are my favourite nieces? Well, I trust? Both of you are in fine bloom, my dears, as is your dear mama, of course.'

Jane was pleased that both girls answered pleasantly and as soon as Phoebe came to say that Mrs Palmer was ready to serve dinner, took his arm and allowed him to lead her into the dining-room.

It was different when they had been young children, she thought, observing the mature good manners of both her daughters. When they were children, Bertram always spoiled them with unsuitable presents, risqué jokes and all manner of dangerous games, some of which involved swinging them round and round until they were in a frenzy of over-excitement. After a visit from Uncle Bertram, it took all Jane Grayson's self-control and patience to calm the girls before bedtime and only his brother Henry's Christian forbearance prevented a family rift.

Bertram was now tucking in to a plump roasted guinea fowl and glanced across at her to say appreciatively, 'Very fine, my dear Jane. And how goes the world with you? What news have you, since I saw you last?'

Observing his pleasant expression and obvious enjoyment

of the meal, Jane returned his smile and offered him more wine sauce. Bertram was no longer the careless rake he had been when the girls were small. Still handsome, he was now inclined to be rather fleshy and as head of the family, a little more serious.

Charlotte and Kitty were eager to tell him about the thunderstorm and the collapse of the chimney and all through dinner, he was regaled with descriptions and speculation by all the family.

'So you see, my dear Bertram, our stay in Sir Benjamin's house has not been without incident,' said Jane.

Sitting back in his chair, replete but censorious, Bertram decided to give his sister-in-law the benefit of his considered opinion on the whole situation.

He was now much given to pomposity and as different from Henry Grayson as it was possible to be. He was relentlessly critical of every aspect of Jane's actions and of the upbringing of her children and frequently bemoaned the fact that his brother had been so unwise as to marry a woman as strong as Jane Grayson and had been so unworldly as to take Holy Orders late in life, when he could have been comfortable as a country gentleman.

'My dear Jane, none of this distressing experience would have happened had you taken notice of my advice and sought out a smaller and more modest residence, more becoming to the widow of a clergyman. I cannot think what possessed you to enter into the leasehold of such an expensive, gloomy pile as this. Poor Henry must be turning in his grave at your excesses.'

None of this cut any ice whatsoever with Jane. She had always had money and Henry was not a younger son. He had also been wealthy and the living a good one. He had felt he had a vocation and she had encouraged him to follow his heart's desire to preach the Gospel and to do good works. She knew that Bertram treated this sort of attitude with the utmost contempt.

'After all,' he argued, 'what had it profited Henry to devote his life to God and die in his early fifties only to leave his widow wasting money in such a profligate way?'

He sipped his red wine appreciatively while continuing to pontificate about the discovery at Westbury Hall and Jane's folly in renting the property from Sir Benjamin in the first place.

Bertram was listened to politely by Jane, who was nevertheless on tenterhooks at the reactions of her daughters, especially Charlotte, who did not suffer prosy fools gladly and was never to be trusted to keep a still tongue. She looked covertly at her as Bertram began to drone on about the folly of purchasing Felbrook Manor, which again would be bound to be too big for her, especially after the girls had married and left home.

'Throwing good money after bad, my dear,' he boomed.

A mutual antipathy existed between her daughters and their uncle, but in spite of this, Charlotte and Kitty both behaved with complaisance and civility towards him. After all, he was Papa's brother and now that dear Papa had passed away, Bertram had assumed the role of head of the family and their mama had always stressed the importance of politeness and respect for elders. Jane was pleased and relieved at the maturity of their behaviour and felt that no argument or disagreement could now spoil the evening.

Dinner being over, the weather had turned cool. Bertram stood with his back to the fire in the drawing-room and addressed his captive audience. He dismissed the strange discovery of the skeleton with a few words. 'I trust Adam Brown has requested the Watch to remove the bones you found and has reported everything to the magistrate in King's Lynn.' Then he went straight on with no preamble, back to the topic nearest to his heart. 'I am at a loss, ma'am, to guess why you can possibly wish to purchase Felbrook when other more suitable, modestly priced houses are well within your means.'

Jane Grayson was calm but firm and replied evenly, 'I have

always had that intention, brother-in-law, ever since dear Henry's untimely death. As you know, we had to leave the vicarage in Lincoln to make way for the next incumbent. That was only right and proper, as you will agree. And I was pleased and grateful to Sir Benjamin Westbury to allow us a year's lease on the Hall. We have been tolerably comfortable here and of course I have had the girls for company. Now a new chapter is about to begin and in two short weeks, we shall at last move into our own home, where you will always be welcome, dear Bertram.'

Bertram looked round him disparagingly. There were abundant signs littered over the table and even on the floor that the ladies had retired to the drawing-room to do their hemming and embroidery, but neither of the girls or their mama was in fact doing any sewing. They were giving Uncle Bertram their undivided attention.

Jane knew that Charlotte Grayson was angry and impatient with her self-important uncle and could barely restrain herself from giving him a set-down. She also knew that Kitty was still slightly nervous of him, but at Jane's warning look, both had schooled themselves to express the utmost decorum and politeness towards him and to listen quietly without interrupting, even though he seemed determined to dominate the conversation.

Mrs Grayson was grateful that her daughters were being so forbearing and gracefully brought the proceedings to an end by rising from her chair and curtsying to him. 'Dear Bertram, I am conscious of how concerned you are, but Henry never made huge inroads into his fortune, you know, even though he was always such a good-living man and never let anyone in need pass by without helping them. As for himself, his life was always restrained and modest and his material needs were few. My own parents left me a comfortable portion so I am well able to afford Felbrook Manor and to see that my own daughters have a decent dowry when the time comes.'

Bertram Grayson, torn between admiration for this foresight in providing for his nieces to make good marriages and his excessively disapproving mind, merely humphed at her and finally took his leave.

While Jane Grayson took up her neglected embroidery again, Charlotte and Kitty playfully reminisced about days gone by when Uncle Bertram used to perform conjuring tricks, or balanced a glass of water on his head while he danced for them.

'Do you remember when Uncle Bertram bought us that Jack Russell puppy, Mama, and it nipped Grandmama's ankle?' Kitty said.

Jane smiled. 'Yes, I do, my dear. But he was very young, barely twenty, and Papa found the little dog a good home with one of his parishioners.'

Charlotte recalled when she had been ten years old and Uncle Bertram had secretly given her an inordinate number of sweetmeats until she was horribly ill and had to be put to bed by Nanny Bull.

Jane sighed. 'Yes, there were always tears before bedtime, when dear Bertram was here, but your uncle likes children and was always so jolly. It is such a pity that he has no little children of his own. He would make a wonderful papa to some lucky boys and girls.'

She sighed again and to break the mood, Charlotte decided that she and Kitty would perform some duets on the pianoforte, giggling a little and making their mother smile by their devastating imitations of the style and content of some of the young ladies of their acquaintance. 'Miss Aurelia Casterton has graciously consented to perform an air by George Frideric Handel,' Kitty announced and Charlotte gave a burlesque performance of Miss Casterton's rendering of the piece, complete with flamboyant arm movements and exaggerated use of pedals until Jane Grayson was obliged to smile at their fun and high spirits. Then it was Kitty's turn and she imitated the style of Ann West, who played and sang in a fashion so quiet it was almost inaudible.

'From *The Marriage of Figaro*, Cherubino,' she whispered and launched into 'Ye who can measure, love's loss or gain,' in such an accurate rendering of Miss West's small refined voice that Jane laughed out loud and immediately ordered them to go to bed.

'I need a little peace and quiet after such an eventful day,' she said. 'And you two drive me to distraction with your jokes and japes. Come now, both of you, give your mama a kiss and get off to bed. It is late.'

Still giggling, they obeyed. They shared a bedroom on the second landing and were so tired themselves that they didn't even spend time talking, but snuffed the candles promptly as soon as Phoebe had departed.

The next morning revealed a shining countryside, washed by further overnight rain, making leaves and blades of grass sparkle with jewelled raindrops. After a dull start, the weather was once more sunny and Charlotte pulled on some old half boots and set off for a walk with Phoebe in attendance. In single file, they went along a narrow muddy footpath which joined two more substantial tracks leading to the village church of St Paul.

A farmer led a herd of cows up the nearby cart track as they walked along enjoying the fine August weather. The sun was strong, even though the air had an almost autumnal coolness, and the animals' breath was steamy as they plodded patiently along with the herdsman. Once they'd rounded the corner and were out of sight, it seemed to Charlotte that steam was now issuing from the hedgerow and billowing along on top of it. Lost in her own thoughts, she was startled when, as the lane seemed to sink lower between the hedges, it began to twist and turn and became very slippery. Many of the stones had washed loose and she began to walk more carefully, shading her eyes with her hand as she looked for the well-known landmarks of St Paul's and the ancient signpost pointing to Felbrook village.

31

Suddenly, she heard the loud drumming of hoofs very close by and almost at once a huge black horse and rider leapt the hedge to her right and landed in front of her right across the foopath. Both Charlotte and Phoebe were thrown sideways and caught off balance by the suddenness of it all. Charlotte fell towards a bank where spindly twigs and yellowing wild flowers were still hidden among the coarse grass. She got up quickly and just in time prevented herself from straightening her bonnet and pushing back her curls with muddied gloves. Her pelisse and the bottom of her gown were equally spattered with the mud and stones thrown up by the rider's horse and she felt damp and uncomfortable. She had stumbled on to one knee against the bank and had a patch of wet earth stuck to her dress. Phoebe fared somewhat better and as she appeared unhurt and only a little flustered, Charlotte turned her attention to the horseman.

He was tall and sat very straight on the huge black hunter and as she looked straight up at him, she could see his eyes were deep blue, fringed by coal-black lashes. He was looking down at her with the utmost disdain. Then he transferred both his whip and the reins to his left hand and for a moment Charlotte thought he was about to dismount and apologize for his churlish and inconsiderate behaviour, but she quickly recognized that this was very far from his mind. Although he was hatless, his riding outfit and countrified nankeen jacket were faultless and of the very best quality. As she continued to look up into his handsome face, she thought him even more attractive for not appearing embarrassed or apologetic. It was she who was embarrassed. She now quite forgot the state of her gloves and straightened her bonnet, leaving a smudge of mud on her face. She was furious at the way his blue eyes, under their black brows, were appraising her coldly and with no hint of polite apology.

The handsome, arrogant stare did not soften in the least as Charlotte burst out impulsively, 'Sir, that was a very foolhardy action to leap in front of us like that. You could have been the cause of a serious accident.'

'And it was a very foolhardy action on your own part, madam, for you and your companion to be meandering along slippery muddy lanes on a day like today. Any accident would have been entirely your own fault.'

He turned a powerful shoulder away from her and gathered the reins as though about to ride away. Charlotte was almost speechless with rage and chagrin. She was totally unused to such ungentlemanly behaviour. She was all the more angry because what he said had a grain of truth even though she was not about to acknowledge it. She frowned at him, taking in the glossy, fashionably cut black hair, the finely shaped lips and square, masculine chin. Her own chin came up and her fine grey eyes were like chips of granite as she glared up at him.

'Furthermore,' he continued relentlessly, 'you and your companion are trespassing.'

'Oh? And who says so, pray?'

'I say so, madam. I am Hugo Westbury, Sir Benjamin's estate manager. This land belongs to my great-uncle. You have no right to be here. Much as I regret your near accident, you should not be on Westbury land at all. I would count it a courtesy, therefore, if you and your companion would take yourselves off.'

'T-t-t-ake yourselves. . . ?' Charlotte had to try and control herself now because she realized that she was almost spluttering with rage. 'I will have you know, sir, we are leasing Westbury Hall from Sir Benjamin and are entitled to walk in the fresh air if we so wish, without seeking permission from . . . from such as yourself.' She tried to infuse her tone with the righteous superiority of a ladylike legal tenant over a mere estate manager and failed signally in the attempt.

He merely scowled silently at this and then began to manoeuvre the huge stallion, in order to turn it along the path towards the nearest cart track. It was difficult. The horse was nervous and fidgety but he did it skilfully, in spite of the fact that Charlotte felt in danger of being flung into the bank once more and glowered at him all the while.

With a curt 'Good day', he trotted off along the footpath and out of sight, leaving Charlotte and Phoebe to turn back the way they had come and pick their way back to the Hall through the treacherous mud of the country footpath.

As soon as she arrived home and had washed and changed, Charlotte lost no time in seeking out her mama and pouring out her grievances against the insufferable Mr Hugo Westbury. 'Mama, he was such a churlish boor. He may be Sir Benjamin's heir and the manager of the estate, but he is no gentleman, Mama. He did not even bother to dismount to see how Phoebe and I did, after we were thrown almost into the ditch.'

Mrs Grayson gave a barely perceptible sigh. It was never any use reasoning with Charlotte when she was in this sort of angry mood. No gentleman, indeed. She guessed he would have had precious little chance for gentlemanly conduct in the face of Charlotte's furious verbal onslaught. If only Henry were here. He had the magic touch of always charming their elder daughter out of her bad humour. With no more than a little smile and the gentlest of shared jokes, he could transform her temper into delighted laugher in no time at all. If only she herself had that gift, it would be so much more comfortable. . . .

None of these thoughts showed on Mrs Grayson's face and she didn't allow herself the luxury of taking sides. She neither blamed nor defended Hugo Westbury's actions, but said mildly, 'A most inauspicious meeting, my love. Let us hope the young man improves on further acquaintance.'

Charlotte tossed her head impatiently. 'I tell you, Mama, he is the most arrogant and ill-mannered man who ever lived.'

Her mother tutted sympathetically and seemed to give her full attention to her needlework. Charlotte was angry that her mama was not responding positively to the account of Mr Hugo Westbury's inconsiderate and impossible behaviour and ground her teeth as her mama chose a fresh strand of embroidery silk and began to concentrate on threading her needle. Kitty came in at that moment and the whole story of Charlotte's meeting and near accident with the churlish Mr Hugo Westbury was recounted once more.

Kitty was much more worthwhile as an audience for Charlotte's tale and listened with pleasing attention and indignation to the story of his impossible behaviour. Finally, though, even Charlotte could find no more words to say in denigration of Mr Westbury and gradually the conversation turned to an invitation from Matthew's Aunt Lavinia for them all to go over for dinner on Sunday next.

'So kind of dear Lavinia,' Jane Grayson said, relieved that the storm of Charlotte's anger seemed to have blown itself out. Sometimes, she felt she was treading on eggshells when dealing with her daughter's strong passions, so she was more animated in her praise of Lavinia than usual. 'I shall look forward to it, my dears, and shall wear my new grey silk to church in the morning. It will be so enjoyable to talk over the finding of the skeleton in the cupboard later on and we shall find out what Sir Benjamin thinks about it.'

Kitty agreed. 'And we shall find out from Matthew if Mr Brown has discovered anything new about the mystery.' She sounded excited and even Charlotte was prepared to discuss what Sir Benjamin might think of a hidden skeleton in his family cupboard. No further mention was made of the hateful Hugo Westbury as the three of them began to gather up their sewing in preparation for luncheon.

As Kitty and Charlotte were about to leave the room, there was a respectful tap on the drawing-room door and Robert entered, carrying a small silver tray and bowing respectfully.

'If you please, ma'am,' he said. 'Mr Hugo Westbury presents his card, ma'am, and asks if you are at home, ma'am.'

The effect was electric. Charlotte went bright red and opened her mouth as though to speak. Kitty giggled and

looked mischievously at her mama. Mrs Grayson put a delicate white hand up to her forehead as though she had a
sudden headache and said faintly, 'Oh dear. Yes . . . no . . . that
is . . . I suppose. . . . Very well, Robert, show him up, if you
please.'

She cast a warning look at Charlotte and put aside her
sewing and straightened her skirt as Robert announced, 'Mr
Hugo Westbury,' and then withdrew, closing the door behind
him.

The insufferable Hugo Westbury stepped languidly into
the drawing-room and bowed. He made no attempt to smile
or look pleasant, but was merely civil as he acknowledged
Mrs Grayson's greeting and her polite curtsy.

'Mr Westbury.'

'Mrs Grayson. How do you do, ma'am?'

Mrs Grayson studied him gravely and tried to equate
Charlotte's description of the careless and boorish horseman
with this tall, good-looking young man who wore his beautifully tailored garments with exceptional elegance and whose
handsome face and stylish hair seemed the epitome of the
fashionable modern male.

Kitty stared at him with unabashed youthful curiosity and
only Charlotte remained coldly aloof, her colour high and a
light of antagonism in her eyes.

To Hugo Westbury, great-nephew and heir to the vast
wealth of Sir Benjamin Westbury, Jane Grayson appeared as
the archetypal vicar's wife – ladylike, refined, well meaning,
not the sort of woman who would cause trouble, seek
confrontation or engage in any strong verbal exchange. He
was sure he could get her to agree to an alteration of the
removal date. Unlike her daughter, he thought, allowing his
penetratingly blue eyes to flick disparagingly over Charlotte.
He would have the utmost difficulty in getting *her* to agree to
anything. And the other one was barely more than a schoolroom chit, he told himself.

Aloud, he said smoothly, 'Forgive me for calling at an

unfashionable hour, ma'am. I do not wish to discommode you or intrude for more than a few minutes, but I merely seek to give notice of my great-uncle's intentions. Firstly, ma'am, he will be visiting you himself in the next day or two and will keep you informed of the progress of the inquiry into the mysterious skeleton. More importantly, he has asked me, as the manager of his estate, to inform you that he intends to reside in this place and would deem it a courtesy on your part if you would vacate the premises forthwith.'

He made his long speech politely and in an even tone of voice, but it was obvious to his listeners that he meant every word of it.

Mrs Grayson was a truly Christian woman and her inclination was to help her neighbours and try to be accommodating. She knew that Sir Benjamin and his heir were staying at The Oak in King's Lynn and realized that they must be longing to be settled in their own home, just as she was longing to be settled at Felbrook Manor. Her instinct, however, told her that if she attempted to speed up their departure unreasonably, then everything would be a mish-mash. The servants would be under strain, the packing would be done carelessly and belongings would either be damaged or go missing, leading to recrimination and counter-recrimination. In short, utter chaos. Westbury Hall would need to be cleaned thoroughly, especially now that the rubble had been cleared away from the fall of masonry. Moving out forthwith was absolutely impossible. She needed to be kind but firm with this forceful young man, just as she was with some of the older, more difficult boys at Sunday school.

She gave him a kindly smile and said slowly, 'Well ... I would like to fall in with Sir Benjamin's wishes, sir. After all, he is the owner and has been separated from his beloved home for a number of years ... but ... but we shall need all the time we may garner in order to vacate the Hall efficiently and remove our effects to Felbrook. Indeed, Mr Westbury, we have only a fortnight of the lease still to run and I dare say even a fortnight may prove insufficient time to remove our things and to leave the place as I would wish.'

He was impatient with her but said easily, 'I understand your scruples, ma'am, and in the general way I would agree with you, but with the finding of the human remains and the enquiry it has occasioned, Sir Benjamin feels that this is an exceptional circumstance and that he needs to be *in situ* for any investigations of the skeleton. The panelling will need to be repaired and if you are willing to fall in with his wishes, he can easily summon up an army of domestics to tidy and clean the place. It would only take a day. You need not trouble your-self with such details and I am prepared to make you an excessivley generous offer to vacate the Hall quickly.'

Jane Grayson stared at him. She was the widow of a vicar, not to be swayed by any mercenary interests and certainly not used to being bludgeoned into hasty or unpalatable decisions by a man young enough to be her son.

'On the contrary, Mr Westbury, I am prepared to buy an *extension* of the lease, in order to move house in a more comfortable and leisurely way.'

'Extend it, Mrs Grayson?' His haughty tone was now quite chilling. 'You mistake, ma'am. There can be no question of an extension to the lease. Sir Benjamin wishes me to urge you that owing to this particular circumstance, he needs to reclaim his property as soon as possible.'

Her hands had begun to tremble and she clasped them tightly on her lap. 'How soon?' she demanded. 'It is impossi-ble. The lease has two more weeks to run.'

He smiled. Jane noticed the smile and was sure that both her daughters had noticed it too. He had the most fascinating smile she had ever seen in a man. His blue eyes deepened and sparkled, and little lines radiated from the corners, making them look wickedly amused. His fine mouth curved attrac-tively and he bowed slightly, saying, 'Perhaps you might suggest a compromise, then, ma'am?'

Jane Grayson thought quickly, but said calmly, 'If Sir

Benjamin does not think it too much of an imposition, sir, I suggest we compromise and vacate the Hall after one week instead of two and leave the cleaning of the place to Sir Benjamin's servants. I want no recompense, though, for doing my neighbour a good turn. Perhaps Sir Benjamin might instead give a small donation towards the church?'

'I am sure he would find your compromise most acceptable,' Hugo Westbury said suavely. 'I shall convey your decision to him, dear ma'am, and now that is settled I must take my leave of you. Good day, ladies.'

His eyes flickered over the two girls and expressed no interest in them whatsoever. He ignored Kitty but gave Charlotte a contemptuous glance and was shown out by Robert, leaving Mrs Grayson and her daughters to talk things over. Kitty was intrigued and openly admiring of their handsome new neighbour. Mrs Grayson was anxious that all should go well and that they would be able to honour the new agreement, but she was quietly satisfied that she had done her Christian duty and tried to help Sir Benjamin in his desire to take possession of his old home.

Charlotte was furious at what she saw as Mama's disloyalty in co-operating with such an unpleasant and arrogant bully. He thinks he has won, she thought angrily. Her hands clenched and her lips compressed as she fought the desire to protest at the method he'd used to get his own way. Mama is too soft, she thought furiously. I certainly would not be seduced by his charm. But Mama had smiled back at him with undisguised pleasure and admiration. She was probably just relieved that he was not going to bully her and cause a scene. He *has* won, Charlotte thought mutinously.

'How could you, Mama?' she demanded. 'You know how shamefully he treated Phoebe and me. You should have turned him away after his unpardonable behaviour.'

Jane Grayson was unabashed. She wasn't socially naïve and was shrewd enough to know that Sir Benjamin and his great-nephew would be wishing to renew social connections in the neighbourhood once they were settled in. Of course, Charlotte had a faithful suitor in Matthew King, but there was also dear Kitty to consider. Perhaps through the Westburys, she would meet an eligible gentleman. Someone more to her liking than the curate who was paying her such particular attention.

'But only consider, Charlotte,' she said gently. 'He is to be one of our neighbours. We may find a more pleasant side to his black-hearted nature, if we can but get to know him better. If we give him no chance to redeem himself, how will we ever find out that he has a pleasant side?'

As was Mama's wont, she said it so seriously and with such a straight face that only those who knew her well could tell that she was funning. Charlotte scowled and said no more.

CHAPTER THREE

Sunday dawned dull and misty, but with the promise of some fine sunshine to come, as Jane and her daughters walked to St Paul's and took their places ready for the morning service.

Mrs Grayson was wearing her new lavender-grey silk. She was aware that half mourning was far more becoming to her fair colouring and greying hair than the deep black she had favoured until very recently and she was pleased with the matching bonnet, a modest confection in a slightly more modish style than the one she usually favoured, being of pale lilac straw with matching ruched satin ribbon on the inside of the brim. Once the year of full mourning was over, she'd instructed the girls to be free of their dark clothes and wear whatever was dignified and becoming, 'For your dear papa would not feel it signified if you laid aside deep mourning,' she said comfortably. 'He always believed it is what is in the heart that matters and always said, "Thou my God see'st me". He knew how much you loved him and funereal clothes make no difference to that affection.'

Charlotte and Kitty were pleased by this and with no disrespect to Papa's memory, wore gowns which echoed the mellow colours of early autumn. Kitty had on a soft green velvet dress with matching pelisse and bonnet and Mrs Grayson was secretly amused to see that Charlotte had elected to wear her newest gown, which was of a rich russet colour and flattered her flawless complexion and glossy dark hair to perfection. Charlotte's bonnet was most deliciously fashionable, of fine cream straw with sweet little plumes, curling from the back of the crown. Of course, Charlotte would be seeing her beloved Matthew for dinner at Lavinia King's house, later, Jane thought. Why shouldn't she wear her best clothes? She took a hasty look around the church. Nearly all the pews were now occupied and still there was no sign of Mr Westbury and Sir Benjamin. She saw Matthew King arrive with his aunt and they nodded and bowed as they moved to their places. She knew that everyone was aware of the return of Sir Benjamin and Hugo Westbury and guessed that as soon as Mrs Palmer was told yesterday to empty the attics and to crate up all the glasses and china, except the full service that they used every day, that the lady would inform all those who would listen, that 'Mrs, Grayson was being turned out of the Hall, uncommon speedy, like, and would wear everybody out by her hurried packing'.

There seemed to be an expectant hush in the church now. It couldn't be anticipation of the parson's arrival because he'd arrived ages ago and was in the vestry robing up his thin, lanky body with surplice and cassock. It was the curate, Andrew Preston, who was officiating today and he was a nervous young man with wispy blond hair and a bobbing Adam's apple. The portly vicar, Hector Swift, was more popular with the village folk, but he was visiting his wife's relations in Yorkshire and Andrew Preston was more than willing to stand in for him. A pleasant young man, Jane mused, and from a good family, he had excellent prospects for advancement and a good living if he were to marry. So far, she had deemed him as a possible partner for her younger girl and he seemed more than pleased at the prospect.

She drew back her speculative thoughts as the whispered conversations now suddenly ceased and she knew that this must be because Sir Benjamin and Mr Westbury had entered the church. She was determined not to turn her head but most of the congregation had done just that and were unashamedly craning to see the newcomers.

She observed Charlotte and Kitty very closely, ready to frown at them should they be so vulgar as to turn and stare, but conscious of their mama's gaze, they remained decorously looking to the front.

Sir Benjamin was white-haired and frail-looking. his once tall, strong body bent with age, but he was dressed immaculately as became a gentleman and he used his silver-handled cane with singular grace as he walked slowly to his family pew. Charlotte averted her gaze, refusing to look at the hated Hugo and his great-uncle, but she was the only one who did. Everyone else stared at them with unabashed curiosity, one of the villagers even holding up her baby to look at them. There were few in the congregation who still remembered Sir Benjamin before he went to India but there were many more who remembered the lonely, dark-haired little boy who in the school holidays had been looked after at the Hall by tutors and servants. Jane Grayson observed the nodding plumes of some of the ambitious mamas in the neighbourhood and noticed with a smile that Augusta Casterton was poking her dumpy daughter, Aurelia, quite viciously, to remind her to sit up straight and try to look more graceful.

As the two Westbury men took their places, the Reverend Andrew Preston swished into the church and mounted the steps to the pulpit. His Adam's apple bobbed furiously as he announced the first hymn.

He took as his text for the sermon, 'Love thy neighbour as thyself', which was only to be expected, Jane thought with some amusement.

Afterwards, as everyone trooped out of church, there was much very pointed lingering on the part of some of the local gentry, particularly the women. Mr Preston had welcomed the two returned parishioners very warmly and it seemed as though everyone wished to make themselves known to Sir Benjamin and Hugo and to make them equally welcome. Mrs Grayson knew that the two men would be inundated with visits, cards and, of course, invitations to dine and she conceded to herself that it must be very inconvenient for them not to be in the family home. But it is now only five days, she thought, and then we shall have left Westbury Hall for ever. Matthew and his Aunt Lavinia came up to greet them and knowing he was going to see Charlotte and Kitty a little later, Matthew didn't linger but set off with his aunt for Primrose Cottage.

In view of the bright sunshine, Charlotte decided she would take a detour to make the walk home a little longer, but neither Phoebe nor Kitty expressed any interest in this idea. Kitty was intent on writing to her friend in Norwich and Phoebe was to help Mrs Grayson with more packing of the books in the library. 'I know it is the Sabbath,' Jane said with a smile, 'but I hope the Lord will forgive me my trespasses this once. After all, Papa's books are mainly on godly themes, so perhaps our place in heaven will not be too much endangered. Do not be too late, Charlotte. Remember we are dining with Miss King and Matthew today.'

Charlotte walked slowly along the very path where she'd first met Hugo Westbury and her thoughts drifted towards him in spite of herself. It was incontrovertible that he was to be one of their neighbours. They were certain to meet socially when they had invitations from other families. She wondered whether his behaviour would be different in other circumstances and whether she would get over her instinctive antipathy towards him. She doubted it.

Where the path divided, she met one of the little girls from her Sunday school class, sitting forlornly on a fallen tree trunk and crying, the tears running down her pretty cheeks and clinging to her lashes.

'Why, Lucy, dear. What is it? Whatever can be the matter, child? Come here and let me have a look at you.'

Regardless of the newness of her smart russet outfit, Charlotte sank down on the tree trunk at the side of the diminutive Lucy and put an arm round her, whereupon Lucy began to weep more piteously than ever. Her golden curls were tousled and her old-fashioned sun bonnet was hanging down her back by its ribbons. Charlotte gently smoothed the curls away from the unhappy little forehead and spoke sooth-ingly to her. 'What is it, my little pretty? Has someone hurt you, child? Tell me what is wrong.'

The little girl gulped in an effort to control her sobs and said, 'Please, miss, 'tis my dress. I reached for ... for some blackberries yonder and tore it on the brambles. Oh, miss ... I dursen't go .. home like this ... it'd be awful trouble ... Miss Grayson. . . .' And she gave another hiccuping sob.

'Let me see,' Charlotte said. She gently stood the little girl up and turned her round. 'It is but a small tear, Lucy dear. In my reticule I have my little mending kit that ladies sometimes take to dances. Stand still and I will make it as good as new.'

Lucy had stopped crying and gave a shuddering sigh. 'Oh, can you, miss? Can you truly mend it? Ma will be so mad wi' me if she sees it like this.'

She stood patiently while Charlotte opened her reticule and took out the handy little needle case with a needle already threaded up. Very carefully, she mended the small tear in the faded print frock and said briskly, 'There now, Lucy dear. It is done. No one can tell you have had it mended. Look at me now, my dear, and let us dry those pretty eyes.'

Lucy obediently turned towards her, smiling tremulously now, and that was exactly how Hugo Westbury saw them as he walked alone along the footpath, leading his horse and halting in the little clearing. The child was tearful, he noticed, and he scowled. He hoped the unpleasant Miss Grayson had not been unkind to her. If she had, he would have something to say about that. The little girl was the daughter of one of his estate workers. Then he noticed that the hateful Miss Grayson was actually wiping the child's eyes very gently with a most insubstantial wisp of lace and he took out his own immacu-late handkerchief and stepped forward.

'Miss Grayson,' he said suavely. 'Good morning. Allow me

to offer my handkerchief. I trust you have not been mistreating this little child and making her cry.'

Charlotte glared at him and said coldly, 'Your handkerchief and your presence here are equally unwelcome, sir. Kindly leave us.'

She then proceeded to ignore him utterly. She was now tidying the guinea-gold curls on the pretty little head and replacing the faded old bonnet with a tenderness that was as warm as it was moving. Hugo Westbury caught his breath at the gentle loveliness of her expression as she drew the little girl to her and gave her a hug, saying, 'There, my little darling. Now you are all done and I can see you home to your mama.'

Still Miss Grayson ignored him as she rose to her feet and smoothed out her skirts, ready to take the little girl's hand.

Hugo Westbury was unused to being ignored, especially by women. He cleared his throat and said, 'What is your name, little girl?'

'Please sir, I be Lucy Baker,' she said shyly.

'Well, Lucy Baker, how would you like to ride home on this horse?' he said. Charlotte frowned at him. What game was he playing, offering the child a ride like that?

'Where do you live, Lucy?'

'Over yon, sir, in the village, I do. And I would like a ride, so I would.'

'You trust me to give you a ride home, then?'

'Yes, sir, I does,' she whispered shyly and to Charlotte's utter amazement, she showed not the slightest nervousness as he lifted her on to the big black horse.

'Are you sure you trust this strange man?' she asked.

'Yes, miss, cos he's big like my pa and he has smiley eyes, so he has.'

Hugo Westbury gave Charlotte a sideways glance of undisguised triumph. 'Hold on tightly,' he said to Lucy and placed her little hands on the arched front of the saddle and so they set off very sedately, Hugo leading the horse and with

46

Charlotte obliged to walk on the other side, silently fuming at his high-handedness. She would have enjoyed the walk had it not been for the nagging irritation of having Hugo Westbury's presence imposed on her and was determined not to speak to him. She was acutely aware that he glanced at her frequently but addressed his remarks only to Lucy, who was not so much in awe of the fine horse or too tense with the delight of her ride that she couldn't respond. By his gentle conversation and open remarks, he was able to coax the little girl into giving him a lot of information about her family and their house and their dog and even Lucy's Sunday school teacher.

'So, you go to Sunday school, Lucy?' he enquired. 'And who is your teacher?'

'Why, it be Miss Grayson, sir,' she said artlessly.

'And is she very strict with you?'

'Oh no, sir. She'm kind, she is, and I'm learning to read, I am. She'm teaching me my letters, sir.' The little girl spoke innocently and turned to smile at Charlotte as she answered him.

It was now Charlotte's turn to glance triumphantly sideways and this time he made a remark directly to her, saying that the child lived in one of the cottages which he and Sir Benjamin planned to re-roof before the winter set in.

'And of course, Sir Benjamin and I are desirous of improving Westbury Hall, once it is vacated. Some of the carpets and curtains desperately need replacing to make the place more comfortable.'

Charlotte met his mocking, blue-eyed gaze unflinchingly. 'We have been quite comfortable living at the Hall,' she informed him with the utmost conviction. She could tell that he was not pleased with her answer but went on stubbornly, 'However much you desire the refurbishment of Westbury Hall, sir, I still think it reprehensible of you to turn out a widow and her family at such short notice.'

His lips tightened into a straight line and his blue eyes lost their mocking smile. 'Sir Benjamin is now in quite frail health,' he said curtly. 'And then there is the added complication of the unfortunate discovery of that skeleton.' He spoke impatiently as though he wished her to be silent, but Charlotte had no intention of considering his wishes.

'It has put an added strain on my mama,' she protested hotly. 'She can barely manage to accomplish all the packing in time, and the servants are finding everything difficult.'

The more heated Charlotte became with her anger, the more coldly furious Hugo Westbury became and his tone was icily civil as he said, 'But I obtained your mother's agreement to vacate the premises a week early. Your mama was agreeable to the change.'

'Mama felt unable to oppose your proposition, sir. She felt powerless to stand up to someone so ... so ... insufferably overbearing as yourself. I would never have agreed to such an arrangement had I been Mama—?'

She broke off, breathless with temper.

'But you are not she, madam, for which I am profoundly thankful. And as we are speaking plainly, I would find it intolerable to conduct business with such a termagant as yourself.'

'In business, sir, it pays to abide by one's legal agreement, not seek to gain unfair advantage and then resort to verbal insult.'

'That, coming from a skilled practitioner such as yourself, is rich, madam.'

Her colour high, she turned her head away from him and pressed her lips together, determined to say no more. They'd now reached the outskirts of Felbrook village and Lucy, who had been quiet during Charlotte's heated exchange with Hugo Westbury, suddenly raised one of her hands from the saddle and pointed excitedly.

'Oh, see there, miss, 'tis Ma come to meet me.'

Charlotte was obliged to turn towards him as he slowed the horse to a halt. 'Kindly lift her down, Mr Westbury. Her mama is waiting for her. Now, Lucy, say "good day" to Mr Westbury and thank him for the ride.'

She waited, stiffly silent, while Lucy obeyed. Then she clasped her hand and the little girl skipped beside her to her waiting mama, her torn dress completely forgotten as she told her mother of the magnificent horse and the kind gentleman who'd given her a ride.

When he'd gone a little distance from them, Hugo Westbury turned to look back and was oddly moved at the sight of the tall, dark-haired young woman walking hand in hand with the golden-haired little girl, before he rode off in the opposite direction.

To her relief, Charlotte didn't run into Hugo Westbury again as she made her way back to Westbury Hall, but he dominated her thoughts all the same and she pondered on the recent events as she walked on slowly. What a puzzle the man was; so arrogant and domineering and yet so careful and sensitive with Lucy that he'd won the little girl's confidence in next to no time. Finally, she sighed and had to acknowledge that he was extremely handsome and would no doubt become the heartbreaker of the neighbourhood.

Back at the Hall everything was still in a spin about the removal to Felbrook Manor. Papa's books were now all safely packed in crates and Kitty and her mother were having a light luncheon in the breakfast parlour. Charlotte's high colour and restless hands did not escape her mama's notice, but she said nothing except, 'Should you like a little luncheon, my dear? There are no hot meats as we are going out to dinner, but Mrs Palmer has prepared a splendid selection of cold cuts and a trifle, if you should wish for anything.'

Charlotte realized then that she was hungry and did justice to several slices of ham and beef with some of Mrs Palmer's homemade bread to accompany it. She said nothing of her meeting with the obnoxious Mr Westbury, but spoke instead of little Lucy Baker and how pretty she was growing.

They were all pleased at the prospect of visiting Lavinia King and Jane declared cheerfully that apart from their clothes and personal effects, everything was now ready for Jimmy the carter lad, who could take the various boxes and trunks in stages to Felbrook Manor.

It was late afternoon when they all met at Primrose Cottage, to a warm welcome from Lavinia and Matthew.

'Adam is expected any time now,' Lavinia said with a blush, which added to her youthful appearance. 'He is riding over from King's Lynn so it is hard to say precisely how long it will take. But come, my dear Jane, and tell me all the news of Felbrook Manor and of Westbury Hall, of course. How goes the remove?'

Jane laughed and said in a very carefree tone, 'Nothing to tell, Lavinia. We are packed and ready to go. It only remains to oversee the carter and to take ourselves to our lovely Felbrook. After all the frenzied activity, we shall not know how to sustain the next five days. There is nothing more to be done now, except to dust down the walls and windows and return the keys to Mr Hugo Westbury. Even the stables have been cleaned out. The horses have been taken to Felbrook by the stable lad and seem already to be quite at home there. Mr Westbury has even seen to the repair of the library wall and everything is neat and tidy.'

'Why, that is famous progress indeed,' Lavinia said. 'What an admirable organizer you are, Jane, to have accomplished so much packing in such a short time.'

Charlotte bit her lip and said nothing as she listened to this conversation. She thought instead of the fuss she'd made to Hugo Westbury about the lease. What must he think of me, she wondered? Then she raised her chin and told herself defiantly that she didn't care what he thought, but it was obvious to Charlotte that her mama was far from being the downtrodden widow as she'd portrayed her to Hugo Westbury and was, in fact, full of optimism and energy, completely ready for the move to Felbrook Manor.

It was towards six o'clock when Adam arrived at Primrose Cottage and as this was the first time that Jane and her daughters had become aware of the deepening relationship between Matthew's aunt and their lawyer, they observed them closely. Although they didn't discuss it with each other, Jane and her daughters all had their own opinions and perspectives on the romance between Adam and Lavinia.

Jane had been extremely happy with her unworldly husband and had no wish to venture into matrimony for a second time, but she knew that Adam had been married briefly, long ago and that his young wife had died of influenza after less than a year of marriage. She thoroughly understood his wish to share his rather solitary life with someone as attractive as Lavinia King and wished them well, particularly as it seemed that Miss King's nephew, Matthew, would not be left high and dry, but was almost affianced to her elder daughter, Charlotte. After all, what was to stop Lavinia and Adam from living happily ever after, once Matthew and Charlotte were wed? She sighed and glanced across at Kitty. Her younger daughter was so different in personality from the forceful Charlotte, so much more shy and lacking in confidence. Perhaps the diffident curate, Andrew Preston, would prove to be the perfect match for her, if he were able to engage her interest, that is.

Charlotte viewed the romantic friendship between Lavinia and Adam without much interest. She liked Matthew's aunt and Adam seemed a suitable suitor for her.

As for Kitty, she was totally indifferent to the idea of a mature couple such as Adam and Lavinia finding love. In her eyes, they were old and long past the magic of romantic passion. They'd had their day, whereas she was still young and desperately, hopelessly, in love with someone who was totally unattainable.

Adam approached the ladies very pleasantly and both Kitty and her mother were persuaded that they would enjoy a look round Lavinia's garden, while Lavinia herself went to the kitchen to see how the dinner was progressing.

Matthew and Charlotte were left alone and for the first time since she'd known him, Charlotte felt somewhat ill at ease with him. Their friendship had been thus far so relaxed and easy-going. They'd seemed always to enjoy each other's company and felt carefree when they were together. Now, for some reason, Charlotte was uncomfortable and almost critical of Matthew's open expression and somewhat ingenuous remarks. There kept popping up into her mind's eye the incredibly handsome face of Hugo Westbury, now smiling, now angry, but always arresting and interesting. She wondered what he was doing now. Probably gloating over his victory at getting Mama to move out early from the Hall, she thought bitterly.

She was roused from her thoughts when Matthew took her hand and tucked it into his arm.

'Come, Charlotte, what do you say to a walk round Aunt Lavinia's garden, while the evening is still so fine?' he said.

She acquiesced willingly to this and they joined the others in the cottage garden, created painstakingly and lovingly over the years by Matthew's beloved aunt. Here were traditional cottage flowers, interspersed with decorative runner beans, and divided by arches covered in sweet-melling climbing roses, and having here and there little secluded arbours with quaint seats and arches overrun with fragrant honeysuckle. There was much to see and admire and gradually Charlotte's mood calmed and she sat for a few minutes on a stone bench with Adam Brown, chatting about the journey from King's Lynn, while Matthew took Kitty to see Lavinia's giant sunflowers, all turning their faces to the mild, late summer sky.

As Matthew stood beside her, he ran his eyes over Kitty as she smilingly lifted her own face to the sun. She never changed at all, he decided; still the bonny, good-natured girl he'd known ever since she'd come back to live at the Hall. She was such a gentle young thing. He would like having her as a sister, he decided.

As they walked among the roses, they chatted about the riding party which was to take place later in the month. Her two best friends Aurelia Casterton and Ann West had planned the whole thing, she informed him.

'But of course, their mamas are behind all the organization,' she said seriously.

These two young ladies were close friends with each other and almost inseparable. They were known collectively as 'the girls'.

'And how *are* the girls?' Matthew asked, smiling mischievously.

'Ann has just become engaged. Did you not know? To Squire Thorpe's son, over near Walsingham way. He is very good-looking and is an only son. Ann's mama is delighted.'

He imagined he saw a wistful expression in Kitty's honest grey eyes. 'No, I had not heard,' was all he said. He was surprised. The girls were both the same age as Kitty and he hadn't imagined they would be thinking of marriage yet.

'Good Lord! I thought she was still a schoolroom miss. Not old enough to be married.'

'She is eighteen,' Kitty said rather stiffly and once more he thought he saw both envy and disappointment in her expression.

He smiled. He'd known 'the girls' for a long time and knew that even when Aurelia was a little girl, she'd been deliciously chubby, probably because she was always able to persuade her nurse to give her unlimited sweetmeats and delicacies. She'd somehow always been the one who secured the best of everything for herself and was seemingly sublimely indifferent to the needs of others. Ann West was quieter and more modest.

'So, Matthew, if you are coming to the riding party, you will be able to see her for yourself and Robert Thorpe too, I expect,' Kitty said, her face expressionless.

Mention of the riding party brought back a memory for Matthew of a similar event when Charlotte and Kitty were very new to the neighbourhood. Kitty really had been hardly out of the schoolroom then and, greatly daring, had given him a very girlish and inexperienced kiss. It had come as a surprise to Matthew, himself not skilled in the art of kissing, and he had been somewhat embarrassed. He wondered if Kitty remembered the schoolgirl kiss as well and, glancing up at her now, he saw that she was looking directly at him and smiling. Good Lord, she was remembering it too, he thought with a shock, but at the same time he smiled back at her, thinking what a very likeable girl she was.

Aloud, he said, 'Yes, of course I should like to come. Nothing would keep me away, unless Adam has found another skeleton for me.'

They laughed together and then Lavinia called them in and greeted them with wine and little ratafia biscuits and made them so welcome that soon everyone was in the right mood for a delicious dinner. Lavinia had seated Matthew next to Charlotte and opposite Kitty and she and Jane were all set for a cose, as the young people chatted among themselves.

Just as the soup was being served, Adam Brown, bright-eyed and enthusiastic as usual, smiled round the table and said, 'I am so sorry if I was a trifle late, Lavinia. But listen to this, Matthew, because after you left the office, I was able to collect together some papers for your perusal. I am not sure whether they will be of any practical use to us, but I think they might throw some light on the origin of the skeleton. You may be interested to read them.'

'Yes, only later, Adam, after dinner,' Lavinia said firmly, but Charlotte noticed that she gave him a most loving smile as she said it.

Everyone seemed in high humour, including Jane, in spite of having been so distracted with packing and complaints from servants. Charlotte was struck anew at the good humour and energy that her mama put into the most mundane and everyday activities and at how youthful and exuberant was her smile. Thinking back again to her encounter with Hugo Westbury, she felt faintly uneasy that she'd been so out of temper as to insist that her mother was a victim of the landlord's oppression. But still, she thought, he is such an unpleasant man, it is only too easy to be out of sorts with such as he.

Neither Matthew nor Adam wished to linger over glasses of port once the ladies had left the dining-room and soon they were all of them settled in the drawing-room, agog to hear what Adam Brown had to say.

'The first item I found in the strong box is a letter writ to my own papa, Edward Brown, nigh on sixty years since, when Sir Benjamin was about to set off for India. Read it to us, Matthew, if you please.'

Westbury Hall
Norfolk

My dear Mr Brown
I write in haste as I am to sail for India in the morning. Acting on your advice, I shall take no further interest in the actions of my brother George. He seems to be intent on self-destruction, via drink and gambling. Both he and my youngest brother, Charles, now seem to be at daggers drawn over Lady Mary Spence, a great beauty and from a noble family. God pity her. I believe she is a most amiable and pleasant young woman as well as lovely.

As for myself dear Edward, my trusted friend, I find myself pleased to be leaving England for foreign climes, where I shall have the comfort of action and a change of scene. I find I can no longer abide either London society or even the quiet of Norfolk. My desire is to put as much distance between myself and my brothers as possible. I hope I shall remain in touch with you and, meanwhile, believe me to be your friend and client,
*   Benjamin Westbury*

There was a silence after Matthew had finished reading and finally Charlotte said, 'It certainly lets us imagine the family tensions of sixty years ago, but it explains nothing of the dead body and the little child in the picture.'

'And would not Sir Benjamin take exception to our having access to his correspondence with your father, Adam?' Lavinia asked uneasily.

'No, my dear,' he said gently. 'Sir Benjamin has instructed me to act in any way that I think fit and that could aid in the resolution of the mystery.'

'But no one here could possibly have the sort of knowledge to aid you in your enquiries,' Jane protested. 'Even I was not born when Sir Benjamin went away.'

'But it can be invaluable as an *aide-memoire*,' he said quietly. 'You and Mr Grayson were born in Norfolk and there must be memories of little things your parents might have said that you can recall to mind.'

Jane Grayson looked thoughtful at this and then said slowly, 'Yes, I do remember my own mama telling me of a dreadful accident . . . I think it befell Charles Westbury but my dear mama's stories were legion. I recall none of it except that the whole family perished at sea.'

'But how could that be?' Lavinia asked.

Adam Brown said gently, 'They appeared to be on their way to Holland and were overtaken by a sudden freak storm which resulted in the loss of all the passengers and most of the crew. According to the newspapers for 19 November 1757, that day, there were severe storms all around Boston and King's Lynn and from the wreck of the *Golden Maiden* there were but two who survived. But not all the family perished. The baby in the picture was Hugo's father, Humphrey, and he had been left in the care of his nurse.

'Let us pause there, while Matthew reads you another letter, this time from my own father to Sir Benjamin in Mysore.'

Dear Benjamin,
It is with great regret that I write to inform you of the deaths
of your brother Charles and his wife, Lady Mary. They suffered
with other passengers and crew when the Golden Maiden
capsized in a terrible storm off the coast of Cromer. Not all the
bodies have been recovered and no one seems to know why your
brother and his wife were making the journey to Holland, but
whatever the reason, they were tragically young for such a fate.
Fortunately, Humphrey, the young baby, was left in the charge
of his nurse. The memorial service will be at the end of this
month and no doubt you will wish to return to England as
soon as may be. There are certain legal formalities to be gone
through, now that your brother is dead. My condolences to you
and Mr George Westbury.
        Edward Brown

'But, Mr Brown,' Kitty demanded, 'if the baby in the picture
did not perish with his parents, what did happen to him?'

'I know that he was cared for by one of the relatives until
he was of age. He married Isabel Andrews, an American lady,
and Hugo Westbury is his son, the grandson of Charles. Lady
Mary's body was recovered from the wreck of the *Golden
Maiden* but Charles was apparently lost at sea. I know not
what happened to the other brother, George. Perhaps the one
person to explain the mystery must be Sir Benjamin Westbury.
He hopes to be back at the Hall on Friday next and I think that
would be the time to visit him.'

The discussion ended there for the moment and the party
continued with cards and some music provided by Kitty and
Charlotte, who sang very prettily and were accompanied by
their mother at the pianoforte. Even Lavinia was persuaded
to give them one or two songs in her rich and distinctive
contralto voice.

Imperceptibly, the evening was darkening into dusk and
while his aunt was singing, Matthew sat side by side with
Kitty near the window.

'It was quite a surprise to hear of Ann West's engagement, Kitty,' he teased her. 'You shouldn't let her beat you to the altar, you know. You ought to bring some lucky young man up to scratch yourself.'

He expected her to laugh and disclaim coyly at his gentle teasing, but to his utter astonishment, Kitty flushed deeply and lowered her eyes miserably. There was a silence and then she said unhappily, 'Mama thinks I would do well to accept Andrew – Mr Preston, that is.'

Matthew thought of the gawky young curate with the bobbing Adam's apple and felt uncomfortable as he realized that Kitty, the normally open and cheerful Kitty whom he liked so much, was hurt and upset by his crass remarks. He tried to make light of it by saying, 'Good Lord, and here was I thinking you'd be the bride of an earl at least.' She glanced at him quickly, her full lips trembling a little, but said nothing because Lavinia had been persuaded to sing one last song and everyone was quiet.

Afterwards, as Annie served the tea, he continued the conversation with Kitty very briefly. 'I am surprised by what you have told me, Kitty. I cannot recall the Reverend Preston ever singling you out particularly.'

Kitty said bitterly, 'Oh yes, we see him at church every Sunday, of course, and Charlotte and I are both Sunday school teachers. Mama and the vicar, Mr Swift, are on the board of governors at the workhouse in King's Lynn. Nothing has been said yet, but he seems in favour of Andrew Preston's suit and Andrew often visits us after evensong on Sundays.'

Matthew thought again of the wispy-haired curate with his spindly legs and worthy but dull personality. 'Good Lord, Kitty,' he exclaimed impulsively, 'you cannot marry him. It would be a disaster. The fellow is an absolute bore.'

'I know,' Kitty said, twisting her fingers in her lap. 'But Mama says that the other ladies in Felbrook all like him.'

'Then let one of them marry him,' Matthew said, smiling at her.

'It is all very well for you to say that, but Uncle Bertram is also in favour of my accepting Mr Preston. He thinks that Mr Preston has excellent prospects for advancement. According to Uncle Bertram, we are soul mates.'

Her pretty lips twisted scornfully and Matthew said with some concern, 'You are not engaged to the fellow, are you?'

'No,' Kitty said, but she said it with the sort of hopeless sigh which implied that it was only a question of time before the masterful Uncle Bertram would get his own way. 'Uncle Bertram thinks that if a young lady does not take sensible opportunities for an eligible marriage, she will end up at her last prayers.'

'What fustian,' he said reassuringly. 'But still, do not concern yourself, Kitty. He cannot force you to marry if you do not wish it.'

'He can wear down my determination, though, and I may run out of reasons for resisting.'

'Have no fear,' he said, patting her hand reassuringly. 'I shall think of a resolution to the problem.'

'Will you indeed, Matthew?' She looked up at him tremulously and he saw her eyes were filled with tears. Quickly she turned away and dabbed her eyes with her lace handkerchief. In the past year, since he had been friendly with the Grayson family, he had never known Kitty to cry and he was surprised at the compassion she aroused in him. He patted her hand awkwardly, searching for words of comfort for her, and with a visible effort Kitty tried to smile.

'I am so sorry to be a watering pot, Matthew. I expect you hate missish girls who cry?'

Kitty was such an appealing little thing, he thought, and although he had never before felt any attraction for her in that way, when he had seen her tears, he'd felt a keen desire to help her.

But thinking along those lines was not going to provide him with an answer to the problem of Mr Preston and Uncle Bertram's desire to see Kitty safely married. He must try and calm her and not let her become agitated by the pressures which were being forced on her. He set himself out to be gently amusing and chatted to Kitty of the various clients that he had dealt with lately, all of whom were characters he found entertaining. Before Annie came to offer them both some tea, Matthew had succeeded in calming her and Kitty had regained her composure long before it was time for the Graysons to leave.

CHAPTER FOUR

The day of the riding party started with exceptionally splendid sunshine, even for an Indian summer.

'I know that this weather cannot last,' Jane Grayson sighed. 'Make the most of it, my dears, because tomorrow is removal day and we shall be too busy to think of such fripperies as riding parties for days to come.'

Both her daughters smiled at this, knowing that their mama's consummate organizing ability would make the removal almost painless, and then they continued with their preparations for the picnic. John Dean had brought the horses from Felbrook Manor and by two o'clock, both Charlotte and Kitty were dressed in smart velvet riding habits and were ready to go.

Augusta Casterton was a widow and her only daughter, Aurelia, was her life. Tall, commanding, with advanced social aspirations and very wealthy, Augusta's most burning ambition was to see Aurelia well married. She privately despised Ann West's parents for allowing their daughter to accept an offer of marriage from Robert Thorpe, who in her opinion was but a modest country squire. True, he was wealthy but he would never be a member of the *ton* and Ann would never be accepted in the top echelons of society. Aurelia, on the other hand, would never be allowed to throw herself away on such as he. Since the return of Sir Benjamin and his heir, she'd decided that Hugo Westbury would fulfil the role of her future son-in-law to perfection.

He had graciously accepted her invitation to join the other young people of the neighbourhood for a ride round Mrs Casterton's estate, followed by a lavish and luxurious alfresco meal, but she had seen his acceptance as nothing to signify. Augusta Casterton was a very astute woman of the world. She knew that Mr Westbury would be accepting many invitations and mixing socially with Felbrook society, especially once he was settled at the family home and able to return such hospitality. She guessed that with Sir Benjamin in frail health, Hugo Westbury would soon be seeking a wife. But not just yet, she thought cynically. He would give himself time to survey the possibilities and to play the field.

Perhaps none of the young damsels in the area would please him. Except Aurelia, that is, her one and only chick, in whom she had invested such time and emotional effort and money, of course. Aurelia was sure to please the most exacting gentleman. So Mrs Casterton bided her time and refused to see anything exceptional in his agreeing to attend the picnic. There would be many more invitations for him, especially in the lead up to Christmas, as the other mamas urged their darling daughters to set their caps at such a prize, and she was not going to allow Aurelia to appear to be too eager for a husband.

Even Bertram Grayson had accepted an invitation. Although not riding with the other young people, he arrived exquisitely dressed in a very modish outfit and proceeded to devote himself entirely to Mrs Casterton.

Bowing over her hand, he murmured, 'Charmed, my dear ma'am. A most felicitous day for your outdoor venture. And the sun is set to shine on you and dear Miss Aurelia. So kind to invite an old fuddy-duddy like myself. I am sure I will enjoy being in such gay and youthful company.'

He gave her the benefit of his most attractive smile, while seeming hardly to notice Aurelia's existence. Mrs Casterton liked him on sight. No fortune hunter here, she decided to herself, nor fuddy-duddy either. Rather, a handsome, worldly wise but modest young man who was putting himself out to be civilized and obliging. She immediately entrusted dear Aurelia into his care while she hurried off to check the catering arrangements yet again. Aurelia didn't seem inclined to ride just yet, so Bertram offered his arm with a polite bow and led her off on a decorous walk round the gardens.

The other riders were all young and most of them were acquainted with each other already and all were looking forward to the afternoon picnic. All except for Kitty, that is, for as she and Charlotte had smilingly ridden together to meet Matthew, she'd caught sight of the curate, Andrew Preston. He was mounted on a fine chestnut mare and unlike the other young men of the party, who were in casual country nankeen jackets and breeches, he was dressed rather formally in his dark parson's clothes. Matthew had also noticed him and swiftly positioned himself between Kitty and Andrew Preston, so that the curate's view of her was obscured. In spite of her sweet nature, Kitty was not without her own strategies for dealing with her unwanted suitor and as he called 'Good afternoon, ladies' in his light tenor voice, she took the opportunity to spur her horse a little further away from him and she and Charlotte cantered round a little patch of scrubby trees, closely followed by Matthew King.

'Mrs Casterton has said that we may ride where we will until three o'clock and then we shall meet back here again for a picnic,' Kitty informed Matthew.

He glanced towards Mr Preston, who did not appear to be lacking for female company, and said quietly, 'Should you care to ride towards the park? I have never had the chance to explore the woods on the boundary of Mrs Casterton's estate, where it joins Sir Benjamin's land.'

Both girls were eager. Charlotte knew that it was perfectly in order for her to wander with Matthew when accompanied by her sister and Kitty had no compunction at playing gooseberry if it meant avoiding Andrew Preston.

They had a swift canter as far as the woods and then slowed to a walking pace as they followed the path in single file, ducking to avoid overhanging branches and enjoying the peace and the sweetness of the birdsong. All three of them were quiet as they arrived at the edge of Mrs Casterton's parkland, which adjoined that of Sir Benjamin Westbury and was bounded by a narrow stream. To Charlotte's surprise, they were not alone. There in front of them was Hugo Westbury's great black horse, Gypsy, his long, glossy neck stretched low over the water. She froze as the hated Hugo came into view, walking at the side of Aurelia Casterton, who was on horseback, and her Uncle Bertram. Bringing up the rear was Aurelia's maid.

Charlotte took all this in instantly and would have turned and fled had not Ann West and her brother also arrived, both mounted on glossy chestnut mares. Matthew said with a smile, 'Miss Casterton, Miss West. Gentlemen. Good day.'

Bows and polite greetings were exchanged while Charlotte remained fuming with impatience to be gone from Hugo Westbury's hateful presence. Matthew had no notion of her feelings and was very affable in inviting the others to join their group at the picnic. Ann and her brother declined, saying they were promised to keep company with Robert Thorpe and his party, but Mr Westbury accepted very politely, without even a glance in Charlotte's direction, and so they parted very amicably.

The picnic was planned for three o'clock and Charlotte and her sister were able to have an exhilarating gallop along the boundaries of the Casterton land with Matthew, before they returned to the picnic spot and chose a place under the spreading shade of a large tree. John Dean, Mrs Grayson's groom, helped the girls down and tethered the horses nearby. He spread the picnic rugs and Mrs Casterton's footman came forward with suitable napery, glasses and cutlery and prepared to serve them with some of the delectable food provided by their hostess. The sisters sat with their backs against the warm, gnarled trunk of the tree and Matthew lounged at his ease near to them, plying them with a little of each new delicacy being served by the footman, until they both laughingly cried, 'No more!'

This is how Hugo Westbury saw them as he walked across the grass, followed by a groom leading his huge black stallion. He knew hardly anyone at the picnic, although he recognized Matthew, the young partner in Sir Benjamin's firm of lawyers. Oh, and the unpleasantly aggressive Miss Charlotte Grayson, of course, he thought to himself sardonically. She looked very attractive, laughing in the sunshine, but he noticed that her laughter faded as he approached. Definitely a young lady to be avoided at all costs.

Matthew was the first to greet him and rose to shake his hand. 'Mr Westbury, I am so pleased you have come to join us, sir.'

Hugo bowed civilly to the two girls and he and Matthew joined them on the grass, both young men eating with hearty appetites. Mrs Casterton had an ice house and the lemonade was pleasantly cold as was the chilled white wine and all four of them sipped appreciatively, until finally, their appetites satisfied, Matthew smiled at the newcomer and said, 'Let me raise my glass to you, sir, and welcome you back to Felbrook. I know you will be moving into the family home very soon. Your continuing good health, Mr Westbury, and I hope you will prosper as the manager of the Westbury estate.'

Both Charlotte and Kitty listened to this with conflicting emotions. Kitty, noticing Mr Preston hovering on the edge of their little group, studiously avoided looking at him and hoped his presence would not be noticed. Instead she gazed at Mr Westbury with a very pleasant expression and raised her glass obediently for Matthew's toast. Charlotte, still feeling absolute dislike for the arrogant and obnoxious Hugo Westbury, lifted her glass with a noticeable lack of enthusiasm and didn't smile. None of this was lost on Hugo Westbury, who made a point of being affable to Matthew while ignoring the sisters.

'And how are the investigations continuing, Mr King?'

'Well, some progress, sir. My partner Adam Brown has now definitely identified the unfortunate young man as your late grandfather and he will be able to tell you more when you meet us in the office.' He lowered his voice and said gently, 'Mr Brown has arranged for the remains to be moved to the coroner's office at King's Lynn, where a closer examination may be made.'

Hugo Westbury said, 'I see.' And that was all.

Watching him, Charlotte was fascinated by the expression on his face. Sadness, certainly, and puzzlement as well. As though aware of her scrutiny, he composed his features into an expression of sardonic amusement and said, 'And what about you, Miss Grayson? The deceased was obviously a relative of mine. Do you have any theories as to how the poor fellow could have met his end?'

'No, sir, only what Mr Brown and Mr King here have guessed at.' She spoke stiffly, all the pleasure of the picnic now having been destroyed by the presence of Hugo Westbury and the reminder of the grisly find at Westbury Hall.

He sensed her antipathy and decided to taunt her a little further. 'I trust you are now completely over the shock of your macabre discovery, Miss Grayson, and are ready to move out of the Hall tomorrow?'

His eyes were mocking but she refused to give him the satisfaction of seeing her anger. 'Why, yes, Mr Westbury,' she said in a fair imitation of Ann West's sweet voice. 'Mama has moved heaven and earth so that we will be out tomorrow.' Her raised chin and glinting eyes belied her gentle tones and she gazed at him just as challengingly as she had done when he'd caught her meandering along the muddy path and had narrowly avoided an accident. It was obvious that this angry and unreasonable young woman was determined to cross swords with him yet again. She would regret it, he thought grimly. The female who was able to get the better of Hugo Westbury had not yet been born. He turned towards Matthew King, deliberately cutting her out of the conversation, and proceeded to talk about estate business, the state of the crops and his ideas for the repair and renovation of some of the cottages. This gave Andrew Preston the opportunity he needed to greet Kitty and Matthew King and to sit down near the sisters. They had to greet him politely and, unusually, Charlotte actually welcomed his presence. After all, she could effectively cut out Hugo Westbury now by conversing animatedly with the young curate.

He was most unsuitably dressed for the occasion with his starchy dog collar and the damp, wispy hair was flattened against his brow with the heat. It was obvious that he was eager for an opportunity to chat with Kitty and gradually Charlotte withdrew from conversation with him and looked instead at Matthew and Hugo Westbury. Their conversation had also petered out and they both lay back, relaxing in the warm sun, holding half-empty wine glasses.

Although Hugo Westbury had pointedly ignored Charlotte, he was reclining next to her on the picnic rug, his eyes closed against the glare of the August sun, and she was able to study him unobserved. She took note of the bronzed hands, one of them still languidly holding the glass, the fingers long and slender for a man, his white shirt casually unbuttoned at the wrist and rolled back slightly. Her eyes moved higher to watch the steady rise and fall of his powerful chest. Like all the young men present, he had dispensed with a cravat and there was a sprinkling of fine, dark hair showing through the immaculate shirt, which was open at the neck, revealing the strong, tanned column of his throat. Charlotte studied his profile, the prominent, almost beaky nose and firm, shapely mouth. His cheekbones were aristocratically high and his black lashes hid his unusual blue eyes. One lock of black hair had fallen over his brow and she had a sudden impulse to brush it back. He was frowning slightly because of the sun and she was very conscious of the warmth of his body so near to her own. His grasp on the glass had now become slack. His other hand supported his head and it almost seemed as if he were asleep.

Suddenly, he opened his eyes and for one startling moment her own eyes were locked into his incredible blue gaze. Then, as the warm colour flooded her cheeks, she quickly glanced away and looked instead at her sister and Andrew Preston, still talking stiltedly and seemingly oblivious of her interest in Hugo Westbury.

Hugo Westbury was equally affected when he realized how intense her gaze had been. As he rolled over and sat up, the look he directed at Charlotte was unfathomable. He rose unhurriedly and bowed politely, but with an almost sneering expression as he took his leave of her. Definitely a young woman to be avoided, he told himself.

The atmosphere now became very uncomfortable. Kitty was too polite to express how bored she was with Andrew Preston's conversation. Matthew was puzzled at Charlotte's sulky silence and Andrew Preston, feeling that he had neglected others in his congregation, excused himself and went to greet some of his parishioners.

Hugo sought out his hostess, Mrs Casterton, and her daughter.

He found them seated under an awning erected by Mrs Casterton's indefatigable servants. Mr Bertram Grayson was with them, lolling at his ease on one of Mrs Casterton's delicate gilded chairs. He noticed that Mr Grayson seemed to be very much approved of by the hostess, and was indeed making himself utterly charming to her. Hugo was used to moving in society, and he recognized the polish of one as experienced in polite circles as Bertram Grayson. His dress was the epitome of modern fashion and his figure, although a trifle portly, was undeniably graceful. His address, though a little pompous, was perfectly sophisticated.

Bertram rose as soon as Hugo approached and greeted him smoothly, as though he were in charge. 'Ah, Mr Westbury. Well met, sir. May I direct the footman to bring you some refreshment?'

Hugo noticed Mrs Casterton's beaming approval of this and glanced at Aurelia. Her rather plain little face was set in a satisfied smile. It was obvious that like her mama she was pleased with the attentions of Bertram Grayson. Mrs Casterton was a widow, he reflected. To have a surrogate husband or son, or indeed any male substitute for family support, must be very gratifying for her. Bertram Grayson was obviously fulfilling that role very satisfactorily.

Augusta Casterton had been extremely busy in organizing this event. The catering arrangements, the difficult butler in charge of the wine cellar, dear Aurelia's smart outfit, all the invitations and the replies; all these responsibilities had fallen on Augusta's shoulders. She was pleased and grateful that, as a widow, without a man about the house, she seemed able to count on Bertram Grayson.

Hugo took in all these observations, while accepting a glass of chilled white wine, and watched as Bertram Grayson bowed before Miss Casterton and her mama, asking if they would care for any refreshments. Aurelia's heavy expression softened into something more pleasant and her mama positively beamed as Mr Grayson snapped his fingers imperiously to the footman, glorying in such masterful charge of their comfort and pleasure.

Hugo chose a seat next to Aurelia and set himself the task of being polite and pleasant to her. Not a very obviously attractive chit, he thought to himself, but perhaps he should take the trouble to get to know her. She and her mama were, after all, now his neighbours. He hoped there was more to Miss Casterton than at first appeared. He was amused to observe the charm and gallantry lavished on both mother and daughter by Mr Grayson and after some further polite conversation, he took his leave.

Charlotte and Kitty didn't linger for very long after the picnic. Pleading their need to help dear Mama with last-minute packing, they made their way back to Westbury Hall, accompanied by Matthew. In spite of Mrs Grayson's warm invitation to him to stay for supper, Matthew was firm in his resolve not to impose on her at such a busy time and left, promising to come round early to help with the move.

Both Charlotte and Kitty were somewhat reticent about the riding party and answered their mother's questions briefly and without enthusiasm. Finally, Jane Grayson laughed and said, 'You seem to have had a dismal time of it in spite of so looking forward to the occasion. What was wrong? I can hardly believe Augusta Casterton penny-pinched on the food and refreshments. The weather was a little cooler this afternoon, I suppose. Was it that the company was uncongenial?'

'No, of course not,' Charlotte snapped. 'And Matthew stayed with us all the time.'

'What, then?'

'Aurelia Casterton has turned into a real flirt-gill just lately,' Charlotte complained. 'And Hugo Westbury was as unpleasant as ever. . . .'

'And Andrew Preston would not stop talking,' Kitty chimed in.

'Dear, me,' Mrs Grayson laughed. 'What a miserable time you had, to be sure. And not even the solace of a good supper. Mrs Palmer has given notice that it will be only a cold collation this evening. She will start breakfast very early in the morning so that all the vegetables and victuals will be packed up for the move.'

The girls were unaccountably subdued and even the excitement of moving failed to enthuse them.

On the next day, however, with their usual youthful exuberance, they were up betimes and waiting, ready and impatient for John Dean to bring round the horses. Jimmy the carter had already loaded their movable pieces of furniture and crates of books and china. He would be making the journey to Felbrook Manor as many times as was necessary to remove everything from Westbury Hall. Hugo Westbury was as good as his word and before the furniture had even reached the Hall gates, a small army of domestics, recruited from the village, was moving purposefully up the drive. All were armed with brooms, mops and carpet beaters, ready to clean the Hall in preparation for Sir Benjamin and Hugo Westbury, and Charlotte scowled as she passed them.

Jane Grayson's childhood home had originally been a working farmhouse and when they reached the gate, the two girls were very surprised to see that there were none of the outbuildings and barns usually associated with animal husbandry.

'Well, dears,' Jane said. 'In the days when transport and communications were unreliable, my grandfather's prosperous estate had provided all the necessities of life. Gradually, however, the estate became less self-sufficient and as roads and waterways improved, luxuries from abroad, like Madeira wine and bohea tea, became essential to ladies and gentlemen of quality. My own parents found that servants were not so easy to keep as they had once been and so the dairy, brewhouse and bakehouse were done away with even before my dear papa died. Of course, the stables have been kept.'

Charlotte and Kitty could only vaguely remember Felbrook Manor from their own early childhood and they spent the first hour in their new home exploring. The entrance hall led to a gracious panelled and papered staircase and on the right of the hall was a small sitting-room that their mama had designated as Mrs Palmer's. The library and study were combined and the kitchen had a separate game larder, where game birds could be hung and prepared for the table. Both the dining-room and the drawing-room were very spacious, the dining-room able to seat twenty and the drawing-room with deeply curved cornices around the ceiling, beautifully decorated with moulded flowers and swags of plaster foliage. Both the girls were enchanted by the delicate rose- and cream-coloured carpet, ordered by their mama well in advance of the move. Jane Grayson had also ordered new beds and various pieces of fine drawing-room furniture from a reputable cabinet maker in Norwich and these items had already been delivered to their new home.

'Now come and see your bedrooms, girls. A surprise for you. We are so spacious here and you have your own rooms.'

This was indeed a surprise. They'd never had a room each at the vicarage and the rather gloomy bedrooms at Westbury Hall had been so full of dark antique furniture that Charlotte and Kitty had got the two hired men to move various pieces out of the pleasantest room, to make more space, and they had shared the large four-poster bed.

'Luxury indeed,' Charlotte said. 'Thank you, dearest Mama. It is so thoughtful of you to know what we wanted.'

'Yes. Thank you, Mama,' Kitty echoed dutifully, but Charlotte saw the faintest shadow cross her sister's pleasant, open face and wondered with a pang if Kitty really did want her own room and whether her sister felt quite ready to sleep alone. It wouldn't be so easy to have their late-night confidences or fits of girlish giggles now, she thought.

But Kitty's expression turned so quickly into smiles of admiration for the delicate new side tables and wash stand that Charlotte thought that perhaps she had imagined it.

The morning passed very quickly with all the unpacking and arranging of the furniture. With Matthew's help, Mrs Grayson had directed the hanging of the curtains in the main bedchambers before luncheon. This meal was merely a picnic of cold meats and wine in the grand dining-room, but as usual in the Grayson household, it had been enjoyed with much pleasure.

Afterwards, Matthew helped Charlotte to unpack the books and arrange them on the library shelves, while Kitty helped her mother to make up the beds.

'This is such a good job done, Kitty darling,' Mrs Grayson said. 'And tonight we shall be so comfortable in our new house. Now we have finished for the moment, run down and ask Mrs Palmer if she needs any help with anything.'

Kitty duly ran down, but Mrs Palmer was as always too prideful to admit to needing help with anything, especially from a young lady, who was in her opinion 'just a young lass' and not used to hard toil. Easier to do it with Phoebe, she thought, especially as her mistress had engaged another maid to help with the work and she was due to start first thing in the morning. She thanked Kitty very graciously. 'I shan't be needin' yer, Miss Kitty,' she said. 'Much better for you to help your ma, wi' the beds.'

Kitty ran back up the stairs, only to be told by Mrs Grayson that the men had come to help with shifting the furniture and arranging the drawing-room. 'Perhaps you could look in the butler's pantry and see that the cutlery and china are safely stowed, my love,' she said, and with the help of a little stable lad, Kitty had accomplished this in less than an hour. She went over every item of cutlery with Robert's special cloth and stored them away safely and then sent the lad to help John Dean. It seemed a long time since luncheon and even longer to dinner and Kitty felt sleepy. She settled down on the soft cushions of the window seat to have a little rest. Her eyelids drooped and without being aware of it, Kitty fell asleep, one arm dangling over the edge of the cushions with the silver cloth still clutched in her hand.

She was awoken by a light touch. Matthew had been sent down for another pair of scissors to release the string on a pack of books and finding Kitty asleep, tried to remove the cloth without wakening her, and replace it on the sideboard. She awoke immediately, flushed with sleep and unable at first to remember where she was.

'Hello,' Matthew said gently. 'You are obviously sleeping on the job and that could mean instant dismissal if you are found out.'

She sat up, struggling to regain her composure and smoothed her gown. 'I . . . I must have fallen asleep . . . What time is it? Where is Charlotte?'

'It is after four o'clock. Charlotte is still sorting books. She needs these scissors. We shall soon be finished.'

He stood in front of her, without picking up the scissors, but merely staring down at her as though it were the first time that they'd met. Kitty looked up at him, smiling innocently and meeting his eyes with her clear gaze. 'I suppose you were up very early,' he said. He was surprised by the feelings that Kitty had aroused in him when he'd come across her asleep and so vulnerable, like a child, he thought. He was startled by a sudden feeling of wanting to love her and look after her. He turned his thoughts away from these emotions immediately. He had no business feeling like that about Kitty. After all, he was practically betrothed to Charlotte.

'Mama did not need me and . . . and the silver and china is all put away now. I must have fallen asleep. . . .'

'And that is a hanging offence,' he laughed softly, feeling an overwhelming desire to kiss her.

She immediately joined in with his pretended censure. 'But please do not give me away, guv. I shall not do it again. Word of honour.' She stood up, still smiling at him, and Matthew took her hands in his, looking down into her steady grey eyes.

'Very well. I will not tell. Just this once,' he said smiling.

She didn't look away, but met his gaze innocently. He continued to hold one of her hands to steady her as she swayed slightly, her face still upturned to his, her lips gently parted. He raised her hand and kissed it, determined that this little interlude should stop before it went any further, but he was unable to prevent himself from planting a light kiss on her soft lips, and then he drew back, astounded at what he had done.

'I think we should go and find Charlotte and your mama,' he said gently and Kitty turned obediently, although her head was drooping a little. They both went to the library to help Charlotte with the last of the books. Neither of them spoke again until Matthew finally took his leave and went home to Primrose Cottage.

The night wasn't as comfortable for Kitty as Mrs Grayson had foretold. She couldn't help thinking of Matthew when he'd found her asleep in the dining-room. She had longed for him to be a little less of a brother and be a little more loving, but it was hopeless. Charlotte was so beautiful and vivacious, he couldn't help caring for her, she realized that. She turned over restlessly in the brand new comfortable bed and caught her breath on a sob. No! She must not cry. Crying never helped. She loved her sister and wanted her happiness. She wiped the tears from her lashes and tried to go to sleep, comforting herself with the thought that Matthew had wanted to kiss her as much as she had wanted it herself.

Meanwhile, Matthew's silent preoccupation with his own thoughts had not passed unnoticed by his loving Aunt Lavinia. She had made little progress with any conversation during supper and attributed his silence to tiredness, an opinion which was strengthened by his early retirement to bed, without even their usual game of cards.

In spite of his early night, Matthew also slept badly. He had no wish to make Kitty unhappy, she was such a dear, good girl, so innocent and vulnerable. In spite of her appeal for him, he was as good as betrothed to Charlotte and he could hardly tell her that he no longer loved her. Whatever he did or didn't do, he was bound to hurt someone. He cursed silently, turned over again and tried once more to sleep.

CHAPTER FIVE

Charlotte was awake early the next morning and was somewhat startled to be served her morning chocolate not by Phoebe but by a young girl she had never seen before. She blinked at the handsome country girl, with her rosy cheeks and fine black eyes.

'I do not think I know you,' she said as she sat up and took the cup from her.

'Nell, Miss Grayson,' the girl said briskly. 'I got a place wi' your mama and very glad I am, miss. I worked for Squire Perkins' wife for three years, but it were dull, Miss Charlotte, them being elderly, like. Your ma says I'm to wait on you and Miss Kitty and I'm pleased about that. I hope as I shall give satisfaction.'

'I should not think you will find it dull with my mama,' Charlotte said. 'She is a positive whirlwind of activity and there is always so much to do when you move to a different house.'

'Yes, miss, I've noticed that; it's why I'm so pleased to get a place here. And no gentlemen in the house to be a nuisance, either,' she added as an afterthought. 'I shall go and get your water now. I were not expectin' you to be up and ready, see, or I would have done it sooner. Are you wishing to get up now, miss?'

Charlotte decided she liked young Nell and got out of bed straight away. It was a peach of a morning and she determined to go for a walk before breakfast.

Twenty minutes later, dressed in her newest and most becoming blue walking-dress, she crossed what had once been the laundry court in days gone by and walked over the crescent lawn to a little creaking old gate, set snugly in the mellow brick wall, and then she was out in the green lane which led directly to the village. She wondered how Lucy Baker did. She knew Lucy had recently had a new little brother and she'd taken care to put a bright gold sovereign in her reticule for the latest Baker child. Perhaps it was a little early to call at the Bakers' cottage, but if she saw Lucy playing out on the lane. . . .

Thoughts of Lucy immediately put her in mind of Hugo Westbury. How she detested him, especially when she remembered the arrogant way that he had stepped forward with his handkerchief to stem poor little Lucy's tears. Still, the child had seemed to trust him and had accepted a ride on his huge black horse without appearing to be nervous—

Her train of thought was cut off abruptly and she gave a start of horror as she neared the Bakers' cottage. Coming towards her was none other than Hugo Westbury himself and beside him Aurelia Casterton, simpering up at him and then turning to wave with smiling condescension to little Lucy Baker and her beaming mother who both stood at the cottage door. Aurelia's maid trailed behind them, holding a little bundle of clothes suitable for a new baby. It was too late to turn and go back and so she was forced to greet Aurelia and her companion as calmly as she could.

Hugo Westbury bowed politely and wished her 'good morning' but Aurelia, triumphant at managing to gain such a handsome and eligible escort, smiled patronizingly on Charlotte and said with false brightness, 'Miss Grayson. Good morning. Is it possible that you have the same errand as ourselves? Mama heard about the Bakers' new baby and discovered that they are tenants on the Westbury estate. She has prevailed on dear Mr Westbury to escort me to the cottage to offer a little christening gift.'

Charlotte noticed that 'dear Mr Westbury' was gazing at the Bakers' yew hedge with studied indifference as though he wished to be elsewhere and she quickly cast about in her mind for some way of escaping from her situation. It was impossible. She couldn't meet two of her neighbours at the Bakers' cottage and pretend that she wasn't visiting the family.

There was a tense silence, which even the gushing Aurelia seemed unable to break. Hugo Westbury now turned his sardonic gaze on Charlotte, fully understanding her discomfiture and waiting to see how she would resolve it. She seemed determined to avoid his company but at the same time to carry on some semblance of politeness and good manners. In spite of his unwillingness to admit it, he found her completely lovely. Her hair, under the brim of her charming little straw hat, curled round her face in a way that made her grey eyes seem softer and more luminous. Her blue walking gown clung enticingly to her slender curves, its rather severe style accentuating rather than hiding her femininity. Compared to the dumpy and girlish Miss Aurelia Casterton, with her round face and rather indefinite features, Charlotte was a coolly beautiful and extremely desirable young woman.

As if sensing his gaze, Charlotte turned to look at him, slight colour staining her cheeks. Her eyes met his as challengingly as usual and a sudden disturbing awareness of desire shot through him. He tore his eyes away from hers with difficulty, wondering what the devil was wrong with him. He broke the uncomfortable silence himself, by saying stiffly, 'I think we should not impose our company on the family at such a busy time. Miss Casterton and I will not stay longer than five minutes. Should you care to accompany us, Miss Grayson, I am sure Mrs Baker will not think that three is the proverbial crowd.'

Two playful kittens suddenly shot out of the cottage,

pretending to fight, and he gave her one of his rare, unexpected smiles. 'And if you could use your influence as a Sunday school teacher to prevail on little Lucy not to let her cats claw my coat, I would be eternally grateful.'

'Yes ... yes, of course I will.' Surprisingly, and much against her will, Charlotte found herself smiling back at him. She heard his sharp intake of breath as their eyes met and she forced herself to look away.

The moment was broken by Aurelia who, displeased at being ignored, took the baby clothes from her maid and flounced up the path to Mrs Baker, who welcomed them into the tiny cottage. 'Ain't not much room to sit, my lady,' she said to Aurelia, and she swept a bench by the side of the fire with her hand. 'But our Lucy's that glad to see you, Miss Grayson. Come you forward, Lucy, and bid Miss Grayson "good day", my dear.'

Lucy stepped forward, smiling shyly, and put a finger under her chin as her mother had taught her and bobbed a charming little curtsy.

'Why, that was very well done, Lucy,' Charlotte exclaimed and, cupping the little girl's face in both hands, she kissed her gently on the forehead. The only other chair in the room was dragged forward for Hugo Westbury and in no time at all Charlotte was nursing baby Billy and Lucy had fetched Bruno, her favourite little kitten, to show to Hugo. Aurelia was noticeably quiet and after giving the baby clothes to Mrs Baker, sat and stared at nothing in particular, obviously bored and wishing to be somewhere else. Lucy danced excitedly round Hugo, reminding him of the ride she'd had on Gypsy and obviously longing to repeat it, and he involuntarily glanced at Charlotte. For some reason, the sight of her holding the baby was so extremely tender and beautiful he could hardly bear to look away. But Lucy had by now given him Bruno to hold and as his eyes again met Charlotte's, he gave her a little comical signal with raised eyebrows and an almost helpless expression. Involuntarily she returned his signal with an understanding grin and a raised eyebrow of her own. It was as though they were communicating in a secret language across the room which only they understood. She knew exactly what he wanted, which was rescue from Lucy's friendly kitten. Having put Billy tenderly in his cradle, the sovereign tucked under his blanket, she moved over to Hugo and tried carefully to pick up Bruno, who refused to move. Hugo was acutely aware of her and of her soft perfume as she held the kitten in one hand and began to gently disengage its tiny claws from the expensive superfine cloth of his fashionable jacket with the other. Her nearness was so seductive that for a moment he closed his eyes, breathing in the scent of her and feeling her gentle fingers fumbling against his chest. He felt the soft flesh of her arm brush against his cheek and opened his eyes again. A mistake. Her lovely peachy face was now so very temptingly near to his own, it would take only a second to move his lips to hers, but beyond her, he could see Miss Casterton, expressing rigid disapproval in every line of her body. He attempted to break the tension by saying, 'Have I now been finally extricated from Bruno's wicked claws, Miss Grayson?'

'Yes, indeed, sir,' she said. For some reason she felt a trifle breathless. She'd been very conscious of the way her arm had brushed his cheek and of the hardness of his body beneath the smart coat as she'd disengaged the little kitten from him. He had felt in no way tense or aggressive, but utterly relaxed as though he were enjoying it, in spite of not wanting his coat to be ruined.

She gathered herself together with an effort and said coolly, 'Now come, Lucy dear, and take Bruno to his mama, for we must be going.'

Aurelia sprang up with alacrity, and Mrs Baker ushered them to the door, smiling and waving. Lucy danced down the path ahead of them and looked up at Hugo adoringly. 'And please, sir, Mr Wessb'ry, sir, can I have another ride on Gypsy?'

'That depends on whether Miss Grayson is available to accompany us,' he said gravely.

Charlotte's eyes flew to meet his, but his face was expressionless and for once, she was unable to think of anything to say.

'We shall have to see, Lucy dear,' was all she could come up with.

She noticed Aurelia's lips tighten angrily and was glad when they reached the turning to Felbrook Manor and she bade them farewell.

When she arrived home, order had succeeded whatever chaos had reigned on the removal day and although it was obvious that her mama was a little weary, she was nevertheless in good spirits. 'Uncle Bertram is to visit again tomorrow,' Jane Grayson said. 'And this morning while you were out, we had an invitation from Mr and Mrs West to the betrothal ball for Ann and Robert Thorpe, a week on Friday. We must think of a gift, girls. I am sure I wish them happy, but I think there are those who feel that dear Ann could have set her sights higher than the son of a country squire.'

'But if she truly loves him. . . .' Kitty murmured.

Charlotte looked at her. What did Kitty know of love, she wondered? She'd noticed Andrew Preston's attempts to gain Kitty's interest at the picnic, but she couldn't believe that Kitty had developed a *tendre* for the gawky curate. Surely not. She had a sudden mental image of Kitty walking in Lavinia's garden with Matthew, raising her open, young face to look up at him, just like one of his Aunt Lavinia's sunflowers, she thought, and she wondered fleetingly if in fact Kitty was in love with Matthew.

Miraculously, Felbrook Manor was now almost straight. The kitchen was arranged to Mrs Palmer's liking with every pan and dish washed and stowed in its rightful place and the two maids, Nell and Phoebe, had unpacked their modest belongings in the attic bedrooms and were already at home in their new situation. Charlotte and Kitty had supervised the disposal of their own clothes and belongings, so that the tireless Jane Grayson could see to the arrangement of the furniture and have a bedroom prepared for Uncle Bertram, who was not expected until the early evening. They were now free to relax in a cosy room on the ground floor which had once been a spacious study. It was a light, airy room with several comfortable chairs and a substantial fireplace and after lunch the three of them gathered there to read and sew.

But they were not relaxed for very long. Robert, acting as butler, came in with a small silver tray on which was a card from Sir Benjamin Westbury, presenting his compliments and begging to be allowed to call on the following day at 11 a.m. Jane Grayson was now all of a twitter to check that the house was truly fit to entertain a visitor of such standing as Sir Benjamin Westbury. Finally, reassured that the drawing-room was pristine, that the decanters were sparkling and that there was a good selection of biscuits and sweetmeats with which to entertain guests, she sank back into her chair and resumed her sewing, until such time as Uncle Bertram would arrive. He was rather a mixed blessing, Jane reflected placidly. Although Bertram was still young and good-looking, she realized he was becoming very pompous and self-opinionated, almost offensive, in fact. And yet . . . and yet her poor dead husband had loved him dearly. They had been devoted brothers and though the hard-headed and rakish Bertram had often scoffed at Henry's idea of taking Holy Orders, Jane knew that he was basically a kind man and had been inordinately proud of his brother's calling. She sighed. Unfortunately the girls were both too young and inexperienced to recognize Bertram's decent human qualities beneath his bombastic exterior. She wished with all her heart that Bertram could find a suitable young woman and settle down. She was sure he would make a kind and loving husband and father, if he met the right one. It was so unfortunate that Charlotte and Kitty were impatient of their uncle's unsuitable jokes and patronizing opinions. There was always tension when he came to stay as though they were all just on the verge of a violent argument. She'd just have to do her best to avoid family conflict, she decided, as she cut off her embroidery thread with a decisive snap of the scissors.

Adam Brown arrived at 10.30 the following morning and at precisely 11 a.m. the drawing-room door opened to show Robert bowing lower than usual as he said very respectfully, 'Sir Benjamin Westbury and Mr Hugo Westbury to see you, madam.'

From earliest childhood, Jane Grayson had known of Sir Benjamin Westbury, who had once lived 'up at the Hall' and had heard vague though impressive tales of his wealth and power and the animosity between his two younger brothers, but even her steady grey eyes widened somewhat to behold what had become of this rich nabob, who had built up a second massive fortune in India. The tall, powerful, most revered and respected landowner in the county was now a shambling wreck. The disabilities of his old age were far more pronounced than they'd seemed when he'd entered the village church the other Sunday. His white head was bowed and he leaned far more heavily on his stick than he had done when he'd attended Sunday service. His other hand clasped the arm of the tall, handsome Mr Hugo Westbury.

'Brown, introduce me to all here, if you please.'

The voice, though soft and almost feeble, was yet so compelling and full of authority that Jane Grayson and her daughters were each unable to take their eyes off him.

'Sir Benjamin, may I present to you Mrs Jane Grayson, and her daughters, Miss Charlotte Grayson and Miss Kitty Grayson. You may perhaps have some recollection of Mrs Grayson – Saunders, as she then was – who resided here until her marriage?'

'Hardly, hardly, I am afraid, Brown,' sighed Sir Benjamin, sinking into the armchair which Adam Brown pulled forward for him. 'Although, now I come to look at the eldest girl. . . .

Yes . . . I have a recollection of you, Mrs Grayson . . . you must have been very like her, my dear.' He sighed again and surveyed Charlotte carefully from under his bushy white brows. It was a keenly searching glance that lingered over her beautiful, proud young face, passed over her slim body and paused at her dainty satin slippers and then up again to the brilliant grey-green eyes which met his own so fearlessly.

Hugo Westbury had remained standing and, although feigning indifference, was watching Sir Benjamin's reaction to Charlotte Grayson with interest.

'Please be seated,' Jane Grayson said and there was a moment's activity as her daughters and the visitors disposed themselves about the room.

Adam Brown cleared his throat and said, 'I have taken the liberty of inviting Mr Harry Bunfield to join us today, ma'am. He is staying at The Brook in the village and I think he will be invaluable in helping us with our enquiries into the sad death of Mr Charles Westbury.'

No one spoke. Sir Benjamin merely nodded, his face expressionless and everyone present appeared to be waiting for some guidance from the lawyer.

Matthew King moved to sit by Charlotte in the window. There was an expectant pause.

At that moment, Robert appeared once more to announce, 'Mr Harry Bunfield from Bow Street, ma'am,' before retiring once more.

Bunfield was a powerfully built man in his early forties, a neat and tidy person with crisp white collar and trim blue coat, his boots polished to perfection, and he carried a short staff with a discreet crown at the end, as a symbol of his authority. His eyes, as he surveyed the room, were as bright as the buttons on his red waistcoat and were of a glittering blue.

'Your servant, ladies and gentlemen,' he said and gave a bob of his head, halfway between a nod and a bow.

Jane Grayson indicated a seat for him and Adam Brown

opened the proceedings with greetings for Bunfield and further introductions. 'Well now, Mr Bunfield,' he said. 'We would very much like to hear your report concerning the recent ghastly discovery at Westbury Hall.'

'Mr Brown, sir, the Felbrook constable attended the preliminary inquest held at The Swan in King's Lynn on 18 August when Mr Bates declared a provisional verdict of "Murder by person or persons unknown". Further evidence will have to be gathered and presented to the examining magistrate if the culprit is ever to be identified.'

He took out a somewhat battered notebook and read from it. ' "From enquiries already carried out, the body has been identified as that of Mr Charles Westbury, youngest brother to Sir Benjamin and grandfather to Mr Hugo Westbury, who died of a fatal stab wound to his back, delivered with some force, if the coroner's surgeon is to be believed." '

'How shocking,' Jane Grayson murmured.

'Shocking indeed, ma'am.'

'And there is no doubt as to the identity of my grandfather?' Hugo Westbury spoke very quietly. 'And yet, we, my parents, that is, were led to believe that my grandfather and his wife had perished on the *Golden Maiden* in a terrible storm off the coast of Cromer, notorious for the sandbanks which lurk beneath the waters.'

'There seems no doubt of the identity of the deceased, sir, but I shall be making further enquiries there.'

He turned to Sir Benjamin, whose frail shoulders seemed to be drooping more than ever. 'They were on their way to Holland, as I understand it, sir?'

'Yes. The child, Hugo's father, was left with his nurse, but I know not the purpose of their voyage.'

'It was to sell some diamonds, Sir Benjamin.' Harry Bunfield spoke quietly, but took note of Sir Benjamin's deliberately blank expression. 'And the contemporary reports of the sinking of the *Golden Maiden* state that not all the passengers and crew were accounted for. There is no record of Mr

Charles Westbury's body being recovered, so he was lost, presumed drowned, but I expect you knew that, sir?'

'Yes, of course,' Sir Benjamin said reluctantly. 'At the memorial service for my brother and his wife, hers was the only coffin.'

There was a silence, broken again by Harry Bunfield. 'There were two other known survivors, sir, and they were Mr Tobias Todd, a tutor from Lynn Grammar School, and a young sailor, name of Ted Rudkin, and happen if they're still alive, I shall definitely pay them a visit, Sir Benjamin.'

Adam Brown passed across to Hugo a small roll of velvet fabric containing the signet ring and the battered silver watch. 'The coroner has agreed to release the body for burial, sir, and has requested that I give these remaining items to you, as the next of kin.'

Charlotte looked curiously at Hugo Westbury, but apart from a strained whiteness round his mouth, he gave no sign of any of the shock and horror that Mr Bunfield's investigations had produced.

Sir Benjamin seemed to have shrunk even smaller and his shoulders were more bowed than ever. He sighed as he spoke. 'Alas, my poor dear brother, Charles. He was the youngest and most handsome of us . . . the most loved . . . the most blessed. He shall in due season be honourably interred with his dear wife in the family vault. Hugo will make the funeral arrangements.'

It was at this point that Jane Grayson rang for Phoebe, who brought in wine and refreshments. Jane noticed the way that Charlotte had looked so intently at Hugo Westbury and, without appearing obvious, she positioned herself near to him, offering him a glass of red wine and saying in a voice of utmost concern, 'I am so sorry that you should have had such a sad shock at your homecoming, sir. Please accept my condolences.'

He gave her a smile of great sweetness. 'Thank you, ma'am. But these things happen and at least he may be given a Christian burial.'

With her skill as a good listener and receiver of confidences, Jane Grayson remained silent and looked at him so sympathetically that he was moved to add, 'I have no recollection of my grandparents and my mother and father both died young, so it is not so devastating an experience as it could have been.'

Jane Grayson took the liberty of pressing his hand in silent commiseration and tactfully signalled to Phoebe to refill his glass. What an attractive and sensitive young man. What a pity there seemed to be so much animosity still between himself and dear Charlotte. She looked across at her eldest daughter and could tell by the carefully composed expression of indifference on her face that Charlotte had listened to every word of the conversation and Jane smiled to herself. Perhaps, she thought, Matthew was not, after all, the right one for Charlotte. . . . She looked speculatively at her beautiful, spirited elder daughter and then back to the darkly handsome Hugo Westbury. What an attractive couple they would make, to be sure.

Hugo, also acutely conscious of the beautiful Miss Charlotte Grayson, looked across at her over the rim of his wine glass. She was listening respectfully to something Sir Benjamin was telling her and her lovely head was bent towards him, so she could catch what his thin old voice was saying. She offered Sir Benjamin a ratafia biscuit and refilled his sherry glass. All this was done with the utmost kindness and solicitude. What a contrast to her usual confrontational attitude, Hugo thought. She looked so beautiful and womanly, he was forced to make a comparison between her and the insipid Aurelia Casterton, who lacked all Charlotte's address and grace and could only gaze up at a fellow with those limpid, vacant eyes.

To the devil with his decision to stay away from Charlotte. At the next brief lull in the conversation, Hugo turned to her and said quietly, 'The weather seems set to remain fine, Miss Grayson. Perhaps you could be prevailed upon to grant Lucy Baker's wish and come for a ride with us on Sunday? If her mama agrees, I thought a short ride on Gypsy, after Sunday school, perhaps?'

He made his request with such polite deference that she looked at him with suspicion. It was true he had acted the perfect gentleman all morning, but speak as you find, she thought grimly. Her memory of the arrogant way he had dealt with the lease of Westbury Hall still rankled.

He was waiting for her answer, politely patient, one black eyebrow raised in amused enquiry, then he said softly, 'There is no need to look so serious, Miss Grayson. I am merely inviting you on a little outing to please the child, not a public hanging.'

'Odious man.' But she was obliged to smile and thought quickly of the little muslin dress she was making for Lucy. If she worked at it, she could have it finished for Sunday and that would be two pleasures for the child.

'Well?'

'Well, what?'

'Well, am I going to have the pleasure of your company, Miss Grayson? If so, I shall approach Lucy's mama for her approval.'

'Very well, I thank you, Mr Westbury. I know Lucy has very few treats and I am sure she will enjoy it.'

'And you, Miss Grayson?'

'I beg your pardon?' she said stiffly.

'Will you also enjoy it?'

She looked at him in surprise. In spite of herself, she knew she was colouring up. His eyes, incredibly blue in the morning light, were crinkled with amusement. She was surprised at allowing herself to be talked into this proposed treat for little Lucy Baker so easily. But of course, from the first, it had been impossible to deny Hugo Westbury anything that he really wanted. She wondered ruefully if it would always be thus, but she answered coolly enough, 'I hope to do so, sir. And Lucy's enjoyment will be most important, of course.'

'Of course.' He said it without a trace of irony.

'Very well, then, we are agreed. Sunday at three outside the church, unless Mrs Baker refuses permission, of course.' She kept her voice light and smiled, knowing Mrs Baker would be only too pleased for Lucy to have such a treat. Then she excused herself politely to go and chat to Adam Brown, who was standing with Harry Bunfield, still discussing the shipwreck of the *Golden Maiden*.

Hugo turned towards Kitty and enquired politely how she did, and praised the smooth way that the house move had been effected by the two girls and their mother. Kitty tried valiantly to keep her end up, but was somewhat overawed by him and faltered in her replies, until she was rescued by Sir Benjamin, who, raising himself painfully from his armchair and leaning heavily on his stick, came to say that he and Hugo must be going and to bid farewell to them all.

It seemed almost impossible to settle down to some sewing again, but Charlotte at least had an incentive now and took up the little dress that she was making for Lucy with the intention of finishing it by Sunday. It was a white muslin with a pale blue dot, made from a piece of material in Jane Grayson's fabric box. She knew it would suit Lucy's blonde prettiness to perfection and she planned to take it round to the cottage as soon as it was finished so that Lucy might wear it as her Sunday best.

All was peaceful until such time as Uncle Bertram arrived, beautifully dressed as was his wont, and as always more than ready to do justice to the ample dinner served up by Mrs Palmer.

'Although, as you see, 'tis a bit of a force pot,' she declared as she set the steaming dishes on the table.

But Uncle Bertram waved her apologies away most affably. Not only was he being treated with the kindness and consideration that was usual from Jane Grayson, but the news of Sir Benjamin's visit added a decided stimulus to his already inflated feeling of self-importance. Bolstered up by a most substantial meal and several glasses of mellow port wine, he took up his customary stance in front of the drawing-room fire and prepared to hold forth to his captive audience. He was determined to inform Jane and her daughters of the procedures to be followed when an inquest was arranged. Jane's efforts to avoid this melancholy subject were in vain. Although she tactfully sent Kitty and Charlotte on a couple of tasks to try to get them out of the room, while their uncle proceeded to discourse at length on the unsavoury details of the murder, he refused to take the hint. When the girls returned, he was still in full flow about the inquest.

'Bates is the county coroner, you know, Jane, and he routinely holds inquests in public houses.'

Jane was silent and Bertram took this as a sign that she was interested in the macabre subject.

'Good idea, really,' he continued. 'There needs to be a room, you see, where the body can be laid out and where it can be viewed by the jurors. I know the landlord at The Swan is always happy to oblige – the jurors always need drinks and refreshments after their unhappy ordeal. I suppose Bates called Dr Armstrong to view the body, but from what you have said, there was no doubt precious little of it left to view and of course Armstrong will have been paid his expenses. A sorry business, my dear, but, still, Bates will have had to assign a cause of death. I wonder when the funeral will be?'

Kitty shuddered and said that she hoped it would not be until after Ann West's betrothal party. Uncle Bertram said pompously that these important family occasions took some time to organize. There were important people to be contacted. Distant, even far-flung relations who must be given notice and opportunity to attend the ceremony. The family vault would have to be prepared, accommodation made ready at Westbury Hall. A thousand and one things would be required to be organized by Sir Benjamin's great-nephew in preparation for the obsequies of his grandfather, Charles.

Charlotte remained silent, her head bent over her needlework, wondering if she could find a nice piece of wide ribbon in Mama's sewing box to make a sash for Lucy's dress, while her Uncle Bertram continued to pontificate about the funeral. And so the evening passed pleasantly enough, with Jane and her daughters, as if by mutual consent, giving minimum encouragement to Uncle Bertram's speculations.

Charlotte was not the world's best needlewoman, being too impatient, untidy and not remotely interested in sewing, but she was determined to make the dress a success.

As it happened, it was finished well in time and she took it round to the Bakers' cottage before the Sunday school.

'Oh, look, Ma, at what Miss Grayson's brought for me!' Lucy flew across the room to hug Charlotte, watched smilingly by Mrs Baker, and she said excitedly, 'Oh, thank you, Miss Grayson. And look! Ma's bought some ribbons from the gypsy woman.'

Charlotte looked at the small, heart-shaped face, the smiling lips and bright eyes. Even the gold curls bobbing about on the smooth, babyish forehead seemed to quiver with the excitement of it all and Charlotte was glad that she'd made the effort to finish the dress.

At three o'clock, Lucy was outside the church, hopping excitedly from one foot to the other when Hugo Westbury arrived. After the formal greetings, the groom held the horse's head and Hugo lifted Lucy up on to the huge black hunter. Charlotte had decided to have Nell to accompany her, rather than Phoebe, and they set off in silence.

Not so Lucy Baker. She kept up a constant stream of chatter, mainly directed at Hugo. 'I love this horse, Mr Wessb'ry,' she said, 'and I love my new dress what Miss Grayson has made for me.'

'It is very pretty and smart,' Hugo Westbury murmured. There was no hint of patronage in his tone.

'Yes, she'm kind, Miss Grayson is.'

For some reason, Charlotte looked across at him and was disconcerted to find that he was looking at her. His eyes were smiling, full of humour in the brilliant afternoon sunshine, and with the well-remembered fine lines radiating from the corners.

'I had not thought of Miss Grayson as merely kind,' he said, still smiling. 'Difficult, argumentative, impossible, perhaps . . .' he said softly, looking at Charlotte all the while, until she blushed and looked away.

But Lucy was now feeling more confident and sat up higher in the saddle to say imperiously, 'And over yonder is the stream. Gypsy could have a drink and I could get down for a minute, I could.'

Hugo immediately slowed the horse and lifted her down. The groom led Gypsy towards the stream and Lucy began to dance and pirouette in the little grassy clearing. 'And look at me, Miss Grayson,' she cried. 'I can dance in my new dress, I can.'

She danced and skipped and twirled and then at last went to lean against a tree. 'But I can't dance like grand ladies do, Miss Grayson. Show me how to do it proper, miss. I want to do the waltz, Miss Grayson.'

Charlotte laughed and, taking both Lucy's hands in hers, showed her the basic steps and the rhythm, pulling her gently along.

'Well, it is like this, Lucy. Forward side, together. Forward, side, together. And if you dance with a gentleman, you must go backwards and still keep in step.'

'Mr Wessb'ry's a gennelman. Dance with Mr Wessbr'y then. Show me. Show me!' she cried.

Charlotte stood silent and a little nonplussed, not quite sure how to deal with this request, but Hugo stepped forward and echoed Charlotte's words smoothly, saying, 'Well, Lucy, it is like this. The gentleman bows to the lady and says, "May I have the pleasure of this dance, Miss Grayson?" and the lady puts her hand on his.'

Charlotte looked up at him, startled, but as if in a dream, she obediently put her hand on his. 'Then,' Hugo said, 'he puts his arm about her waist and when the music starts, they dance, forward, side, together, forward, side, together.'

Still in a dream, Charlotte gathered up the folds of her gown and then looked ruefully down at her feet. She had on her sturdy half boots, just right for a walk in the country. 'I fear I am not wearing my dancing slippers,' she said, smiling.

'Nor I,' Hugo whispered. 'I must take care not to step on your toes.'

He continued to murmur, 'Forward, side, together,' a few more times and then as they became more confident in each other's steps, he began to hum a waltz, very softly and in a pleasant baritone voice. Soon, their steps matched perfectly and at the edge of the little clearing, Hugo led her perfectly to execute a graceful turn and, still humming, brought her back to Lucy, who clapped her hands in delight.

'That were wunnerful, Miss Grayson,' Lucy squealed excitedly. 'Oh, do some twirls again, Mr Wessb'ry. Please.'

'Very well, but only one more,' he said. 'Miss Grayson has had enough of dancing for one day.'

But Miss Grayson hadn't. Her eyes were closed as she listened to his soft humming, allowing him to guide her and, after the final twirl, bring her gently to a full stop. His hand moved from her waist and he held both her hands in his.

They stood facing each other for a long moment, and he didn't release her hands. Charlotte had opened her eyes, but her head had fallen back and she was looking up at him as though in a trance. He bent his head towards her and for one heart-stopping moment Charlotte thought he was about to kiss her and, rather belatedly, she attempted to break free.

Even Lucy was quiet now and Charlotte became aware of Nell, standing still and silent on the edge of the grassy clearing, and of the groom leading Gypsy from the stream, ready for the journey back. She turned her head and stepped away and, reluctantly, Hugo was obliged to let her go.

CHAPTER SIX

Before completing the formal funeral arrangements, Hugo decided he would visit Cromer himself and try to find Ted Rudkin, the most promising survivor of the tragic shipwreck, who had been a young sailor on board the *Golden Maiden* at the time of the disaster. For some reason, he felt restless and ill at ease after his outing with Lucy Baker and Charlotte Grayson. Lucy Baker was always a delight and one half of him had been charmed by the whole spontaneous experience of dancing in the open air with a beautiful young woman like Charlotte Grayson. He was unable to forget the touch of her cool hand, her grey eyes, large and clear in the sunlight, at first smiling up at him and then closed in concentration as he hummed the waltz. Most of all, he couldn't forget his urgent overwhelming desire to kiss her when he'd had his arm around her slender, lissom waist.

Schoolboy stuff, he told himself cynically, and yet he'd sensed that Charlotte would not have objected. He thought of his earlier resolution to have nothing to do with the troublesome Miss Grayson and decided once more that he must be sensible and keep away from her. Besides, he told himself, if Aurelia Casterton were to be believed, Charlotte Grayson was practically engaged to young Matthew King. He shook himself mentally and went to find Sir Benjamin.

The old gentleman was in the library, looking through some papers, his thin white hair made into a halo by the sun streaming through the window.

'Hugo,' he said, his eyes alight with pleasure and affection. The cards have arrived from the printers in King's Lynn, so this evening perhaps we could draw up a list of people we wish to attend the burial service.'

'Yes, sir,' Hugo said. 'And tomorrow, if you agree, I plan to travel to Cromer to see if I can trace Ted Rudkin.'

Sir Benjamin looked a little startled. 'But Harry Bunfield. . . .' he said.

'Yes, I have spoken to him, sir, and he will come with me. At present he is pursuing enquiries round here and he hopes to be able to interview relevant people at the funeral.'

'I see.' Sir Benjamin looked alarmed at this, but then sighed and said bravely, 'Well, I have no objection to what you propose. I expect you find the Bow Street Runner's investigation a little slow?'

'A little, sir,' Hugo said and grinned.

'Well, take care, my boy.'

'I will and I am pleased to take Bunfield with me. I think he would be a good man if there is trouble.'

Sir Benjamin looked even more alarmed but said merely, 'Well done, my boy. Come and see me in the morning, before you set off.'

And he returned to his papers.

Hugo was up betimes in the morning and visited his great-uncle in his bedchamber to wish him farewell. His man, Latimer, had packed the minimum of clothes, toiletries and neckcloths, suitable for a young gentleman who wished to spend two or three days from home, and Martin brought round the curricle promptly at nine. Hugo Westbury's curricle was modern, lightweight and speedy and they reached Cromer well in time for lunch. Bunfield, who knew the place, suggested a decent but modest inn called The Royal Oak. 'It bein' a place where we could find out where to seek for Mr Rudkin, sir,' he explained.

He took the horses into the yard and got chatting immediately with two of the ostlers who strongly recommended the landlady's steak and ale pie and also her tap room as a comfortable and friendly place in which to eat it. Neither of them had heard of Ted Rudkin, but suggested The Jolly Sailor as being a promising place to ask after a seafaring gent.

Hugo did no better. The landlord's wife ushered him to a private parlour and spread a snow-white cloth on the table, before telling him of a slow-cooked lamb shank, the topside of beef and a large ham done with creamed onions. She poured out a large glass of red wine for him, while he was still making up his mind, and then disappeared swiftly to the kitchen to oversee the cooking. Neither she nor her husband had ever heard of Ted Rudkin, but they had both heard of the sinking of the *Golden Maiden*.

'My pa were one o' them as were drowned,' the landlord said. 'And most of the town come out to try and rescue 'em, but t'were useless. Most poor souls had tried to get to the shore, but there was no survivors as I knowed to.'

'What about Ted Rudkin?'

'I don't know, sir. I were but a little lad of six years when my ma told me as the angels had come for my pa. You could ask at The Jolly Sailor, sir. A lot of old tars gathers there.'

There were indeed, a lot of old tars gathered in the The Jolly Sailor; in fact, fact, business was much brisker than at The Royal Oak. Hugo had the forethought to remove his smart jacket and elaborately tied cravat and he had rolled back his shirt cuffs. This in no way constituted a disguise. He was obviously a toff and recognized as such, but still, the customers of the ale house appreciated his effort to leave class distinction at the door. He left a young lad to stand by the horses' heads and guard the curricle and sauntered into the inn with Bunfield. It was not to be supposed that a tall, handsome member of the *ton* and his stocky companion would be able to sidle unobserved into such a close-knit group and Hugo knew that, in spite of the adjustments he'd made to his dress, he was still conspicuous. He made no attempt to mingle with the crowd round the bar and having secured two tankards of best home-brewed ale, he looked round the room ready to catch the first friendly eye. He hadn't far to seek. A very old fisherman sitting alone in a corner drained his glass very pointedly and made room for Hugo and Bunfield on the pine settle.

'Aye, young man, my name is Enoch Benton and I'll join you in a pint if you be offerin', sir.'

Hugo smiled and immediately procured him a drink before sitting down beside him. The buzz of talk in the tap room, which had lessened and almost died, started up again as Enoch Benton began to quaff his ale. His astute old eyes were fixed on Hugo's face.

'You two b'ain't from round here, sir. Be you lookin' for someone, sir?' he asked.

'Yes,' Hugo said simply. 'I am hoping to find Ted Rudkin, a sailor from these parts who survived the wreck of the *Golden Maiden*.'

'Ted Rudkin, you say? Why he'm getting on now and he don't live here no more. Ten year back, he went to live Brancaster way, wi' his sister, Nancy.'

'Brancaster, you say?' Hugo sighed, slightly exasperated.

There seemed nothing for it but to travel the thirty-odd miles back along the road to Brancaster. There they had better luck and found good lodgings at the The Queen's Head. It was already getting dark by the time Hugo had got a stable-hand to see to the horses and they had been shown to their rooms.

Later, Bunfield said diffidently, 'What do you say to *me* trying to find Ted Rudkin, sir? Then you could think a bit afore you goes to see him,' he pointed out.

'I think that is an excellent idea,' Hugo said warmly. 'And you may be able to find out more about him by not speaking to him directly. For now, let us have some supper and you can try to find him tomorrow.'

*

The next day, Bunfield asked no directions of anyone, but sauntered round the village and drifted towards the beach, where fishermen mended their nets and crab baskets were brought in on fishing smacks to be unloaded on the quay.

To all intents and purposes, he was just another drifter, perhaps looking for work, perhaps just idling his time away. No one knew who he was and although they were guarded, the men were not unfriendly. He took out a pipe and offered his tobacco pouch to an old salt in a thin, worn jersey, who was threading up his fishing line. His gesture of friendship was received very civilly and they puffed for a few moments in silence. A young fisher lad ran by, his trousers rolled up and his feet bare. He called a cheerful greeting to the old man, who merely waved his pipe at him. This was the opening Bunfield wanted.

'I expect you knows most folk round here,' he said.

'That's right. I've lived here, man and boy, for sixty year.'

'A long time. Would you perhaps know a fellow name of Ted Rudkin?'

'Aye, that I do. Lives wi' his sister, Nancy. Up the old beach road and on to Field Cottages. He tapped his pipe on the heel of his shoe and looked up with a smile. 'And who wants to know, then?'

'My master's interested in the sinking of the *Golden Maiden*. Seems as one of his distant family died in the storm, is all.'

'Well, I knows as Ted were lucky, but so many perished. I knows no more'n that.'

'So, where might I come across Ted Rudkin?'

He grinned. 'Well, I knows he goes in The Black Lion. A famous place for some of the old salts, is that.'

Bunfield slipped him some coins. 'You have been more than helpful,' he said. 'Thanks.'

He reported back to Hugo and that evening they set off for The Black Lion. It was easy enough to find. The shutters were open and light spilled from the windows on to the village street. It was a much rougher and more low-lived place than

The Jolly Sailor, being a flash tavern where the local criminal life were wont to meet and mingle with more respectable customers, so this time the adjustment that Hugo made to his dress was more radical. He borrowed clothes from Bunfield and combed the expensive Brutus styling from his hair, leaving it tousled and *au naturel*. He took care to rub his hands in the dirt in the yard so that his nails no longer looked so pristine and well cared for.

The landlord was an enormous man, as fat as a bacon pig, with great jowls and a bloated, mottled nose. He carried a huge belly.

'Welcome, gents. What would be your pleasure?' he asked them. His small eyes, set in pouchy lids, darted shrewdly between the two of them.

'Two tankards of your best home brewed, landlord, and whatever you would like yourself.'

The landlord relaxed visibly. 'Why, thank'ee, sir, that's uncommon civil of you.'

There was silence for a time and in spite of the number of rough seafaring types in the tavern, the bar was not so busy. Bunfield swigged his ale appreciatively and said, 'Does Ted Rudkin come in 'ere of an evenin', landlord?'

The publican paused and wiped his mouth with the back of his hand to gain extra thinking time. Then he said, 'He might do, sir. Who wants to know?'

'Oh, friends,' Harry Bunfield assured him. 'If we could meet him, he might hear something to his advantage.'

Intrigued, the landlord leaned nearer. 'He ain't in this evenin', but I could give you the nod if he was to appear, like.'

Hugo smiled and slipped him some coins. 'Much obliged,' he said softly and the two men drifted across the room to stand by the window, where they could observe both the tavern regulars and the street outside.

They hadn't long to wait. A small, thin man rushed into the tavern and ordered a drink with obvious impatience.

'Hold yer 'orses, Ted,' the landlord said. 'It won't come any quicker by frettin'.'

He laid the foaming tankard on the bar and turned his head towards Hugo and Bunfield, giving them a meaningful stare and imperceptibly jerking his head towards Rudkin.

The two of them watched as Ted Rudkin carried his tankard to a comparatively quiet corner near the door to the kitchen. Then by mutual consent, they drifted casually towards him.

'Good evening, sir. Are you by any chance Ted Rudkin?' Hugo's voice was soothingly soft and he gave the man a pleasant smile. Even so, the small skinny Rudkin started as if he'd been shot.

His head jerked up suddenly and he said aggressively, 'Who wants to know?'

'My name is Hugo Westbury and I'm making enquiries of a kinsman of mine, who it is thought may have perished in the wreck of the *Golden Maiden*.'

Rudkin's small piggy eyes almost became crossed with his repressed anger; he pursed his thin lips and turned his shoulder away from the two men. 'It's in the past,' he muttered. 'All over and forgotten.'

'But there could be a decent reward for information as to the whereabouts of my kinsman.'

'Dead, I expect, after all these years.' The words were wrung out of him as though he could hardly talk.

'Yes, more than likely,' Hugo said softly. 'But still, a decent reward is worth having.'

Rudkin's eyes now swivelled towards him. 'A kinsman, you say? He must be cold meat by now.' He thought for a moment, pinching his bony chin between a grimy thumb and forefinger. 'How much you say were the purse?'

'You would have to name your price,' Hugo said, smiling. 'But for definite news of him, two guineas would be on the table.'

Ted Rudkin still pondered, rubbing his filthy stubble with an almost obsessive stroking. His whole body expressed his indecision as he rocked on first one foot, then the other. 'Two, you say? Suppose I axed five?' His small cunning eyes looked upwards and sideways at the tall young man opposite to him.

Hugo knew intuitively that Rudkin didn't wish to talk about the shipwreck and had named the impossibly high price just so they would walk away.

'Well, suppose you did name five. It would still be worth my while, but it would have to be on the basis of reliable information.'

Whatever the reason for Rudkin's reluctance, this was an offer he couldn't refuse. He pulled out a couple of rickety chairs. 'Let's sit then, gents,' he said, and Bunfield went to get him more ale.

'My grandfather was Charles Westbury and his body was never recovered,' Hugo said. 'But his poor wife was definitely drowned.'

Rudkin was thoughtful. 'Aye, I mind the lady and gent you be meanin'. They was on the way to Holland to sell diamonds.'

'How do you know that?' Hugo said, intrigued.

Rudkin tapped the side of his nose. 'There was Dutch diamond merchants aboard and I 'eard the gent talkin' to 'em. Sailors allus 'ears a lot on account of not bein' noticed by the nobs.'

Hugo was silent, hoping Ted Rudkin would reveal more.

The man's eyes seemed almost to have disappeared as he relived the wreck once more in his imagination. He spoke slowly and haltingly, as though he had not been used to recalling his terrible experience for many years. As Bunfield placed another foaming tankard in front of him, Rudkin said, 'The *Golden Maiden* were a brigantine, see, one o' the smallest o' the two-masted ships and she were Captain Woodford's pride and joy. She weren't too big, see, and was easy managed under sail. She 'ad a good turn o' speed, sir, and the voyage to Holland should a' been plain sailin'. John Woodford were from Yarmouth and 'e weren't expectin' no trouble, but that

101

night over a 'undred fishin' smacks an' coasters was wrecked between Cromer and Southwold and nary a man saved. . . .'

He closed his eyes very tightly as he took another swig of his ale and Hugo waited a moment and then said quietly, 'And what of the *Golden Maiden*?'

'When the storm began to blow, Captain Woodford took every precaution. 'E reduced sail to barest minimum and hove to wi' 'is anchor . . . but bein' unladen, yer see, sir, she were 'igh in the water. 'E thought as we could get back to dry land safely, steerin' along the channels between the sand banks. But all of a sudden, the wind blew so 'ard that the *Golden Maiden* strained on 'er anchor, 'er cable parted an' she drifted rapidly at the mercy o' wind an' current. . . .'

If Hugo was impatient with these details, he gave no sign, but waited while Ted had another gulp of his ale and wiped his lips with the back of his hand.

'She were blown out o' the safe channels and into the shallows where the sands stretch out far from the shore. Then, there bein' no point in everyone stayin' on board, as the heavy seas smashed into 'is ship, the long boat was hoisted and 'e saw most of the passengers safely on board. He were still confident they could get to dry land even though the sands was covered in places by the tide which had started to sweep in. . . .'

Ted gave a convulsive gulp at his drink and was silent.

'And then?'

'Captain Woodford told the coxswain to unload the passengers on to a big flat rock so as they could wade ashore and the long boat could go back for the others. He were concerned about some o' they Dutch passengers, see. They was in a panic and he 'ad to restrain 'em from jumpin' overboard. . . .'

Hugo was patience itself. 'So, how did the situation resolve itself?'

'Well . . . the wind suddenly changed direction and blew with such force as no cable nor anchor could hold a ship agen' it. The *Golden Maiden* was blown on to the dreaded sand banks, to be 'eld fast an' hammered by the towerin' waves. I knows that those as were watchin' could see poor survivors as 'ad taken to the riggin', but then another great wave would come poundin' in and when they looked agen, the riggin' was empty. . . .'

Hugo restrained himself and asked politely, 'And Mr Westbury and his wife?'

'Captain Woodford thought it best for everybody to wade ashore while the tide was ebbing. It seemed straightforward and they all set off, but the women grew tired and although the men tried to help them, the sea crept up and they was drowned, sir.'

'And the survivors?'

Ted Rudkin paused, seemingly at a loss, then he said slowly, 'Only myself and, yes, Mr Westbury and one other person made it to the shore and we was exhausted, sir. The *Golden Maiden* were battered to pieces.'

Hugo was thoughtful, then he said, 'And who was the other person?'

Rudkin blinked rapidly and then looked away. Finally, he said slowly. 'I know naught of him, sir. He'd been a school-master, as I recall, quiet and steady an' disappeared as soon as 'e reached Cromer.'

'You recall Mr Westbury's name. Do you recall the name of the quiet gentleman?' Bunfield asked him.

Ted Rudkin looked shifty and then said, without looking at either of them, 'No, sir.'

'You have been more than helpful, Mr Rudkin, and here, this is for your trouble.' Hugo laid the promised guineas on the table and with a last furtive look round, Rudkin pocketed them. With a muttered farewell, he slid out of the inn and disappeared rapidly.

Left alone, the two men looked at each other and grinned.

'That Ted Rudkin ain't no nodcock, sir,' Bunfield offered. 'It was a slow start, but he took the money fast enough.'

'That is true,' Hugo said. 'But if nothing else, he has served to confirm that the dead body is indeed that of my grandfather, though I cannot begin to guess how he came to be at Westbury Hall, or how he met his end. Come, Harry, if you have finished your drink, let us return to The Royal Oak. Find the landlady and tell her you and I will sup on a nice piece of topside, followed by the ham and white onion sauce. We shall be returning to Westbury Hall in the morning.'

Hugo reflected that he had at least learnt something of his grandfather's fate and he knew the name of the third survivor, even if he had not discovered all the circumstances of Charles Westbury's death. The next morning they travelled home and found the village of Felbrook buzzing with the planned betrothal of Ann West and Robert Thorpe. In fact, the preparations were advancing apace. Both Charlotte and Kitty had decided on new gowns and even Jane Grayson was persuaded to follow suit, although she laughingly protested that as she would be sitting with the old dowds, no one would notice how she looked.

'Nonsense, Mama,' Charlotte said firmly. 'You are so pretty and have so many more qualities than the other ladies, you owe it to yourself to shine at Ann's Party.'

Once this had been decided, the coming celebration at the Wests' family mansion occupied all their thoughts.

Early on Wednesday morning, they were surprised by a knock on the front door, which heralded an unexpected visit from Hugo Westbury, who they'd thought to be still on a visit to Cromer. He was as handsome and well dressed as ever, but was looking worn rather than rested.

The three ladies were as usual chatting and laughing instead of concentrating on their needlework. Charlotte in particular was on the top doh as she gave a wicked imitation of the imagined scene when Ann West's father formally announced her betrothal. Charlotte mimicked everyone – Ann West, the bluff young Robert Thorpe, Ann's gentle, languid, die-away mama, even old Grandmama West, who approved of nothing and disapproved of everybody. Hugo

Westbury caught them in a delightful little cameo, the three Grayson ladies, mother and daughters, as he was ushered into the drawing-room by Robert.

'Mr Westbury, good morning.' Jane Grayson pulled herself together quickly but the amusement still lingered in her pleasant smile as she offered her hand in greeting.

Both girls greeted him politely and Jane Grayson rang for Phoebe to bring some refreshments. 'To what do we owe this unexpected pleasure, Mr Westbury?'

'I have heard, that is . . . I understand . . . that you will be without a carriage on the occasion of Miss West's betrothal party.'

'Yes, that is true,' Jane sighed. 'My brother-in-law is not sure whether he will be returned from King's Lynn and we have no carriage of our own. We scarce had occasion for anything so grand when my dear husband was alive. But I was thinking to purchase a barouche and meanwhile, we could perhaps hire a coach from Fletcher's in King's Lynn . . .'

'I hope you will not do so, ma'am. I come to offer to convey you there in Sir Benjamin's coach. I trust you have not yet made other arrangements for the occasion?'

'No, not at all,' Jane Grayson said faintly. 'But I understood you were away from home, Mr Westbury.'

'Well, I travelled to Cromer on family business,' he said smoothly.

Charlotte, looking at his rather worn expression, said impulsively, 'The journey seems to have tired you.'

He eyed her with some amusement, aware of her wicked pleasure in seeing him looking rather weary. 'Why? Do I seem exhausted?'

'Not exactly, but a few days away is supposed to be restful.'

'A few days away,' he observed languidly, 'can be quite the opposite of restful. But I drove with all speed yesterday, knowing I am engaged to attend Miss West's betrothal party on Friday and I understand that it will be the social occasion of the year.'

'That is true, Mr Westbury, and we are all looking forward to it,' Jane Grayson said, gently interrupting their conversation.

'Capital. Then you will be willing to go in Sir Benjamin's coach?'

'We would be very glad to accept your kind offer, sir.'

Hugo Westbury smiled. He saw it as a small victory, that the Grayson family were to ride with him to the party. Charlotte Grayson was so challenging and she had continued to be so scornful of him since their very first meeting. He guessed that her proud nature made it difficult for her to accept any kindness or favours and it amused him that her mama had taken the decision out of her hands. He could tell by the way that she studiously kept her face averted that she too recognized this minor triumph. After all, he was not unaware of his attractiveness. He was used to women doing what he wanted. Why should Miss Charlotte Grayson be any different?

Besides, if Aurelia Casterton and various other eager young females and their mamas thought he was fixing his interest with Miss Grayson, it might serve to free him from their attentions.

Aloud, he said, 'Then, if you agree, I shall come for you at six-thirty, as we are engaged to be there at seven.'

Kitty and Charlotte were silent. It was again their mother who answered for them. 'That is very kind of you, Mr Westbury. We shall be pleased to accept.'

He bent over Mrs Grayson's hand. 'Until Friday, then,' he said, and flashed her his charming smile. 'Good day, ma'am. Miss Grayson. Miss Kitty.'

He spoke very pleasantly, but Charlotte's grey eyes met his own so grimly that he involuntarily took a step backwards. 'Till Friday, then,' he repeated. He bowed and left.

Jane Grayson was the first to break the silence after his departure. 'It is very civil of Mr Westbury to be so concerned as to offer us a ride in the carriage, is it not? Such a fortuitous offer, my dears. Matthew is one of the few young gentlemen in the neighbourhood who has a professional occupation and I know he is out on business with Mr Brown on Friday.'

Charlotte turned towards her mother with a glare that would cause hell to freeze over. 'Even if Uncle Bertram is not on hand to escort us to the party, Mr Brown has offered Matthew the use of his own carriage,' she said tersely. 'Mr Westbury's offer is surplus to requirements.'

Jane thought how difficult and wayward Charlotte could be when she was in one of her prickly moods, but she merely said gently, 'Well, Charlotte, Uncle Bertram has not said definitely whether he can or cannot convey us to Wycliffe House and dear Matthew might find it a struggle to return from his work and change for the evening before taking us up. I think it is easier for him to meet us at Wycliffe House, then it will be of no consequence if he is slightly late for the party.'

Charlotte said nothing, but took up her neglected needlework and continued to scowl. Jane was put in mind of the old nursemaid they'd had when the girls were little. Old Nanny Bull used to meet these scowling black looks by saying that Charlotte would stay like it if the wind changed. Jane smiled to herself as she thought of old Nanny Bull and, seeing the smile, Charlotte gathered up her sewing and flounced out of the room, completely destroying the atmosphere of playful fun that they'd enjoyed before Hugo's visit.

Although she was outwardly calm, Jane groaned inwardly, hoping that Charlotte would have recovered her good humour before Friday.

CHAPTER SEVEN

True to his word, Hugo arrived on time and greeted the girls courteously, gently refusing Mrs Grayson's offer of wine and instead exchanging pleasantries about the weather. Kitty was not quite ready, Nell having mislaid one of her evening gloves, and in spite of being silent, Charlotte was at least not looking as cross as she had done the last time they'd met. His cool gaze swept over her as they exchanged polite bows and he took in her exquisite bare shoulders, rising from the rounded neckline of her evening dress. She was dressed in a gown of palest *eau-de-Nil* silk, simply styled almost to the point of plainness, yet which flattered her beautiful body to perfection. It was decorated very simply with Bruges lace at the hem and her satin dancing slippers had been dyed to match it exactly. Charlotte Grayson, he reflected, would be able to wear a cotton duster on her head and still look superb, but this evening, her glorious hair was fastened up in a Grecian style, with grey-green ribbons, matching her magnificent eyes exactly. He noticed that the front of her hair had been cut much shorter and encouraged into soft feathery curls, which framed her brow so enticingly that he looked away so as not to be thought staring. He had a sudden mental picture of her, angry and dishevelled, that day when they'd first met. Even with her muddy dress and a smudge on her pretty nose, she had looked wholly beautiful, he thought, and was obliged to smile to himself as he moved towards a seat near the window.

Charlotte noticed his attractive smile and she was determined not to react to him, but even she was startled at how
handsome and charismatic he looked. She'd never seen him
quite so grandly dressed before and the impact of his splendid appearance was obvious as he moved across the room.
His black evening coat fitted perfectly over his pale brocade
waistcoat, as though moulded to his muscular body. His shirt
points were fashionably high without being ridiculously so
and his cravat was a masterpiece of the sartorial art. His
breeches and stockings seemed designed on purpose to show
off his powerful thighs and Charlotte's heart gave an unaccountable sudden lurch as he rose to greet Kitty, who was
now quite ready. He escorted Jane to the waiting carriage and
then returned and offered an arm to each of the girls. Kitty
smiled sweetly up at him but Charlotte was determined to
reject any of his overtures. She shot him a look that was
almost angry as well as unfriendly as she took his proffered
arm. Hugo could hardly hold back a smile as he walked them
to the carriage. Plenty of women would be delighted to take
his arm and be escorted to the betrothal party in such a smart
carriage. Charlotte Grayson looked positively murderous.
She was a very unusual lady, quite outside his experience of
women, Hugo thought, but he had to admit to himself that
she attracted him and the novelty of her outright rejection
intrigued him. Between the fine cloth of his expensive
evening coat and the exquisite fabric of Charlotte Grayson's
white evening glove, there was no real physical contact at all.
Not like their visit to Mrs Baker's cottage when her bare arm
had brushed so softly and seductively against his cheek. At
the vivid memory of that encounter, Hugo felt a sudden rush
of heat which had nothing to do with the mildness of the
summer weather. He handed both girls into the carriage and
as Charlotte raised the hem of her gown slightly to negotiate
the step, he was treated to the sight of a trim ankle and a
gracefully arched foot encased in a satin slipper, and had a
repeat of that unaccountable rush of warmth. Impatient with

himself, he cursed inwardly. Confound it. He was in control here, not the rebellious Charlotte Grayson. He settled himself opposite to her and the coachman folded up the steps and they were off.

Charlotte studiously avoided his gaze and instead looked about her. Papa, in spite of his affluence, had abhorred all worldly wealth and show and it was some time since she'd been in such an elegantly appointed vehicle. The scent of the soft leather upholstery and the smell of oiled mahogany impressed her with their luxury and opulence. She felt like a princess on the verge of an exciting adventure and she was obliged to give a wry grin at the thought that the rather mundane conversation in the carriage did not at all reflect these feelings, in spite of the fact that this evening, Mr Hugo Westbury had all the appearance of the handsome prince in a fairy tale.

Her mother, meanwhile, was chatting seamlessly to Hugo and not even attempting to coax her daughters to join in the conversation. Both she and Hugo had noticed Charlotte's half smile and both of them had chosen to disregard it.

'And how are the funeral arrangements progressing?' her mother asked in a gentle voice.

'As well as can be expected, given the particular circumstances of my grandfather's death,' he answered sombrely.

He found he liked Jane Grayson. She was sympathetic but not maudlin in her interest and he wondered if his own mama would have been like her, had she lived. He wondered what the two women would have talked about if his dear mama had been going to the party with them. He still had some childhood memories of his mother's beautiful face and elegant clothes, her soft voice and that American way she had of almost drawling her words.

Jane interrupted his reverie very gently.

'Will there be many of the Westbury family able to attend?'

'George, the other brother of Sir Benjamin, is also dead, but he has a grandson, Alfred Westbury, who has been informed of the discovery of my grandfather's remains. My American relatives would be hard pushed to attend, even if I were able to get in touch with them. Most of the mourners will be friends and business contacts of my Great-Uncle Benjamin.'

Jane thought of the lonely little ten-year-old boy spending all his school holidays in Westbury Hall and sighed.

Aloud, she said comfortably, 'I am sure there will be many of your neighbours and estate workers who will also wish to pay their respects.'

There was a silence after this and seeing the number of carriages lined up to discharge their passengers at the front door of Wycliffe House, Charlotte reluctantly admitted to herself that she was pleased that her mama had accepted Hugo's offer. No one of any consequence would have arrived at the party in a hired vehicle. As it was, the fact that they were seen to be escorted by Mr Hugo Westbury, in Sir Benjamin's carriage, must lend them some social distinction. She recognized grudgingly that it was good of him to be so thoughtful when his mind must be distracted by the funeral and other considerations.

She glanced at him from under her eyelashes, obliged to admit that she admired what she saw. It was unbelievable that she should be so conscious of his attractiveness, almost impossible to think that she should actually begin to like him. . . .

There were now only three carriages in front of them and Hugo said to her, 'It is bound to be a sad crush, Miss Grayson, but may I be allowed to have the pleasure of a dance with you?'

Charlotte knew that her mama and sister were pretending not to hear what was being said and she felt herself colouring a little. Common courtesy decreed that she should accept, especially after the way he had considered their comfort and convenience.

She swallowed and said politely, 'Yes, sir. I should be pleased to dance with you.'

Hugo smiled, trying to disguise the triumph that he felt. He would solicit the hand of the most beautiful woman there and dance with her in full view of all the hopeful young virgins and their ambitious mamas who were gathered at Ann West's party. He now saw the conquest of Charlotte Grayson as something of a challenge. His own affections were not engaged, of course, but it would amuse him to see if he could make her fall in love with him. She might be stubborn and difficult but he knew she was not unaware of the impact that their arrival would have on the other guests. She would see it as a triumph that so notable a person as Sir Benjamin Westbury had put his opulent coach at their disposal, and not only that but had made his very eligible heir available as their escort. Without any undue conceit, he knew he was attractive to women and could make her fall for him. Perhaps this would settle Charlotte Grayson's arrogant confidence once for all. By just becoming a fool in love she might learn some humility, he thought grimly.

He escorted the three Grayson ladies up the gracious staircase of Wycliffe House and they passed along the line of the West family, who were waiting to greet their guests, before proceeding to the reception room where liveried flunkeys circulated with wine and light refreshments. In no time at all, Hugo was surrounded by admirers, male as well as female, and the Grayson women were soon on the edge of this group, with only old faithfuls and the immature young friends of the prospective bridegroom to entertain them. Partly to escape the crush in the great hall and partly to secure an eligible partner, guests were now entering the ballroom, where there was a dais at one end for the musicians. The famous chandeliers of Wycliffe were ablaze with myriads of candles and there were small gilded chairs surrounding the dance floor.

'For the old dowds,' Jane said laughingly, as she excused herself from the girls and went to greet one of the elderly ladies from the church.

Charlotte looked about her. Andrew Preston was chatting

to a group of ladies who seemed to be hanging on his every word. People were grouping and regrouping as they greeted each other. The musicians now began to strike up and the first country dance was announced. Hugo Westbury was squiring a hopeful young female on to the dance floor and she noticed that Uncle Bertram had arrived, looking extremely elegant in his formal evening clothes. She watched curiously as, not looking to either right or left, he made a beeline for Miss Aurelia Casterton and bent over her hand, obviously requesting the pleasure of a dance. Not letting the grass grow under his feet, Charlotte thought. So far, neither Matthew, Lavinia nor Adam had arrived, and one of the prospective bridegroom's friends asked Kitty to dance and she smilingly acquiesced, so Charlotte was left alone. She watched the dancers and saw that as Aurelia's dance with Uncle Bertram ended, Aurelia immediately accepted Hugo Westbury in the next one. Charlotte's heart skipped a beat as she watched Hugo. He had such a distinguished air of almost careless grace as he danced with Ann West's best friend, and she was angry with herself for feeling a little envious of Aurelia, who was obviously enjoying being his partner. She saw the flash of his white teeth as he smiled politely at the rather stodgy young woman, who looked as if she were too dazzled to answer him. She noticed the glossy sheen of his dark hair, highlighted by the brightness of the chandeliers, and the confidence with which he moved to the measures of the dance. Charlotte was more than a little envious, she acknowledged to herself; she was suddenly, fiercely and quite irrationally jealous of the young woman whom he had chosen to partner. She watched as the dance ended and Hugo escorted Aurelia from the floor, then she deliberately looked away from them and concentrated instead on the intricate design of flowers and songbirds on her fan.

'Good evening. May I have the pleasure of the next dance?'

It was Matthew's calm and quiet voice and Charlotte smiled up at him, pleased to see him.

113

'Better late than never,' he said. 'Adam and my dear aunt are still paying their respects to the happy couple, so we may take to the floor without them.'

She put her hand on his and allowed him to lead her into a cotillion. She looked up at him and thought that he seemed somewhat strained.

'Ann's parents have put on a wonderful party for her, have they not?'

'Yes. Quite so,' Matthew answered, seemingly uninterested. 'Where is Kitty this evening?'

'Oh, dancing with various young friends of Robert Thorpe,' she said, somewhat surprised at his question. 'No doubt we shall see her at the supper interval.'

'I hope so,' he said. Then he exclaimed, 'Oh, is that Kitty now, standing up with that absurd Andrew Preston?'

'I am sure I have no idea who Kitty is standing up with,' she said with some asperity. What was the matter with him, she wondered?

Matthew's hand tightened on hers and she looked at him crossly.

'What is it, Charlotte?' he asked quietly. 'You are usually such good friends with your sister.'

She began to feel as though this situation was unreal. She was almost dizzy with conflicting emotions as though a chasm had unexpectedly opened at her feet. One half of her knew that she was being unreasonable, but she couldn't help herself. She wanted to dance with the charismatic Hugo Westbury and instead was being partnered by the rather dull Matthew King. Quite irrationally, she longed suddenly to provoke Matthew, to shake him out of his calm acceptance of their prolonged courtship and to anger him as much as he angered her with his persistent attentions to her younger sister. 'If you are so concerned, why not seek Kitty out yourself?' she said tightly. 'I am sure she would appreciate it.'

Matthew's gentle expression hardened. 'Can it be that you are jealous of Kitty, Charlotte?' he challenged her. 'I thought you were the best of friends.'

Charlotte was appalled at herself. She didn't know what to say and they were both silent for a few minutes. It was a silence which seemed full of the tension of what they had said, but also of what they had not said, until Matthew drew a deep breath and broke the silence by saying with an undertone of anger in his deep voice, 'To please you, I suppose I must not pay any attention to your sister, but at the same time, I must remain oblivious to the attentions you are receiving from Hugo Westbury.'

'That is unfair, Matthew. He has no interest in me whatsoever.'

'You are mistaken!'

They had both kept their voices quiet during this exchange, but now Charlotte's anger welled up inside her and her voice rose without her even being aware of it. She was somewhat disconcerted to realize that the music had now stopped and people were looking askance at her. She could tell that the normally mild-mannered Matthew was furious. Wordlessly, he escorted her to the edge of the dance floor. She could feel his anger and tension as she rested her hand on his arm and she herself felt hurt and frustrated by their sharp and painful exchange. She had no opportunity to mend the rift between them because Hugo Westbury was now approaching with Aurelia Casterton on his arm.

'Why, Miss Grayson,' Aurelia said with feigned sweetness. 'I have not seen you since we visited the Bakers' cottage. How are you?' She didn't wait for a reply but continued, 'How fortunate to have met you. Perhaps dear Mr King would agree to us changing partners. Mrs West has decided not to have dance cards, so I hope you do not think it amiss if I solicit Mr King in the next country dance. You two are such old friends, I am sure you could spare him, dear Miss Grayson.'

Charlotte glanced quickly at Hugo Westbury and saw the same mocking smile that she had noticed before when they'd encountered Aurelia Casterton. She struggled to contain her temper, but before she could think of a polite reply, Matthew smiled at Aurelia and said, 'Of course you may solicit my hand in the next dance. I should be honoured, Miss Casterton. Miss Grayson and I are indeed such old friends she will hardly miss me. Your servant, Mr Westbury.' He bowed to Charlotte and Hugo and, offering his arm to Aurelia, he led her away.

Charlotte stood rooted to the spot, absolutely outraged at Matthew's uncharacteristic behaviour. She was still aware of Hugo's quizzical gaze as she beat down the anger which was welling up in her and fought for control.

'Should you care to dance, Miss Grayson?' he asked gently. 'Or should you prefer to walk on the terrace for a few minutes. It seems very warm in here.'

Charlotte watched Matthew attending Aurelia so solicitously and allowed Hugo to lead her into the dance. Their conversation was of necessity rather stilted and lacking in continuity as they parted for the different figures in the dance and then met with different partners, only to return once again to their set places.

At the end of it, by mutual consent, they moved over to the open doors where the light summer breeze cooled the air somewhat. The terrace was at that moment almost deserted as the musicians took a rest and guests drifted towards the supper room.

Hugo was aware of the tension about her and guessed that it had to do with her friendship for Matthew. He noted her shaking hands clasped tightly round the delicately painted fan and on an impulse he covered her hands with his own. He felt her instinctive resistance but at least she didn't move away from him. Hugo Westbury was skilled in the art of seduction and knew how gently he had to proceed. He studied the shapely finger tips emerging so delicately from her evening gloves and he waited patiently for her to regain her calm.

Once, trading with some Portuguese merchants in Goa, Hugo had wandered down to the beach and had gazed at the myriad of seashells washed up on to the sands. The ones in particular which had caught his eye were of an opalescent pink, edged with pearly white. So like the perfectly formed nails on the ends of Miss Grayson's elegant slim fingers, he thought. For all their delicacy, they were not weak or useless hands, but expressive and purposeful. He thought of the way she had so tenderly held the Bakers' baby and of her gentleness with Lucy Baker. Very carefully, he parted each finger in turn and kissed it lightly. Then he raised his eyes to look into hers. 'You have very beautiful hands, Miss Grayson,' he said softly.

Suddenly, his gentle seduction was shattered when Charlotte snatched her hands from his. 'How dare you, sir?' she gasped.

He smiled slightly. He'd never imagined even the spirited Miss Grayson would be so indignant over such a trifle. So she wasn't impervious to him after all. He stepped back a little and bowed politely.

'I beg your pardon, Miss Grayson,' he said. 'I should not have taken such a liberty. Would you like to go into supper?'

He could feel that the hand she placed on his arm was still trembling, but his face remained blandly impassive as he escorted her silently to her mother and Kitty. Once they were in the supper room, he bowed and went across to greet Robert Thorpe and offer his felicitations on the betrothal. Charlotte had eaten very little dinner before coming out and had thought that she was more than prepared to do justice to the superb supper. Now, suddenly everything seemed to be turning to dust and ashes in her mouth. There was no sign of Matthew; she could only suppose that he was in the card room. She glanced covertly across at Hugo, who seemed to be laughingly trying to resist all solicitations from Robert Thorpe to join himself and Miss West at their table. There was still no sign of Matthew; perhaps he was no longer on speaking terms with her.

'It would be a mistake,' Hugo was saying disarmingly, 'for a grumpy, confirmed bachelor such as myself to play the gooseberry on the eve of your betrothal celebration.'

Both young people laughed and insisted, so eventually Hugo subsided gracefully into one of the vacant chairs, still smiling and protesting. It did not escape either Charlotte or her mama's notice that Aurelia Casterton appeared suddenly, as if from nowhere, and slipped into one of the remaining chairs at Hugo's side. Just as if it had been reserved for her, Charlotte thought bitterly, and pointedly ignored her. Almost immediately afterwards, Uncle Bertram, who had escorted Aurelia into the supper room but had paused to greet one of his friends, joined her. From time to time Charlotte caught Hugo's eyes on her and refused to look away, but returned his regard steadily. It was obvious, she thought bitterly, that Aurelia Casterton was setting her cap at Hugo Westbury. Perhaps she was using Uncle Bertram to try to make Hugo jealous.

And then, as though with deliberate insult, Hugo turned to Aurelia and gave her his devastatingly attractive smile and she, quite dazzled, gazed back at him adoringly. Charlotte and her mother both watched with interest as Aurelia fluttered her eyelashes and smiled demurely in response to all Hugo's polite conversational overtures. Uncle Bertram appeared not to notice and instead engaged Ann West in conversation, but Charlotte was incensed at Hugo's flirting.

What a reprobate, she thought angrily and quite lost her appetite. Once the covers were removed and the hothouse fruits were produced, she merely toyed with a luscious peach and sipped her wine, furious with herself at letting the unpleasant Hugo Westbury affect her emotions like this.

Robert Thorpe's cousin, Richard, begged to be allowed to join Mrs Grayson and her daughters and then Charlotte was able to exact some revenge on Hugo Westbury by flirting openly with a young man who was obviously already smitten by her beauty and eager to dance attendance on her, fetching her chilled champagne cup, selecting dishes of sweetmeats, for her and begging earnestly for the pleasure of a dance with her after the interval. Charlotte was inclined to be gracious, bowing her beautiful head gracefully in acknowledgement of his admiration and thanking him prettily for every attention he paid her. Glancing under her lashes at Hugo Westbury, she was gratified to see that he had noticed her young admirer and the encouragement that she had given him and had forgotten his assumed pleasant, smiling expression, allowing a black scowl to dominate his handsome face. Flirting was not so difficult after all, she reflected, and it had certainly seemed to halt for the moment the effortless smiles that Mr Hugo Westbury had been bestowing on Miss Aurelia Casterton. Uncle Bertram now seized his opportunity and whisked Aurelia off for another dance. Charlotte accepted Richard Thorpe's arm and they moved back to the ballroom. The musicians struck up and suddenly, feeling refreshed, the guests were ready to dance again and came out of the supper room in groups to take their places.

'Would you care to dance, Miss Grayson?' Richard asked humbly.

'Thank you, sir,' Charlotte said.

He was stiff with youthful nerves and embarrassment, but had been well schooled in the dance steps and didn't hesitate or stumble. She smiled encouragingly at him and he seemed a little more at ease. As the dance progressed, they changed partners and to her surprise, she found herself taking Matthew's hand as she moved down the set for the next figure.

He still seemed at odds with her, but as his fingers closed firmly around hers, he gave her his familiar open smile. 'Well, Charlotte. I trust you're feeling in a better humour now that you have had supper.'

'Yes, Matthew. I . . . I am sorry I was so ungracious earlier.'

'And I am sorry that I was not able to escort you to the party in person,' he said.

119

And so they seemed to have patched up their disagreement, Charlotte thought, as they parted once more and the dance ended. Uncle Bertram begged for the pleasure of a dance with her and Charlotte was pleasantly surprised at how less pompous he was now that they were out on a social occasion. She'd noticed the attentions he'd been paying to Aurelia and it had given her food for thought. Although it is difficult to think of an uncle objectively, he was, she reflected, a good-looking man and not too old for matrimony. He was also very well dressed and an accomplished dancer. No wonder Mrs Casterton had been keen to have him on her guest list.

'Shall you be staying to the end, Uncle Bertram?' she asked, wondering if so countrified an entertainment as Ann's betrothal ball would interest someone as sophisticated as he.

'Of course,' he replied heartily. As though reading the thoughts behind her question, he went on, 'One can become very jaded with city life, my dear. The pleasures of one's youth do not always satisfy a man's deepest desires.'

'Deepest desires, Uncle Bertram?'

'Yes, Charlotte. There comes a time in a man's life when the frivolous pleasures enjoyed by the *ton* begin to pall. A man wants substance. A settled home life ... an established family. . . .'

'A family, sir?'

'Yes. Do not look so askance, Charlotte. You are still young. You still crave excitement. Balls. Pretty clothes. Romance, perhaps. But when you get to my age. . . .'

'What then, Uncle?'

He laughed. 'Stop encouraging me to speak like some old dodderer, niece. When you get to my age, even you will have calmed that fiery temper of yours, Charlotte, and you may long for the quiet haven of a happy marriage.'

'Marriage, Uncle Bertram?' And she gave him a mocking smile. 'I shall only marry, sir, when I am too old to do anything else and am at my last prayers.'

'We shall see,' was all he said, as the dance ended.

She noticed that Hugo Westbury did not seem so enamoured of Aurelia Casterton that he could allow her to distract him from his interest in the card table. Mrs West had set up several card tables in a separate room, mainly for mature or married gentlemen, hoping that the younger and more eligible bachelors would offer their attentions to the young ladies. Hugo was aware of this, but had decided to avoid the opportunity to converse or socialize with any single young women, especially Charlotte Grayson. He had to admit to himself that he found her very attractive and was determined to keep up his cool manner with her. He set out to win as much of the modest stakes as he could and emerged from the card room an hour later, feeling pleased with himself, being several guineas in profit. He felt unaccountably furious to observe Miss Grayson in close embrace with Richard Thorpe, dancing the waltz, and turned away to address some civil remarks to Kitty, who was nervous of being asked by Andrew Preston and was sitting out this particular dance.

Hugo was not the only one to observe Charlotte and her partner. Matthew was also aware of her lively conversation and graceful movements. He sighed and sought out Kitty. In spite of her avoidance of the young curate, Kitty had not lacked for partners among the young men of the neighbourhood, who were only too willing to ask her for the pleasure of a dance. She was so sweet, so charming, her eyes so soft and gentle, and Matthew thought that the curves of her girlish figure were shown to advantage in her modest white gown. She was a good dancer, always keeping to the correct rhythm of the dance and never attempting to lead her partner, and as she placed her hand in his, Matthew was conscious of a feeling of satisfaction and the rightness of the two of them together as a couple. Soon, he completely forgot his disagreement with Charlotte in the pleasure of dancing with her sister.

*

121

It was half past midnight before the carriages were called and Hugo escorted the Grayson ladies from Mrs West's triumphant soirée, Bertram having decided to make his own way home. Everyone agreed that it had been a great success and the whole occasion would be food for the gossips for weeks to come. After courteously handing the ladies in, Hugo remained sunk into his own corner of the carriage. Even Jane Grayson was silent and as for Charlotte, she was determined to press herself back into her own corner, resolving to offer no conversation, no intimacy towards a man who, she thought, found Aurelia Casterton's person and her fortune so irresistibly attractive.

The truth was that Hugo was afraid to move too freely in case he should inadvertently come into contact with his beautiful companion. The overwhelming attraction that he felt for her should have been stifled long before, when she was displaying all her aggressive contrariness and when he still thought of her as a confounded nuisance. He realized now, especially when they'd been on the terrace and he'd captured her hands in his own, how strong the temptation had been to take her into his arms. To think that he could cold-heartedly entice Miss Grayson to develop a *tendre* for him while remaining cool and unmoved himself was the merest fairy tale, he told himself. Now that he recognized this, he regretted having spent the whole evening so far away from her and yet he had no intention of becoming involved with someone so forceful and opinionated, however beautiful she was.

If only Aurelia Casterton were so alluring, he thought. She was insipid and biddable and although she was rumoured to have £60,000 as her dowry, one would tire very quickly of such a moon-faced weakling. He sighed and stirred slightly in his seat, hoping that Charlotte wouldn't notice his restlessness.

But Charlotte was only too aware of him. In the dim light of the carriage, she could see the outline of his head and shoulders and, as he glanced out of the opposite window, the movement of his eyes. She refused to let herself think of the blueness of those blue eyes, their provocative humour and the intensity of his gaze when he'd kissed her fingers on Mrs West's terrace.

Her mother was now offering a final conversational opening to the unaccountably silent Mr Westbury. 'I would like to thank you, sir, for your kind attention this evening. Your offer of the carriage has made the occasion most agreeable.' She paused slightly and then said in a quieter tone, 'I suppose the next time we meet, it will be on a much sadder and more mournful occasion.

'Yes,' he said tersely. 'The funeral of my grandfather on Thursday next.'

'Quite so.' She was almost whispering now. 'Thank you again, Mr Westbury. Why, here we are, already! Can I persuade you to partake of some refreshment before your journey home?'

'I thank you, ma'am, but I am anxious to return to Sir Benjamin.'

The atmosphere felt strange and tense and even her mother seemed pleased and relieved to be standing on the gravel of the drive. No one was inclined for polite chat as Hugo bade them a courteous farewell and got back into the carriage, his expression totally neutral.

CHAPTER EIGHT

Sir Benjamin rarely rose before noon but today was the day of the funeral and he was in the dining-room, viewing the immaculate person of his great-nephew from head to foot. He sighed.

'You are so like your poor grandfather, and yet with your tall figure and blue eyes, you favour your dear mama also.'

Hugo smiled slightly and inclined his head as Sir Benjamin went on, very quietly, 'Tell me, Hugo, is your obnoxious cousin Alfred intending to favour us with his presence this morning?'

The young footman who was waiting on them had retired to stand by the sideboard and could not possibly have heard Sir Benjamin's question, but even so, Hugo kept his voice equally quiet as he said, 'I fear so, sir. His equally obnoxious man has made it known among the servants that his master has been fitted out for his funeral clothes by no less a tailor than Weston of London.'

'That does not surprise me,' Sir Benjamin murmured. 'In spite of his resentment that you are my chosen heir, he seems determined to create a good impression among the other mourners.'

'Well, to be fair to my cousin Alfred, his grandfather was more senior than my own and he feels he has a greater claim on your estate, sir.'

'True,' Sir Benjamin sighed, 'but being a childless bachelor,

I may dispose of my fortune as I please.'

He looked more penetratingly at Hugo, his once-handsome face falling suddenly into sad folds, and then his keen eyes clouded over and he gave a deep sigh 'Do not allow yourself to be left to a lonely old age, my boy. Marry and have children. The sooner the better.'

Hugo said nothing to this. He was spared the necessity of a reply to Sir Benjamin's broad hint by the entrance of his cousin, Alfred, who had arrived at Westbury Hall the previous evening, fortunately after Sir Benjamin had retired for the night.

Alfred had made a nuisance of himself to Hugo, with his demands for the best accommodation for his valet and complaints to the housekeeper that he needed extra pillows on his bed, and an insistence that brandy should be brought up to his room at gone midnight, when the servants should be able to expect some rest. Hugo had dealt politely but firmly with his difficult behaviour and had even been able to view his unpleasant criticisms with good humour, but he was all the more determined to avoid his cousin Alfred at all costs and not to allow him to take any further liberties with either himself or any of the servants.

Alfred now seated himself at the breakfast table, smiling with airy nonchalance, as though his churlish behaviour had never happened. He was indeed dressed to advantage by one of London's foremost tailors and his cravat was a positive miracle of creative fashion, of which he was only too aware. He held his chin proudly high of its lightly starched, intricate folds. His shapely lips were stretched somewhat unnaturally in a condescending smile and his elegant white hands were spread gracefully before him, as though he were hesitating politely before he started his breakfast.

The two cousins were quite unlike, Mr Alfred Westbury being of a much lighter colouring and with rather close-set amber-brown eyes. He was neither as tall or as muscular as his cousin but, nevertheless, Hugo had to acknowledge that he was a good-looking man and carried himself with the arrogance of one who had some standing among the *ton*. They very rarely met socially, but he'd heard that Alfred was an inveterate gambler and was often badly dipped at cards. Not that he cared, Hugo thought sarcastically. As far as he was concerned, Alfred could go to the devil. The sooner the better.

'Dear Sir Benjamin, I fear my presence is at a most inopportune time, coming as it does at the interment of your poor brother,' Alfred said, as he helped himself to a generous portion of the luscious rashers of pink bacon and some coddled eggs.

'True,' Sir Benjamin murmured. 'A most sad and mournful occasion, to be sure. Only my great age is helping me to come to terms with it.'

Alfred Westbury waited for the footman to finish serving him and when the young man had retired once more to his position near the sideboard, he continued to smile as he said in his soft, oily voice, 'It further grieves me to have to tell you, sir, that there are some ugly rumours circulating about the . . . mmm . . . er . . . discovery of Hugo's grandfather behind the panelling in your library.'

'I believe so,' sighed Sir Benjamin.

'You believe so, sir? Those words hardly do justice to such a particular circumstance. The words "dreadful", "ghastly" and "horrifying" would be more suitable.'

'And your point, Alfred?' Sir Benjamin said with exemplary patience.

'Why, sir, that the discovery of a family skeleton in a cupboard, where he was presumably thrust so violently all those years ago, must, shall we say, throw some suspicion on his immediate family?'

Although his tone remained soft and quiet, Alfred's amber eyes darted meaningfully between Sir Benjamin and Hugo, and gleamed with ill-concealed malice.

Hugo remained silent as his great-uncle laughed softly and said in a deceptively gentle voice, 'How well I know you, my dear Alfred. You are so like my dastardly brother, George. No doubt your father too inherited his unspeakable depravity and evil vices. With your gambling and womanizing, you, sir, are the culmination of that particular inbred evil.'

There was a shocked silence at this and Sir Benjamin smiled again as Alfred scowled and moodily pushed aside his breakfast. Hugo and Sir Benjamin rose from the table together and bade him farewell. 'I would remind you that the funeral service for Hugo's grandfather, your late Great-Uncle Charles, is at eleven o'clock in St Paul's Church,' Sir Benjamin said coldly, but Alfred maintained a sulky silence as they left the room and he continued to scowl at his rejected breakfast plate for some minutes.

Other family guests were present at the ceremony, including a couple of aged aunts and a friend of Hugo's from his Oxford days, whose father had known Charles Westbury. Mostly, though, the mourners were village folk who came to pay their last respects, as was traditional for tenants on a large estate. After the ceremony, attended by the few remaining family members, Hugo noticed that Jane Grayson's brother-in-law, Bertram Grayson, was among the congregation in church for the service of remembrance, escorting Mrs Casterton and her daughter, and afterwards, at Westbury Hall, as his great-uncle's elderly butler served wine and refreshments.

Uncle Bertram seemed to be at pains to avoid them, Charlotte thought, but it was inevitable that Alfred should meet Jane Grayson and her daughters during the luncheon for the mourners. Amidst the tinkle of delicate china and the clink of crystal glasses, Alfred was introduced to the three ladies by Matthew. The conversation was conventionally restrained and low-key, but this didn't stop Alfred from presenting his most gallant and polished persona. He paid particular attention to Charlotte, having heard that she could expect a decent portion from her deceased papa's estate, on the occasion of her marriage. He managed to separate

Charlotte from the rest of her party and was quite determined to put himself out to charm her, exerting all his considerable skills as a dashing blade and an out-and-out regency buck.

Charlotte, however, steadfastly refused either to be charmed by him or to make any attempt to charm him in return. In fact, to his chagrin, he noticed Miss Grayson's eyes following the tall, elegant figure of his cousin as Hugo circulated among the guests, greeting newcomers and gracefully accepting condolences from among his neighbours. Alfred was politely ignored and after some while he became less confident and indeed quite despondent. With a last desperate attempt to gain Charlotte's attention, he said with false brightness, 'Do you care to walk, Miss Grayson? Perhaps I may crave your mama's permission to take you and Miss Kitty walking in the gardens at Sheringham? They are so peaceful with such everlasting beauty amidst the tranquillity of silence. . . .' His voice tailed off at this point as he realized that his pretentious attempt at poetic language had been overheard and from just beyond Charlotte's shoulder, he met Hugo's darkly scowling gaze.

Noticing his sudden silence, Charlotte glanced behind her and she was also aware of Hugo's black looks. She made a sudden irrational decision and said demurely, 'You may be sure that I shall be guided by whatever Mama says, sir, but yes, it would be a very agreeable outing.'

Hugo was angered to see that her face held an expression of both pride and amusement at Alfred's amorous overtures and his scowl became even more pronounced. Hell! The flirtatious minx was pleased at the effect she was having on him, just as she had been when she'd flirted with Richard Thorpe. As for Alfred, he was ogling her stupidly, like a fish caught on a hook. Hugo felt an unaccustomed surge of helpless jealousy and quickly composed his features into an expression of bland politeness as he greeted them.

'Miss Grayson, Cousin Alfred. It was good of you to come.' He offered his arm possessively to Charlotte and said, 'I must see that you have some refreshments, Miss Grayson.'

With that, he almost marched her to the buffet table and Charlotte was too taken aback by his high-handed actions to protest. Instead she allowed herself to be persuaded to fill her plate with dainty slices of meat and pie, almost as if she were in a dream. The air was suddenly alive with the tension between them and Hugo firmly stifled a desire to give her a set down over her behaviour. Alfred, meanwhile, excused himself quietly and slid back among the other guests, leaving Charlotte and Hugo alone.

'I should warn you,' Hugo said stiffly, 'that my cousin Alfred is somewhat ... untrustworthy where young ladies are concerned. Your mama would do well to forbid you from having anything to do with his rackety invitation to walk in the gardens at Sheringham.'

Damnation! This was worse than giving her a set down. Even to his own ears, he sounded like a pompous ass. As he expected, Charlotte's anger surfaced immediately.

'How arrogant you are,' she said, softly furious. 'Excuse me, Mr Westbury, I must go and seek out my sister.'

He gave her a slow, deliberate smile. It was a wickedly glinting smile, which made Charlotte blush, as he'd intended it should, but he bowed formally as she swept across the room to join Kitty and their mother. Looking at her ramrod-straight back and the proud set of her head as she walked away from him, Hugo's smile faded abruptly.

Miss Grayson had not bothered to hide her obvious antagonism towards him and any idea he'd had of charming her into lowering her guard against him seemed doomed to failure. Meanwhile, there was the obnoxious Alfred to deal with. Hugo hoped he would only be here a couple more days and that Alfred was determined to be vigilant. He would not allow any unsuspecting female of his acquaintance to be put at risk by his unscrupulous cousin. He decided to ask Harry Bunfield to keep an eye on him.

Alfred, meanwhile, had slipped down the wrought-iron

staircase to be joined by Josiah Bennett, his personal servant and valet who, although he was as quietly spoken and soft of foot as his master, was yet not able to detect the soundless approach of Harry Bunfield, who stole after him, unseen and unheard. Bunfield followed him down the magnificent staircase, dodging aside and holding his breath as he waited for his quarry to reach each landing in turn. Alfred finally arrived at the gloomy stone corridor and went through the stair hall leading to the library. Here, Harry Bunfield was intrigued to see Alfred step through the panelling into another dismal passageway which led eventually to a thick wall of greenery. Alfred parted this natural screen and then vanished.

Carefully and soundlessly, Bunfield followed, first peering around cautiously and then crawling out into a shady wood, moving very nimbly in spite of his rather heavy figure. The trees were set closely together and were very high, their branches interlaced to form a roof, effectively shutting out the light. As Harry Bunfield hid behind a tree to watch, Alfred's valet appeared suddenly from the bushes. The man had a furtive expression. His sallow face and the eyes set too closely together predisposed anyone into thinking him untrustworthy. Now, his unnaturally sleek black hair, swept back from his brow like a wet seal, made him look even more of a villain. He stood closely together with Alfred Westbury, and the two of them were obviously completely unaware of the sharp eyes and ears of the silent observer.

Alfred was speaking to the valet in a low, intense tone.

'Bennett, did you try my bedroom door last night?'

'No, sir, I certainly did not.'

'Damn! I could swear someone did. It must have been you.'

'No, sir. I assure you it was not.'

Alfred scowled as though in disbelief and was silent for a while, then continued suddenly, 'And did you hear footsteps last night? It sounded like some accursed sleep walker, creeping about softly and slowly in the dark.'

Bennett answered quietly and patiently. 'No. I have never

heard footsteps in the night, Mr Westbury.'

Although he still kept his voice low, Alfred was petulant. 'Must be a cursed ghost, then. I keep sensing a creeping silent presence in the night, but you say you've heard nothing, damn you.'

Josiah Bennett was as quiet as ever as he said calmly, 'No. Never, sir.'

'Well, no matter. But what of my cousin's doings?'

'Well, sir. I have heard that Mr Hugo returned from a journey to Norfolk shortly before our arrival and immediately offered his services to convey Mrs Grayson and her daughters to a social evening with the West family.'

'Who the devil told you that?'

'I heard it mentioned in the servants' hall, sir.'

'Mm. Devil take their clacking tongues.'

'And I have noticed myself, Mr Alfred, sir, that Miss Charlotte Grayson and Mr Hugo Westbury seem to be ... ever more close ... while her association with the young lawyer, Matthew King, seems to have cooled somewhat of late.'

'Ha. Does it now?'

'Yes indeed, sir.'

'And how the devil do you know that?'

'Mrs West's servant, sir. She observed Miss Grayson in the company of Mr Hugo Westbury on the evening of Miss West's betrothal party. They were alone together on the terrace, sir. Very close, they was, sir ... he was kissing her hands passionately.'

'My God! Is this true, Bennett?'

'So true, sir, that I hesitated to tell you, sir, knowing your own admiration for Miss Charlotte Grayson,' he said unctuously.

'Be quiet, damn you!'

'Yes, sir. I am only telling you what Emily, Miss West's maid, that is, observed for herself.'

'Close, were they?' Alfred hissed between his teeth. 'My

two-faced proud cousin and that lying wanton.'

'Well, sir,' the oily Bennett said softly, 'she is a most beautiful young lady and he would be a happy man who could win her. . . .'

'Cousin Hugo must be taken care of,' Alfred snarled softly. 'He must be given a severe warning that if he refuses to leave the lady alone, he will be rendered incapable of ever pleasing a lady and in no condition for lovemaking. Do I make myself clear?'

'Yes, Mr Alfred, sir. I shall attend to it forthwith. I know of one or two local bruisers who could effectively accomplish that for us, sir, for a consideration, of course.'

'Of course,' said Alfred softly. 'But remember, my man, I have enough knowledge of you to make sure that if anything goes wrong, you could find yourself wearing the hempen cravat, dancing the Tyburn jig, the noose, Bennett, the gibbet, unless you deliver a positive outcome. Be warned.'

'Sir, please. I swear to God, I will always serve you loyally.'

'See that you do. And now, go.'

When Alfred Westbury had returned to the house and his valet had disappeared deeper into the wood, Harry Bunfield turned slowly to retrace his steps, deep in thought and determined to find an opportune time to report to Hugo and Sir Benjamin. He'd been keeping a close watch on Alfred Westbury and even hidden inside the house in order to observe Alfred and his valet, Bennett, at close quarters. All their movements, however innocuous, had been duly entered into Bunfield's shabby, dog-eared little notebook. At the moment, Sir Benjamin and Hugo Westbury were dealing with the visitors and entertaining those who had stayed on for the drinks and refreshments after the interment. This was not a suitable moment to seek a meeting with them. He must bide his time and report back when they were free of the constraints of the funeral party. Meanwhile, he would continue to stalk the unsuspecting Bennett, in an effort to discover the names of the local bruisers whose services

Alfred's valet intended to procure.

It was late afternoon before the last guests had departed and Hugo was aware that his great-uncle was exceptionally weary and jaded, fit only to be allowed to rest and to be quiet with his own thoughts. He'd seen nothing of Bunfield and guessed that the Bow Street Runner was tactfully keeping his distance after the funeral. He was also aware of the absence of his cousin Alfred, but gave it little thought, thankful only that if Alfred was out for the evening, he would not be obliged to make small talk over dinner.

Thankfully, Hugo dined alone, because neither Sir Benjamin nor Alfred appeared and afterwards he dismissed the servants and sat in solitary state at the table, deep in his own thoughts. He had never known his grandfather and indeed his own parents were but shadowy figures after such a long time and yet he had found the funeral service both sad and moving. He must discover once and for all the circumstances of his grandfather's death and who had been responsible for it. He would definitely summon Bunfield tomorrow and talk over his visit to Cromer and put the questions that he still wished to ask about the way in which his grandparents had perished. He remembered vaguely how his mother and father had talked of the shipwreck that had killed his grandparents, but it was all so long ago and he'd been but a boy, taking little heed of their talk. Death had had no meaning for a young lad, full of life, indulged by his parents and cared for by devoted servants. After all, he had never known his grandparents. He had just been happy and contented with his strong, handsome father and his beautiful, vibrant mother. He had never had a brother or sister to love and his tall gentlemanly father and his elegant American mother gave him all the affection he needed. They were his whole world and he'd wanted nothing more.

But that situation had come to an abrupt end when he was only nine years old and both of them had succumbed to typhoid fever and died within a fortnight of each other.

He remembered the sense of unreality at the time. The hushed voices of the servants, his own inability to understand both the concept of death and its inevitable finality. He'd felt immense isolation and bewilderment and remembered long hours spent wandering in the lonely, silent rooms of the great house, which formerly seemed filled with visitors, light and laughter. It was only years afterwards that he'd come to appreciate the quiet affection of his Great-Uncle Benjamin, and the warmth of some of the servants, who'd done their best to heap kindness and comfort on him.

But Sir Benjamin was obliged to return to India and Hugo was sent away to school. They did not always meet in the holidays; sometimes over a year would go by with nothing but letters from Sir Benjamin. These were always informative and gently affectionate, but it was a long and lonely childhood. As he grew towards manhood, he'd looked forward to joining his great uncle and worked conscientiously with him until Sir Benjamin decided it was time to return home. Home. . . . It wasn't really his home. Home was where Mama and Papa were and fond though he was of Sir Benjamin, he didn't feel that Westbury Hall was his home. Even after all these years, he knew very few people and wondered if he would ever settle down and feel comfortable in a place like Felbrook.

He thought of Sir Benjamin's advice to marry and have a family to guard against a lonely old age. He supposed he'd never experienced any problems in attracting women, especially in India where eligible bachelors were highly prized by well-bred young ladies, some of whom sailed out specifically to seek for an eligible husband. But this particular social set-up also made it very easy for him and other young men to form liaisons with an entirely different sort of young woman. He remembered vividly one exotic girl in Mysore, so willing to please and content with so little in return. Then a mental picture of Charlotte Grayson flashed into his mind. Her indignation when they'd first met, her bonnet awry and her lovely face streaked with mud. He smiled again at the memory. And at the Wests' party when she'd been so angry at his gesture of kissing her fingers. He'd not managed any further private talk with her, but they would be bound to meet again soon. It was unavoidable. He wondered if she would still be cross with him and decided he would have to put himself out even more to charm her out of her bad temper. Tomorrow, while he was assessing the various repairs needed to cottages in Felbrook village, he would call at the Manor and see how the family did. Who knows? She might be persuaded to take Lucy Baker for another little ride. In spite of the sombre emotions generated by the funeral, he felt happy with this thought and retired to bed.

CHAPTER NINE

Sir Benjamin Westbury was as usual sleeping late and break-fasting in his room when Hugo went downstairs. It was the sort of wonderfully joyous morning that made him glad to be alive, especially after the mournful discovery of his grandfather and the solemnity of the interment yesterday. No doubt he was demonstrating his own love of life and the feeling of gratitude that he was still here, he thought. Rapturously, wonderfully, vibrantly alive, on such a glorious sunny day, and he began to whistle to himself.

He'd decided to walk and see again some of his old childhood haunts and he swung along the well-worn footpath to the village, picking up a stout stick and every so often taking a swipe at a patch of nettles or thistle, his mind preoccupied with thoughts of Charlotte. He wondered if he would meet her. He knew she was singularly independent-minded and sometimes went walking without her maid. Maybe she would be out walking herself on such a fine morning. Perhaps they would be able to walk together for a while. As he entered the woods, he paused suddenly in his nettle-beating activity. There was not a soul about and yet, despite the very early hour, he had the unwelcome feeling that he was being followed. He looked behind him but could see no one. Whom should he see? Whom should he fear? He was in a safe and quiet country village, not in the dangerous city of London. He could only conclude that it was the strange events of his grandfather's death that had given him this sense of some mystery, which had haunted him ever since he'd come back to live at Westbury Hall. He'd be seeing ghosts and apparitions next. He smiled cynically at the thought and returned to his nettle beating, and it was as well he did, for it meant that he half turned away from the path and, at the same time, from the heavy club which was poised to strike him. It was no ghost or apparition that felled him to the ground, but a man. A large, tough rogue, who bent over him and with arms like huge hams, hauled him to his feet and pushed him roughly against a tree, holding him tightly by the front of his expensive jacket and smart cravat.

A swarthy unshaven face was pushed close to his own and the man hissed into his face, 'Nah listen, my fine swell, and listen good. Unless yer wants to be dead meat, keep yer nozzle out o' what don't concern ye, or next time yer daylights'll be darkened permanent.'

He flung Hugo back against the tree, leaving him to slide down on to the grass, before he ran swiftly away.

As Hugo hauled himself up, he reflected that his instinctive feeling that he was being followed was quite correct and that the only explanation for the attack must be his investigations into the circumstances of his grandfather's murder. He looked down ruefully at his ruined jacket and torn cravat. To the devil with the thug's threats, but still, he'd be more careful from now on. Taking out his handkerchief, he wiped his face and felt gingerly at the painful lump on the back of his head. No blood, thank God, and at least the ruffian hadn't punched him in the face. He straightened his clothes and decided to turn back towards home. He was in no fit state to greet any lady, let alone one as critical and mocking as Charlotte Grayson.

It was at that moment that he saw Charlotte herself, coming towards him along the path, looking as beautifully fresh and smart, as though she'd just stepped out of a band box.

At first, she didn't notice his dirty clothes and torn neck

cloth, but when she drew nearer to him, she exclaimed impulsively, 'Oh, Mr Westbury, what has happened? Have you had an accident, sir?'

'You could say that,' Hugo said grimly. 'An accident in the form of a hired bully boy, who accosted me in order to deliver a warning.'

'A . . . a warning?' she faltered.

'Yes. It seems I must desist forthwith from making enquiries about my grandfather's death or else suffer the consequences!' He smiled wryly to himself at his earlier feelings of light-hearted anticipation at a chance meeting with the beautiful Miss Grayson, which had culminated in a meeting of quite a different kind.

Charlotte had never looked so desirable as now, when she stood in front of him, her clear gaze meeting his own, only her tightly clasped hands betraying the anxiety she was feeling.

'It is obvious then that the ruffian attacked you because of your interest in . . . in the body in the library.'

'Exactly.'

'So . . . what do we do next?'

Hugo registered use of the word 'we' and her look of genuine concern and frowned.

'We don't do anything,' he said. 'I am the one who must act to solve the mystery of my grandfather's murder. As for you, ma'am,' he said sternly, 'take care not to go out unescorted, even in quiet Felbrook.'

'But I was there when the body was discovered,' she said mutinously. 'It would be too bad of you to try and exclude me now! And I dislike feeling helpless. I am sure I could—'

'No, Miss Grayson,' he said more gently. 'You must do nothing to draw attention to yourself. That way you will keep out of danger. For the moment, Bunfield and I will continue our investigations as secretly as possible.' Noting her rebellious expression, he gave her his most charming smile and said gravely, 'I will inform you of any progress that we make and I can always ask for your assistance if I should need it.'

She was silent but continued to look up at him questioningly, her large eyes bright and clear in the morning sunshine. He had a sudden vision of the beautiful Charlotte Grayson in his arms and feeling helpless, but quickly recalled himself to the present. He was about to observe that she was without her maid and was going to offer to escort her home, but then completely lost the thread of what he was about to say and could only gaze silently back at her. He had never felt like this before. Perhaps it was the effect of the blow to his head, he thought wildly. Devil take it, he was acting like some idiot moonling boy. He was disgusted with himself.

Still they didn't speak.

Under the shadow of the trees, her eyes looked so enormous and so deep, he felt as if he could drown in them. God help him, he must be losing his mind. All he wanted to do was take her in his arms and kiss her until she really was helpless and then to protect her and guard her from all danger.

The silence lengthened as they stood there still.

'What .. what is it . . . Mr Westbury?' she said at last, looking at him questioningly, almost fearfully.

With a supreme effort, he hastily pulled himself together. 'Nothing . . . nothing, only be careful, dear Miss Grayson. I would not want you to be in any danger.'

'I will heed your warning, Mr Westbury,' she said, taking note of the 'dear Miss Grayson', and was suddenly demure as she took his arm and they walked sedately back to Felbrook Manor.

He took his leave of her at the gate, intent on not being seen in his untidy state and wishing to return to Westbury Hall as quickly as possible. He would have a meeting with Bunfield and decide on some plan of action. He cursed himself for not going out on horseback this morning. Now he would have to walk back. Tedious and time-consuming. On the other hand, he'd set off in the hope that by chance they would meet and in that, at least, he'd been successful. Then he wondered if it really had been by chance. Charlotte Grayson walking abroad without her abigail, or footman, he reflected, was perhaps indicative that she also had hoped they would encounter each other by chance. Even his thoughts seemed incoherent. He must try and calm himself.

By the time he reached Westbury Hall, in spite of his stiff limbs and a severe headache, Hugo was in a saner mood. He even managed to get to his room without encountering either Sir Benjamin or his hated cousin Alfred. His dignified and discreet valet, Latimer, was his usual quiet self as he picked up the torn neckcloth and discarded, soiled garments which his master had thrown on to the floor of his dressing-room.

Then he said tactfully, 'Forgive me for saying so, sir, but you do not look yourself at the moment. Do you wish me to get the footman to prepare a bath for you?'

Hugo smiled appreciatively. 'How perceptive of you, Latimer,' he said. 'I am stiff and weary and my head is throbbing as though it will burst.'

Latimer laid out a fresh set of linen and then, without looking directly at him, said softly, 'May one enquire what has happened, sir?'

Hugo laughed out loud at this and said, 'An unfortunate accident, Latimer, and I have a very sore head. Be a good fellow and bring me a brandy while I await the bath.'

'Very good, sir,' Latimer replied gravely and returned in no time at all with the decanter and a glass on a silver tray, and then he discreetly retired, leaving Hugo to his warm bath.

It was some time later when Mr Bunfield was announced and Hugo received him in the library.

Bunfield's face was as innocent as ever, his small, twinkling eyes darting everywhere as he stood four square in front of Hugo. He had been summoned to discuss progress on the murder mystery and had his little battered notebook at the ready, but it was obvious that he knew something was wrong.

'Beggin' parding, sir, but you look . . . different, somehow.'

Although Hugo was now dressed in his usual smart style, it was clear that Bunfield's sharp eyes had noticed something amiss. Hugo was obliged to smile at the way the Bow Street Runner echoed the words of his valet.

'I am different,' he said ruefully. 'I was walking to Felbrook when I was set on by a huge ruffian who raised quite a handsome bump on the back of my head.'

Bunfield smiled back sympathetically. 'So you decided to go walking about the countryside, did you, sir? Well, try a bit of grease on it, sir. A little rub o' butter or lard takes the swelling down a treat.'

'Thank you, Bunfield, I shall bear that in mind,' Hugo said gravely. He smiled again as he imagined the horror on Latimer's face if he should catch Hugo ruining his expensive hairstyle by rubbing any sort of animal fat into his scalp.

There was a pause and then Bunfield said quietly, 'I have to admit to being at fault over this, sir. In fact I overheard Mr Alfred Westbury telling his valet to organize just such an attack on you, sir, but before I could intervene, one of my scouts met me with more information about the *Golden Maiden*. I was not quick enough to prevent the attack on you, Mr Westbury. I am truly sorry, sir.'

'Think nothing of it, Bunfield. It was a warning, no more. I shall take heed of it and strive to be more careful in the future. But what of the latest on the shipwreck?'

'Well, sir, one of my informants has told me that after Rudkin was saved from the wreck of the *Golden Maiden*, he became very friendly with the other survivor, Tobias Todd, whose real name was William Ingram. He was a former tutor at the Lynn Grammar School and was seemingly a quiet and respectable man with a scholarly demeanour. No one suspected that he had a past to hide. He generously offered Rudkin a temporary refuge when he became homeless and destitute. There was a degree of planned self-interest in the former schoolmaster's seeming philanthropy, however. Rudkin was not to know this, but Ingram was a villain and a murderer. Ten years earlier, he had robbed and murdered Daniel Theaker of Norwich and had hidden the body in some caves at Heacham. It only came to light years later when Theaker's remains were accidentally discovered. This was the only crime that was proved against him, sir, but it is probable that there were others.'

'It sounds to me as though we should interview Mr Rudkin again, Bunfield.'

'Aye, sir, mayhap we may also hear of other crimes that our Mr Ingram was connected with.'

'Very well. We shall definitely pay Rudkin another visit. I shall take a couple of days to nurse my sore head and then we will get back to him. Meanwhile, please continue with your local enquiries. The ruffian who attacked me was a native of these parts, of that I am convinced.'

'Aye, sir. I am also continuing to observe the movements of Mr Alfred Westbury and his manservant, Bennett. Those two need a close eye keeping on them. I suspect them of all sorts of devilry, sir, but am recording my observations in my little black book. Meanwhile, I shall await to hear from you regarding another trip to Cromer.'

He touched his broad forehead with the carved end of his stick and departed.

Long after Bunfield had gone, Hugo remained in the library, lost in thought. His cousin Alfred was nowhere to be seen and Sir Benjamin, who seemed utterly done up by the funeral of his youngest brother, kept to his room and only appeared at mealtimes. He wondered what Charlotte would think of Bunfield's latest revelations and immediately decided that he might be better to say nothing about it when they next met.

This proved to be at a soirée given by the mother of the other of 'the girls' – Mrs Augusta Casterton. There had been a little coolness between 'the girls' since the announcement of Ann's betrothal and Aurelia's mama, not to be outdone by Mrs West's lavish entertainment, was determined to make a push to land a giant matrimonial prize for her only daughter. In spite of the rumours that the heart of the charming Mr Hugo Westbury was utterly impregnable, Augusta Casterton was going ahead with her plan to help Aurelia to captivate him. She was not the sort of woman who would ever be daunted by such a deterrent to holy matrimony as an impregnable heart. In her book, all wealthy, handsome men were good husband material and her dear daughter must be the one who would change the mind of the excessively attractive Hugo Westbury and turn him into an ideal husband. Position, money and good looks were already his. What he needed to complete his cup of happiness was a wife, in the form of her dear daughter, Aurelia.

That Hugo chose to attend was not to indicate his interest in Miss Casterton, but because he was hoping to see or overhear something that might help him and Bunfield in their investigations. Also, it would definitely be an opportunity to meet Charlotte again and he found himself looking forward eagerly to that. His sore head was now completely healed and he felt somewhat dull and bored with only the subdued Sir Benjamin for company. He found Alfred so uncongenial, he discounted him as any sort of companion.

But, having accepted Mrs Casterton's invitation, he was obliged to offer a ride to Alfred, who agreed promptly and made himself agreeable for once. Hugo decided not to confront Alfred with the fact that he knew Bennett had organized the attack on him, but would see if Alfred would lower his guard sufficiently to reveal himself. Alfred seemed highly pleased at sharing a coach with Hugo and chatted pleasantly and sensibly, without any of his usual oily or insinuating conversation.

Nor was Hugo disappointed when he reached the Casterton's country mansion. One of the first persons he saw when he entered was Charlotte. She was, as expected, accompanied by her mother and sister, but also, this evening, by her Uncle Bertram. Predictably, Matthew King and his aunt were with them. Hugo was only a little behind the Grayson party as they reached the top of the staircase to be greeted by Mrs Casterton and Aurelia. Several people had already spoken to him and it was obvious that on this occasion, Augusta Casterton was determined to make it an evening to remember. She had invited everyone in the county who was of any consequence and now she stood with her daughter, acknowledging all the guests with dignified politeness. Hugo was greeted most effusively by Mrs Casterton and even the insipid Aurelia beamed at him and gave him a warm welcome.

Charlotte was talking to Lavinia and Matthew King when she saw Hugo enter Mrs Casterton's huge drawing-room and, on an impulse, she excused herself and walked towards him, offering her hand in greeting.

'Mr Westbury,' she said. 'How are you?'

Knowing that she referred to his sore head, he smiled openly and unaffectedly at both the pleasure of seeing her and with humour at the implied conspiracy of their shared secret.

'Miss Grayson,' he said, bowing over her hand. 'I am indeed wonderfully well, unless you think that the blow to my head has addled my wits for ever.'

'I cannot think that, sir,' she laughed, 'but will give you my considered opinion at the end of the evening. And, furthermore, I shall not be able to make a judgement on the state of your addled wits unless you are able to escort me into supper.'

She knew she sounded too forward and flirtatious, but how else could she respond to the tumultuous emotions that filled her at the very sight of him? He was so breathtakingly handsome in his formal evening dress and his well-cut hairstyle, which showed no evidence at all of his skirmish with the ruffian who had attacked him. He appeared to be absolutely unaffected by the experience; indeed, seemed calm and confident at the prospect of the pleasures of the evening before them.

Now he laughed immediately and with great pleasure at her obvious invitation. 'My own feelings exactly,' he said softly. 'Indeed, my heart's wish would be to escort you into supper, dear Miss Grayson. I shall hold you to your promise.'

Their eyes met and held and suddenly Charlotte's confidence almost deserted her when she saw the unmistakeable gleam in his dark eyes. She changed the subject quickly. 'Have you found out any more from Mr Bunfield?'

'Well, a few more details of the shipwreck, but it is early days yet and we shall be pursuing further enquiries in Cromer. Meanwhile, I agreed to keep my eyes and ears open for anything that might be significant.'

He was still gazing compellingly at her and this evening Charlotte was feeling in a flamboyant mood. She knew she was looking her best in a fashionably low-cut gown, with her hair dressed high in formal ringlets at the back and more casual curls framing her beautiful face, which at this moment was alight with mischief and pleasure. She flirted her fan at him and Hugo was surprised at the sudden ease that he felt, talking to a woman he had formerly thought of as difficult and aggressive.

He was silent now and Charlotte was suddenly serious. 'I do not know whether it is either wise or safe for you to continue with your enquiries. I only know that I must warn you to be careful.'

'As I warned you, if you remember,' he said, also serious now.

'True. But now we shall have to part soon, or the gossips will be having a field day. It is a pity we have not the opportunity to speak more freely.'

Hugo smiled. '*Au contraire*, I thought we *were* speaking freely.'

Charlotte was also obliged to smile at this. 'Yes, but in very restricted circumstances. If you should think of any way that I might be of help in this, you may visit us at any time. Mama has never been a she-dragon over callers and Papa always used to encourage any down-at-heel waif or stray who came to our house for help.'

Hugo's lips twitched at the idea of himself as a down-at-heel waif or stray, but he answered with admirable gravity: 'I never realized that your mama was so civil to me because she had me down as a waif or a stray. Which am I, do you think? Does "waif" describe me to a tee, or does "stray" fit me more accurately?'

She laughed again. 'Odious man, you deliberately misunderstand me. And now I must go and join Mama and the others.'

Hugo bowed and Charlotte retreated back to Matthew and Lavinia, leaving Hugo still smiling at their exchange.

His smile soon disappeared as his cousin Alfred materialized silently at the side of him, his manner quite changed from what it had been in the coach.

'Quite a looker, ain't she?' He said it with such leering innuendo that Hugo was inclined to plant him a facer. Only his well-bred social discipline prevented it. He said nothing and merely cocked a disdainful eyebrow, but Alfred carried on regardless.

'But she is a bit of a hoyden, coz. Any man brave enough to wed her would be grasping a tiger by the tail, eh? Still, I must go over and pay my respects. She will expect it and might favour me with one of her smiles, or even a waltz.'

He left Hugo, and sauntered languidly over to Mrs Grayson and her daughters, leaving Hugo furious. He'd never liked his cousin Alfred. Even as boys, they were never good friends, and he found that the passing years had made him even more conscious of his dislike of Alfred's oily personality.

As for Charlotte, she was obliged to greet Alfred politely and she allowed herself to be led on to the floor with a good grace, but was impatient, wishing it were time for Hugo to claim her to go into supper. She was obliged to be discreet, however. Her earlier conversation and banter with Hugo would not have gone unnoticed and she must not do any more to draw attention to their sudden and close alliance over the murder of Hugo's grandfather. Her continued thoughts of Hugo Westbury and her preoccupation with his investigations must not be allowed to overwhelm her entirely.

Alfred was as usual dressed in the height of fashion, with more than a hint of the dandy about him and, looking at his splendid waistcoat, she wondered where his money came from. Mrs Palmer, the purveyor of all the village gossip, was adamant that Mr Alfred's pockets were always to let and that he was looking out for a wealthy young bride, 'or even a careless widder', she sniffed, disapprovingly.

It became clear to Charlotte that Alfred was determined to press his attentions on her and she was soon concentrating so hard on not allowing him to pull her too close and in politely fending off his unwanted endearments, that she was unable to enjoy the dance at all.

She'd given no hint of the repugnance she felt at Alfred soliciting her hand for a waltz, merely accepting his invitation coolly, with no sign that she found him so unattractive. Looked at objectively, he was quite a good-looking young man. Not as striking as his cousin Hugo and if Mrs Palmer and others were to be believed, not as tall and strongly handsome as Sir Benjamin had once been. Good-looking all the same. No, it was not Alfred's appearance that she found so obnoxious but some primeval inexplicable woman's instinct that told her that he was dangerous. She didn't need Hugo Westbury's dire warnings to have nothing to do with his cousin; her own common sense warned her not to trust him. She knew in her innermost heart that he was not a good prospect for any respectable woman and she resolved to avoid him as much as possible.

Her instincts were borne out by his behaviour during the dance. She realized regretfully that her foolish acceptance of his proposed trip to Sheringham had been a stupid move. After all, she'd no intention of taking up his invitation, even if Mama agreed to it. As it was, he seemed to have the idea that he held some attraction for her. She bitterly regretted the encouragement she'd given him just to try to anger Hugo Westbury. The embarrassing innuendo of Alfred's softly whispered remarks, the too-tight clasp of his moist hand at her waist and the way he stared fixedly at her bosom in the low-cut dress would make most young women steer very clear of him. Why had she been so stupid as to agree to his suggested Sheringham trip? She dealt with his brazen importuning by deliberately turning her thoughts to more pleasant subjects. She danced mechanically, determined not to respond to his suggestive overtures in any way. Her dogged perseverance in the face of his unwelcome behaviour did not endear her to him and was made the more difficult for Charlotte by the need to remain polite and not cause a scene.

It was obvious that her steady rejection of him angered him far more than any strong protestations on her part could have done, and finally he was moved to remark angrily, 'It is your choice, Miss Grayson, to reject me in favour of my well-to-do cousin, Hugo, who has no more sense than to stick his nose into long-forgotten deeds which do not concern him.'

In spite of her preoccupation with trying to thwart his amorous intentions, Charlotte registered the significance of this remark and stored it silently for future reference. It was difficult for her to give Alfred her full attention in any case, because at that moment she noticed the usually pleasant Matthew glowering from the edge of the dance floor. Even when the dance ended and Alfred escorted her to her seat, he still continued to hang on to her relentlessly, being as charming as he knew how and including her mama and Kitty in the conversation as much as possible.

At last, Matthew led Kitty away to the supper room and George and Lavinia followed them, but still Alfred Westbury held on. It was obvious that he was angling for another opportunity to see her and he floated several ideas, in addition to walking in Sheringham, which included a river trip and picnic and even a riding party in the grounds of Westbury Hall, with lunch alfresco. Charlotte wondered fleetingly whether he'd asked permission from Sir Benjamin for this last idea. She doubted it. She observed that her mama was silent but watchful during several more minutes of his inane conversation. But he finally took his leave, having remembered that he was to meet an old friend in the card room. She was relieved when she saw Hugo coming towards them.

He gave Charlotte and her mama an elegant bow and said, 'Miss Grayson, I trust you have not forgotten our supper engagement.' Then with his most winning smile, 'Mrs Grayson, ma'am. May I be allowed to escort *two* charming ladies into supper?'

Jane Grayson returned his smile with one which was very reminiscent of her daughter's and said, 'I am sorry, Mr Westbury. It is extremely kind of you, but I am to be escorted by Squire Perkins.'

Hugo bowed again and offered Charlotte his arm and led her into supper. He was punctilious in making sure she had what she desired from the buffet table and that the footman filled her wine glass as soon as she was seated.

'Your very good health, Miss Grayson,' he said, and nudged her glass gently with his own.

She responded with a sparkling smile, as he knew she would, and then he said very softly, 'I feared that you were avoiding me when I was attacked by that ruffian. I had been walking towards Felbrook on the off chance that we might meet and possibly see Lucy Baker, of course.'

'Oh,' she said, somewhat at a loss. 'Well, at least if we gave Lucy a little outing, we could perhaps speak more privately.'

He laughed. 'We are alone at this table. No one can overhear us. I wonder what exactly it is, Miss Grayson, that you have to say to me that is so private and confidential?'

She coloured a little but said, 'You know exactly what I mean. Pray do not pretend, sir, to be so lacking in understanding of a woman's ... curiosity ... I want to hear all about that ruffian's attack on you. What had you done to deserve it? What was the object of such a heinous crime in peaceful Felbrook?'

He laughed again, not answering her question directly, but with no trace of condescension or mockery. He found it so easy to talk to her now that their initial antipathy seemed to have worn off.

Charlotte used no subterfuges, was never arch or simpering, like other young women he had known. He'd never found it so easy to converse with a woman on equal terms and he was enjoying it, having quite forgotten now his original intention to win her affection in order to teach her a lesson. He realized he'd forgotten it some time ago. If he hadn't been so accursed high and mighty in the beginning, they would have been friends before now.

Her voice was also low as she said, 'One of the things I most miss about Papa is his conversation. Kitty and I could talk to him with utter frankness on any subject under the sun. In society, it is sometimes difficult for women to speak on matters which ... which ... may even affect us more than most. . . .'

She looked him in the eye. 'I want you to know that whatever you discover about the sad circumstances of your grandfather's death, I appreciate your willingness to share your findings with me. It is just what Papa would have done.'

He was silent for a moment and then he said gravely, 'I am flattered at your interest, Miss Grayson. And now, let us have another glass of champagne.'

Once more, they toasted each other and then he said, 'Perhaps we may meet on Sunday, after Sunday school?'

'On Sunday, then,' she agreed.

CHAPTER TEN

It was not to be supposed that her actions had gone unnoticed and the next morning, Charlotte Grayson received a visit from Matthew King, who was both hurt and angry at the obvious deepening of the relationship between herself and Hugo Westbury.

Jane Grayson, fully aware of the implications for the planned betrothal of her eldest daughter, left them alone and indicated to Kitty that she should go and help Mrs Palmer in the kitchen.

'Really, Charlotte,' Matthew exclaimed as soon as the drawing-room door shut behind them. 'It is the outside of enough that my aunt and I have had to endure all the gossip and sly hints from the neighbourhood tabbies at your reprehensible behaviour last evening.'

Charlotte was coldly polite. 'What behaviour is that, pray?'

'Why, your lengthy tête-à-tête with Hugo Westbury, in full view of the whole neighbourhood.'

'Nonsense,' she said, even more frostily. 'It was perfectly respectable and our conversation was open for anyone to join us at any time. We were not attempting any illicit or unsuitable communication. You were certainly welcome to join us. But perhaps you were too busy with your own tête-à-tête with my sister,' she added pointedly.

Matthew said nothing for a moment. His face went first red and then deathly white. 'That is unworthy of you, Charlotte,' he said, visibly shaken. 'It makes me realize that all my hopes for our future have come to nothing. We can never now achieve happiness together.'

Charlotte was also shaken. For the first time, she was obliged to face up to the reality of a married life with Matthew, a clever and pleasant man, but one whom she did not love. In the last few weeks, she'd come to recognize that the understanding she'd had with Matthew King, which had promised a comfortable and secure future, was now at an end. This thought was somewhat like looking down into an abyss. Suddenly, she felt her whole future was empty and uncertain. She was twenty years old and if the love that she'd been able to count on was withdrawn so absolutely, perhaps she would never meet a suitable husband. Perversely, now that he was crying off, she remembered only the happy times of their relationship and regretted the gap that it would leave in her life. Conflicting emotions filled her. Overwhelmingly, though, her feelings were of relief, as she realized that she'd never valued the promise of their betrothal. In her secret heart, she was unable to believe totally in the idea that she could be wholly happy with Matthew King. Meeting Hugo Westbury had shown her the possibility of a passionate and wholly unconditional love that could be a much more exciting basis for a married life. Even if her secret hopes and dreams came to nothing, she thought, at least her eyes were now widely open as to what a deeply loving marriage could and should be.

She'd remained calm in the face of Matthew's anger and disappointment and didn't allow any of these mixed feelings to show in her face. She kept her expression neutral as she said, 'If that is your wish, Matthew, I am happy to release you from any agreement that existed between us. I hope I will always be your friend, but I am thankful that we were never formally betrothed.'

Ears stretched and abnormally aware of the drama being played out in the drawing-room, Mrs Grayson and Kitty, standing in the kitchen with Mrs Palmer, heard the wall-shaking slam of the front door as Matthew took his leave. Indeed, everyone in the house heard it and it was to be a talking point of Mrs Palmer's for days to come.

Charlotte's mother and sister both felt it would be best not to broach the subject of the quarrel with Matthew and if they noticed that Charlotte was unusually quiet, decided not to comment on it. Jane Grayson did what she always did in times of family crisis. She cooked a special meal, which was Charlotte's favourite – slow roasted lamb with a creamy onion sauce, accompanied by home-grown potatoes and fresh little garden peas. In spite of her rather subdued mood, Charlotte was hungry and anyway, tomorrow was Sunday and she would see Hugo again. As for Kitty, her tender young heart was wrung by her sister's situation and she knew that Matthew must also be suffering. She was the only one who failed to do justice to Mama's excellent dinner.

Matthew made straight for his aunt's cottage after the parting from Charlotte and moodily declined all offers of refreshments or wine. Lavinia could see that he was not his usual pleasant self and surmised, quite rightly, that it was to do with Charlotte Grayson. She waited tactfully until they were seated in her cosy parlour, each with a glass of mellow sherry, awaiting the arrival of Adam Brown, before trying her subtle tactics to encourage him to confide in her.

'Matthew, dear, I have something to tell you.'

'Oh yes?' he said, with minimal interest.

'Matthew . . . you like Adam, don't you?'

'Oh yes. Splendid fellow.'

'Matthew . . . last night, Adam . . . asked me to . . . to marry him. And I said yes, Matthew.'

'Did you, by Jove? Well, Aunt, congratulations. I cannot pretend that it is unexpected.'

'You mean . . . you guessed?'

He smiled for the first time since he had come home. 'A blind man with both his eyes shut could guess, dear Aunt.'

'Good gracious!' she exclaimed, blushing. 'But what of your own courtship, my dear? When are you and the lovely Charlotte Grayson to be betrothed?'

'Never,' he said moodily and scowled at his glass.

'Oh, no, please do not tell me you have quarrelled,' she said, distressed at the finality of his tone.

'More than that. We should never suit, Aunt Lavinia. We both realize it. Please do not be tempted to pursue it. Charlotte and I will be friends only from now on.'

'But how dreadful.'

'Not at all,' he said quickly. 'It is for the best. And do not let it interfere with your own happiness.' He stood up, smiling, and held out a hand to her. 'You look far too young to be an aunt when you blush like that. And now, dearest of aunts, I hear Adam coming, so we must set out to be cheerful and entertain him.'

That same morning, Hugo Westbury had occasion to visit some of the estate cottages, including that of the Bakers and, it not being Sunday, he had no reason to suppose he might see Charlotte, but even so, a little germ of hope lingered within him and he was disappointed not to meet her. Having asked Mrs Baker's permission to take Lucy for a ride with himself and Miss Grayson, he was further disappointed by the news that little Lucy was ill and would not be going either to Sunday school or on any outing, so he returned home. There he found his cousin Alfred ensconced in the drawing-room with a decanter of sherry and some small cakes in front of him.

'Hope you don't mind, old fellow,' Alfred said. 'That butler of yours put me in here. Said you wouldn't be long.' He waved a hand towards the sherry. 'Why not join me in a glass of something, coz? Then I can tell you the latest gossip. Everyone's agog at the way you were getting on so famously with the beautiful Miss Charlotte Grayson at the Castertons' party.'

Hugo had no intention of listening to the gossip and was

already out of temper with both his disappointment at not seeing Charlotte and distaste at finding his cousin still on the premises so long after the other mourners had departed. He merely frowned at Alfred and said nothing, which didn't deter his cousin in the slightest.

'Not only that, but my man has it from someone in the know that Matthew King stormed up to the Graysons' this morning and it ended with the young lady and himself having an almighty row and severing their friendship. What do you think to that, eh?'

'I do not think anything,' Hugo said coldly. 'Miss Grayson's friendships are her own concern and it is not up to me to offer any comment about either her or Matthew King.'

This was not the response that Alfred had hoped for and he said weakly, 'I thought you would be interested, coz, especially as I notice that you seem to be the lady's bosom beau at the moment.'

Hugo's tone was now more icy than ever and said pointedly, 'Oh, you notice that, do you? A pity you have no concerns of your own to notice, Alfred. What of your own life in London and your own social engagements? Will not your friends be missing you?'

'Oh, they don't signify,' Alfred said carelessly. He was disappointed that Hugo had failed to react to his spiteful tittle-tattle and as for returning to his own friends, well, he couldn't care less, because he hadn't any true friends.

Hugo tolerated only a few more minutes of Alfred's nonsense and then he excused himself brusquely and went in search of Bunfield. There was but one inn at Felbrook, aptly named The Brook, and it was there that Bunfield had his lodgings – a single room only, but he was able to make use of the landlady's little parlour downstairs. There were rarely any residents at The Brook and such regulars as there were always congregated in the tap room. It was in there that he found the Bow Street Runner, knocking out his pipe against the chimney back, with eyes lowered and ears open for any gossip.

Once Hugo had ascertained that Bunfield had seen him, he went into the inn yard and lounged casually outside the door. Bunfield came out immediately and both men went into the parlour where they could be private.

'I am pleased to see you, sir,' Bunfield said.

'Yes, I feel that now is the time to investigate things a little further. How about a return visit to Mr Rudkin?'

'Aye, sir. If you feels recovered from your – er – accident, I can be ready any time. The only other thing to report is, I have been keeping feelers out round Felbrook concerning your attacker and my informants state that not only is he local, but he is closely acquainted with your own cousin, sir, Mr Alfred Westbury, that is, and his servant Josiah Bennett.'

'Is he indeed?'

'But I thought we shouldn't apprehend your assailant just yet, Mr Westbury, but just continue to keep an eye on him for the time being. Give him enough rope, sir, and mayhap he'll hang 'isself.'

Yes, and that goes for my cousin Alfred, too, Hugo thought grimly.

Aloud, he said, 'When can you be ready then, Bunfield?'

'When you like, sir. Shall we say in an hour?'

There was no time for Hugo to say anything else, because there was a timid knock on the door. It was the landlady, very red-faced from cooking and wiping floury hands on her apron.

'Beg pardon, Mr Wes'bry, sir, but there's a young lady as wants to see you.'

Hugo frowned at this and she whispered, 'It be Miss Grayson, sir.'

Hugo cursed softly under his breath. Damn! Of course, Charlotte knew he was in close touch with Bunfield. She must have guessed he'd be here.

'Do you wish to be private with the young lady, sir?' Bunfield said diffidently.

'No. It is merely that Miss Grayson was present when the

body was found and she knows you are putting up here, Bunfield. Furthermore, she feels she has a right to some involvement in the mystery. Show her in, Mrs Lacey, if you please.'

Bunfield looked closely at Charlotte as she entered the room. She was dressed plainly, in a dove-grey walking dress, whose very plainness served only to emphasize her very vibrant beauty. He noticed that her maid remained firmly outside the door.

Hugo introduced them and Charlotte gave both men her most brilliant smile. 'How do you do, Mr Bunfield. I am pleased to renew our acquaintance.'

She turned to Hugo. 'Mr Westbury. I had hoped to see you tomorrow, but poor Lucy Baker has a bad sore throat and will not be venturing out to the Sunday school class. I thought . . . I thought . . . that I should tell you and Mr Bunfield of some more information that has come my way . . . . connected to your recent attacker, I mean.'

Hugo was polite and friendly, but spoke with studied coolness. 'I understand and appreciate your interest, Miss Grayson, but I must protest that I do not wish you to endanger your own life in any way by getting involved in this dangerous business.'

But Charlotte was determined not to be put off. She continued as though he hadn't spoken.

'It concerns a man called Jim Butler. He is from Cromer but has lived round here for a number of years. One of the stable lads has told me that he is often backwards and forwards to Cromer. He is without any apparent work and never puts himself forward for employment on any of the farms near here. . . . And yet . . . and yet . . . he always seems to have money. He has a cottage on the edge of the village, very close to Sir Benjamin's woods, and Luke the stable lad says that he is sometimes to be seen in the woods, in conversation with Mr Alfred Westbury's servant. Luke has it that Jim Butler is a man who may be hired to commit violence, by anyone who has the money to pay his fee.'

While she was speaking, Bunfield had been looking at her with his head on one side, his bright eyes never leaving her face. 'I call that valuable information, Mr Westbury,' he said gravely. 'It confirms what my own informers have said about Jim Butler. Sounds as though he might be worth looking into.'

Hugo deliberately schooled his features not to reveal his thoughts. 'I agree, Bunfield,' he said neutrally. 'Thank you for your help, Miss Grayson. It is very much appreciated. We are about to visit Cromer again and could follow up your information. Nevertheless, I must repeat, I do not wish you to expose yourself to unnecessary danger by concerning yourself in this.'

Charlotte felt as though she had been snubbed. She said indignantly, 'But I already *am* concerned in it. When the body of your grandfather was discovered, it was before you even took up residence in Westbury Hall.'

'That may be so,' he said, smiling a little, 'but if we are to get any further, Mr Bunfield and I must be able to get on with the investigation without having to worry about your own safety, ma'am.'

Although he spoke gently, she was aware that he would brook no argument. She caught Bunfield looking at her very gravely and subsided, her bottom lip protruding mutinously. Hugo had no right to tell her not to put herself in danger, especially as he was about to endanger himself by accompanying Bunfield to mix with the low-life of Cromer.

Hugo observed her expressive face as it revealed all her doubts and her unwillingness to do as he'd decided. As he watched the rebellious expression on her beautiful face, he longed suddenly to take her into his arms and kiss the mutinous red mouth into submission.

But he revealed none of these thoughts as he said smoothly, 'So that is agreed then. We shall be ready to depart within the hour, Mr Bunfield. I shall take you up a little distance from here, halfway along Brook Lane, in fact. It would be more discreet, I think, and we will assume a much more lowly appearance when we visit Cromer.'

'But you will be careful!' Charlotte begged him.

'Yes, of course, Miss Grayson,' he said and gave her his most winning smile. 'But I am determined to solve the mystery of my grandfather's death, whatever the cost.'

'It has already cost you a severe blow to the head,' Charlotte said caustically.

Exasperated, Hugo forgot his imposed calm and, turning to Bunfield, he said, 'The presence of a woman always means trouble at a time like this, Bunfield.'

The Bow Street Runner preserved his own bland expression with admirable self-control, but Charlotte said passionately, 'And what about *you*? What sort of trouble are *you* in when you take off on such a venture? You will not be treated as Mr Hugo Westbury when you are mixing with the low life of Cromer, dressed as a lowly common peasant! How will Sir Benjamin and . . and . . . your . . . other friends react when you are murdered by some ruffian!'

Hugo opened his mouth to give an equally forceful answer to her challenge, but when he looked into those brilliant grey-green eyes, he realized she was mocking him, and yes, flirting with him. He wanted more than ever to accept her challenge and kiss away all her resistance.

Instead, he said mildly, 'Steady, Miss Grayson. It would not do to scare poor Bunfield away from his investigations. As for me, you may be sure that I shall do my best to come out of it unscathed, and when I return, I shall hold you to your promise of another outing with Lucy Baker.'

CHAPTER ELEVEN

If Hugo had dressed down for his first foray into The Black Lion, his attire had been princely compared to what it was this time. He had obtained rooms for himself and Bunfield and they had effected their disguises in secret, slipping out of The Royal Oak under cover of darkness.

Both were unrecognizable except in build and stature. Hugo had even rubbed chimney soot on to his well-kept gentlemanly hands and wiped them across his face to heighten the illusion of being a down-at-heel labourer. They entered The Black Lion as unobtrusively as possible and although they were obvious strangers, they were mingling freely in the company of murderers, rogues and vagabonds. Strangers were common in this place, in which felons were up to every criminal ploy known to man in order to earn a dishonest penny, and so no one gave them a second glance.

Bunfield had found his clothes for him. God alone knew where he'd acquired them, Hugo thought ruefully. They were not just poor, they were the rags of someone utterly destitute, their patches and darns bearing mute testimony to the abject poverty of their former owner. Bunfield was similarly attired and both men wore knotted scarves and had secreted pistols in the capacious poacher's pockets of their jackets as a precaution against attack. Their boots were the hard tough boots of farm labourers, cracked with age and caked with dried mud.

Hugo felt that in this disguise, only his drawling upper-class voice would give him away and resolved to let Bunfield do most of the talking. To help him with his rough approximation of an uneducated ruffian's accent, he imagined the cadences and pronunciation of some of the estate labourers and tried to keep them in his brain while he formulated some questions for Rudkin.

He let Bunfield order two tankards of ale and looked round quickly to see if he could see Ted Rudkin. There were all sorts and conditions of criminals in The Black Lion. He could see a couple of common prostitutes, standing just inside the doorway and eyeing up the men, but they were both fat, ugly and raggedy girls and as yet none of the patrons of the inn were drunk enough to become their clients. Crouched in one corner was a one-legged beggar, his face eaten away by ulcerated sores, his shoulders slumped in resigned misery. Some of the men, with rough kindness, had thrust a coin his way and the man was waiting patiently to be served with some gin. In spite of the almost frenetic liveliness of The Black Lion's atmosphere, Hugo felt keenly the despair and misery underlying the falsely convivial atmosphere. Here, he realized, was the flotsam and jetsam of sordid humanity. A most suitable place for Rudkin, he thought.

At that moment, sure enough, he spied his quarry sitting alone in one of the booths furthest from the door. He seemed just as nervous as last time, his eyes darting all around as he drank and his arms and legs jerking as though he could hardly keep a limb still. When Bunfield returned with the drinks, Hugo indicated Rudkin with his eyes and both men approached him very casually.

Nothing could be further from the popular idea of a Bow Street Runner at that moment, as Bunfield lapsed into the coarse speech that was expected in a place like The Black Lion. He adopted a faintly threatening manner towards the surly Rudkin as he growled, 'You and me 'as got a bit o' business to finish off, Ted Rudkin.'

Rudkin looked alarmed but tried to stifle it and appear

confident. 'Wot's your game, cully? I've met this 'ere cove who's wiv you before, and I knows he's a gent. Wot you two want wi' me?'

'We need you to talk to us,' Bunfield said softly, 'and, if a bird don't sing, Rudkin, this same gent 'as ways ter persuade 'im.'

'I don't know what you mean. I know naught, I tell you.' Obviously nervous now, Rudkin had begun to babble, an expression of terror flitting across his weasel-like features.

'We'll soon see about that,' Bunfield said menacingly. 'Drink up, Rudkin, and then on your feet; this gent and I will walk you to somewhere quiet, where we can talk. Start resisting and it will be the worse for you.'

From above the pewter tankard, Rudkin's bloodshot old eyes darted to right and left in an agony of indecision. It was obvious that he wanted to flee, that he could not stay and fight such opposition as either the tall, muscular Hugo Westbury or the stockier but equally formidable Bunfield. It was equally obvious that he could expect no support or succour from the rogues and vagabonds who frequented The Black Lion. No honour among thieves and no help there. He deliberately made his last swigs of ale as long drawn out as he could until, hand in pocket and holding the gun, Bunfield nudged the cold steel into his ribs.

'On your way, Rudkin,' he muttered and the trio made their way outside into the filthy, mean alley behind the inn.

'Now, Ted, lad,' said Bunfield sarcastically. 'We can either do this nicely or we can do it nastily. Which is it to be?'

Rudkin began to shake. 'I don't know what you mean. As God's my witness. . . .'

'Oh, He is. Be in no doubt about it, but so are we.' Bunfield slammed him up against the wall and said brutally, 'Some answers, if you please, Rudkin. First, who were the survivors of the *Golden Maiden*?'

Rudkin's pathetically few teeth were chattering now, but he was too nervous even to rub the lump on his head caused by its contact with the wall.

'I . . . I told you, there was only me and Mr Charles Westbury.'

Hugo stepped forward and pressed one of his hands to the wall on each side of Rudkin's neck, trapping him in an iron cage from which there was no escape. 'But this is not strictly true, is it, Ted?' he said quietly menacing. 'We know, do we not, that there was at least one other passenger who did not perish on the night of the storm?'

'I . . . I . . . well, perhaps.'

'Perhaps?'

'There were a gen'leman walked free an' all.'

'His name?'

Rudkin squirmed and Hugo's hands tightened. 'His name, I said.'

'It . . . it were . . . the schoolmaster. Mr Todd.'

Hugo let out a long breath. 'And what happened to Mr Charles Westbury? Where did he go after he had survived the sinking of the *Golden Maiden*?'

'I . . . he. . . .'

'He what?'

'He were given shelter in The Jolly Sailor. After that. . . .'

Hugo took hold of him by the scruffy collar of his jacket. 'And after that?' he said, between clenched teeth.

Rudkin was silent for a few seconds, which seemed to stretch for eternity. His lips worked nervously, but no sound came. Then suddenly the words poured out of him as though in a torrent. He said in his whining voice, 'It were nowt to do wi' me. Mr Charles Westbury had lost his wife, see, and 'ad been injured wi' a falling mast. Mr Todd reckoned as he knew Mr Westbury's brother, George, and could get help for 'im. He sent word to Lunnon an' a carriage came to fetch the three of us. We looked after Mr Westbury on the journey to Westbury Hall, him being very weak wi' loss of blood an' o' course losing his young wife . . . I had naught to do wi' owt. George Westbury met us at the 'all and paid me for me trouble an' gave me a ticket for the stage back to Cromer . . . I never saw any of 'em after that. . . .'

Bunfield now stepped forward. 'And this Tobias Todd you were in league with, did you know his real name was William Ingram?'

'No. . . . I swear. . . .'

'What happened to him after the rescue?'

'I don't know, guv. I left 'im wi' the two brothers. I swear I had nowt more to do wi' 'em. I went back home and then I were taken on by Captain Mason on the *Pride O' Wells*. I ne'er set eyes on any of 'em agen.'

Bunfield thrust him away in disgust. 'Pah! You're a worthless rogue, Rudkin. You must have known what was to be the fate of that hapless Charles Westbury when you left him with Ingram.'

'I . . . no . . . I never. . . .'

'He was a murderer, Rudkin. After you had been paid off and was away on the *Pride O' Wells*, the law finally caught up with him and he was hanged.'

'I knew naught, I tell you.'

'Well, mark this, Rudkin. After he was dead, his body was hung on the gibbet at Norwich for twelve years, to warn other felons. Think yourself lucky you were rescued by Captain Mason.'

'I'm just an old tar, sir. Never meant anyone harm, so 'elp me. . . .'

'Get out of my sight, you're the scum of the earth. If it were not for your age, Rudkin, I would have you before the magistrate and hanged as an accessory to murder. Go, before I do you a mischief.'

Rudkin scuttled off and both men returned to their rooms at The Royal Oak and discreetly changed their appearance before meeting up once more in the parlour. They ordered brandies and Bunfield lit up a long, old-fashioned pipe. He caught Hugo looking at him questioningly and said, 'Yes, Mr Westbury, Rudkin's confession has given me cause for thought. During my enquiries, I searched the records in Norwich for any mention of Ingram and Rudkin. It is quite true that Ingram was a seemingly respectable schoolmaster at the Lynn Grammar School and he became popular with the boys. He went under the name of "Todd" and was a frequent visitor to the vicarage at Heacham. It was noticed that he was a man of loneliness and mystery, fond of taking solitary rambles along the cliffs, but all who knew him attributed this to his scholarly nature, no one suspecting that he had anything to hide. But William Ingram was a murderer, quite famous in his time as it happens. Some five years before the sinking of the *Golden Maiden*, he had murdered and robbed Daniel Theaker, a wealthy merchant, and had hidden his body in some caves near Heacham. The foul deed only came to light when the body was discovered by a sweep digging for stones to supply his lime kilns. Ingram's young accomplice turned King's evidence and his testimony was enough to condemn the schoolmaster to death. He was arraigned and executed. His body was indeed hanged in chains by the roadside at Norwich, where the gibbet remained for several years as a warning to other wrongdoers.'

Hugo listened in horror to the tale and then said slowly, 'But does that mean, then, that Rudkin and Ingram, or Todd as he called himself, were the last people to see my grandfather alive?'

'And your Great-Uncle George perhaps,' Bunfield said gently. 'Rudkin did indeed go back to sea, but after his voyage with Captain Mason, he never managed another voyage. He's a very old man now, and has not worked for years.'

Hugo said nothing, thinking of Bunfield's horrifying revelations. Until the macabre discovery behind the panelling at Westbury Hall, no one even suspected that his grandfather had not perished at sea. His own parents had died very young, in America, so would have heard nothing of William Ingram. His Great-Uncle George was dead and Sir Benjamin had lived most of his life in India.

He sighed and said, 'It was all so very long ago. Perhaps we will never know the truth of it.'

'Yes, perhaps,' Bunfield agreed and knocked out his pipe against the chimney breast Both of them were silent for a time, each thinking his own thoughts.

Finally, Bunfield said quietly, 'If you agree, sir, I feel we should leave Rudkin for the time being and return to Felbrook. He was never accused of anything when Ingram was arraigned for murder. My guess is that we will not get much more out of him than what he has already told us, unless he has to appear in a court of law, that is, but I think it unlikely. If you agree, Mr Westbury, I think I should continue with local enquiries, especially as regards to that Jim Butler, the man mentioned by Miss Grayson.'

'Yes, very well. I agree,' Hugo said. 'And meanwhile, we should both be discreet but vigilant in gathering information from my cousin's activities.'

And so it was decided and, having settled the tally with the landlord of The Royal Oak, they journeyed home, both of them still deep in thought.

The next day was Sunday and began pleasantly enough. Latimer had discreetly handed Hugo a note from Charlotte as soon as he was dressed and had tactfully disappeared while his master was reading it.

Dear Mr Westbury
I have a message from my small friend, Lucy Baker, who very politely requests another little ride on Gypsy. As Lucy is now completely restored to health, I have deemed it suitable to pass on her message to you, in the hope that you will grant her wish. We shall definitely be at church this Sunday, but if you are unable to oblige Lucy in this, I shall convey the bad news to her myself and think of an alternative little treat for her.

Seeing Hugo's mobile mouth curve into a most joyous smile,

the normally taciturn Latimer ventured to ask, 'Good news, sir?'

'Yes, Latimer. Very good news.' And Hugo went down to the dining-room, whistling.

It being Sunday, there was no sign of his obnoxious cousin Alfred, but Sir Benjamin, despite his frailty, was immaculately turned out and was even partaking of a little breakfast.

'Ah, Hugo,' he said. 'How went the journey to Cromer? Did Bunfield find any more clues to this ghastly business?'

'Some,' Hugo said cautiously. 'We talked to one of the last people to have seen my grandfather alive. He is a very old man now, but was rescued along with Charles Westbury, when the *Golden Maiden* capsized.'

In spite of his frailty, Sir Benjamin's eyes were still keenly intelligent. 'You said "one" of the last people, my boy. May one ask who the others were?'

'Well, unfortunately, a notorious Norfolk murderer and . . .' Seeing his great-uncle's stricken look, Hugo lowered his voice and said gently, 'And the other one may have been my Great-Uncle George.'

There was a pause as the implication of what Hugo had said sank in, but then the old gentleman squared his shoulders and said firmly, 'But you do not know for certain who was with Charles when he . . . when he met his end. . . .'

'That is true,' Hugo said even more gently. 'Ted Rudkin is very old himself and a proven liar. He may or may not have been there when my grandfather was killed. We do not know for certain, sir. Mr Bunfield is still pursuing his enquiries.'

Sir Benjamin's face was impassive. It was difficult to tell whether these latest revelations had any effect on him or not. Neither of them said any more because at that moment, Alfred Westbury walked into the room, smiling as though well pleased with himself, and Sir Benjamin signalled to the footman that he wished to return to his room and after the briefest exchange of civilities with his cousin, Hugo did the same.

In spite of his great-uncle's obvious unease about Bunfield's findings, Hugo was unaffected by it and still retained his earlier mood of cheerful optimism as he ordered the groom to bring round Gypsy ready for his journey to church and a hoped-for meeting with Charlotte Grayson.

CHAPTER TWELVE

Charlotte's day had begun innocuously enough. Although it was rather cold, the walk to the church was a pleasant one and she had been able to persuade Phoebe that as there were so few blooms, Mama might need some help with collecting suitable foliage for the flower arrangements in the church. She was thus able to travel to morning service alone and set off eagerly. She was full of hope and anticipation at the pleasure of meeting Hugo and perhaps an enjoyable outing with dear little Lucy. Her spirits were high as she stepped blithely along the path to the church, lost in a dream of love and romance with the handsome Hugo Westbury. What did it matter if her hopes were unrealistic? She smiled to herself as she thought of him and was full of the confidence and optimism of youth. At that moment, she felt that anything was possible. Remembering the way he had looked into her eyes at Aurelia's party, she was certain that he returned her regard. They would walk the bridle path to the boundary with Wycliffe Manor and would have some chance to talk.

The attack came suddenly and with no warning. A figure appeared from nowhere and a dark blanket was thrown over her head. Immensely strong arms held her fast and although she struggled, it was quite futile. Charlotte lifted her skirts above her ankles and attempted to break away and run along the path towards the church.

It was to no avail. She was immediately caught up and

swung off her feet. She attempted to scream, but a large, rough hand was instantly clapped over her mouth. There was no escape. She could feel the animal strength of his long arms, smell the vile stench of him and taste the filthy blanket next to her lips. The next moment, she felt herself being thrown unceremoniously into a closed carriage. The door slammed and she heard the ruffian leap into the driver's seat and away they went. As they drove off at a cracking speed, the carriage rocked and Charlotte tore off the dark blanket which covered her head. She managed to look through the window and realized that they were just passing the large, imposing gates of Westbury Hall. She made one last desperate bid for freedom by flinging the door open, determined to jump out, but at that moment, the carriage stopped. There in front of her was a familiar face. Thank God, someone who could rescue her, be her salvation.

She gathered up her skirts and prepared to jump, but before she could escape, just like the ruffian who had captured her, he grabbed her roughly and threw her back into the farthest corner of the carriage. Then he jumped in himself and sat beside her.

'Drive on, Butler,' he shouted and then he said softly, 'Miss Grayson, please behave yourself or it will be the worse for you.'

Charlotte was stunned. It was none other than Alfred Westbury – a man she would have expected to be her saviour, to rescue her from the likes of her attacker, not someone who would do her further injury.

No! No! she screamed inside her head. No! Why should Alfred Westbury wish to harm her? Where was Hugo? And how would he be able to help her now?

She forced herself to remain calm and looked out of the side window of the carriage to see where they were going, but immediately Alfred Westbury leaned over her and pulled down the blind.

'Leave it alone,' he growled menacingly, 'or it will be the worse for you.'

As pleasantly as she could, she asked, 'But . . . but where are we going?'

'That is something that you do not need to know, Miss Grayson,' he answered suavely. 'Suffice it to say, you are the proverbial sprat to catch a mackerel and, when I get to your sweetheart, my dear cousin Hugo, you will be disposed of, dear lady.'

'He is not my sweetheart,' she said indignantly.

'Be quiet, or I shall have to silence you.'

The threatening glare that accompanied his words frightened Charlotte so much that she shrank into the corner of the carriage, her mind racing. It was pointless to defy him. He was not only stronger but it was obvious he was a ruthless, nay desperate, character. She tried to think coolly. Which direction was the carriage coming from? In which direction had it been pointing? Was there anyone else involved, except Alfred Westbury and the thuggish Jim Butler, who had bundled her into the coach in the first place? Most importantly, where were they going? Where was Hugo? If she were unable to meet him at the church, would he know there was something wrong and try and find her? How on earth would she be able to escape from this situation?

She clenched her hands in an agony of anxiety and terror, trying to compose her thoughts and failing miserably. She must try to think coherently. Knowing Alfred Westbury and his coarse overtures, she wondered if he'd decided to abduct her with a view to ruining her reputation sufficiently to force her to marry him. But what would happen now?

The last question was answered almost immediately. She heard a muffled curse from the driver and immediately the loud crack of splintering wood as the coach came to a shuddering halt amid loud cries of distress from the horses. The vehicle was struck with such force that it left the narrow country road completely and mounted the bank before it was turned on to its side. Both Charlotte and her abductor were thrown on to the floor with the force of the impact. She heard the scream of one of the injured horses and then there followed a moment's eerie silence. She felt a searing pain in her shoulder; smelled the faintly sickly smell of Alfred Westbury's cologne. The blinds still covered the windows and she could see nothing. The silence was broken only by the faint jingling of a horse's harness. The gentle snorting of a horse still on his feet; the continued harrowing scream of the horse who was mortally injured.

Slowly and painfully, she got herself back on to her feet, gasping at the pain in her head, which had received a terrific bump. She could hardly stand, her legs were like jelly. Her whole body felt bruised and weak with shock. As for Alfred Westbury, she noticed in the dim light of the carriage that he appeared to be completely stunned. He lay on the floor of the coach, very still and with a gash on his head which was slowly oozing with thick red blood. Slowly and stiffly, she managed to raise one of the blinds, starting back in shocked surprise as a familiar face materialized on the other side of the glass.

It was Squire Perkins, his homely red face ludicrously dismayed and contrite, gazing anxiously at the scene within. He was on his way to church in his substantial old country trap, pulled by a horse which was too spirited to be controlled by the fat old gentleman. Squire Perkins was still affected by his prodigious consumption of the brandy he'd taken to ward off the morning chill, and he'd been unable to prevent his ancient vehicle from charging into the side of Alfred Westbury's carriage.

'Anyone hurt in there?' he shouted.

'Yes, Mr Perkins. I am afraid Mr Westbury is injured,' Charlotte replied with exemplary calmness.

This was her opportunity to escape. Alfred Westbury was in need of help. It was clearly her Christian duty to aid a fellow human being who was badly injured, but with a silent prayer to her guardian angel, Charlotte decided to ignore her Christian duty. She was quite determined to run away. This was her chance.

Aloud, she said, 'If you can help me, Mr Perkins, I think I can get out of the coach and go for help.'

'Surely, Miss Grayson, ma'am.'

The door was jammed, but the sudden shock of the accident seemed to have sobered up the old gentleman farmer and he set about the door with his big hands and then used his stout feet to kick it open at last. Even this noise did not waken Alfred Westbury and Charlotte, relieved, allowed herself to be lifted from the carriage and set down gently by the stalwart Squire Perkins. The old gentleman seemed too stunned by what had happened to express surprise at Charlotte riding unchaperoned with Mr Westbury, and said shakily, 'Here's a sad coil, Miss Grayson. I trust you aren't too badly hurt, ma'am.'

'Thank you, I am only shaken,' she said, her voice trembling a little. She looked about her. As it happened, she was at Felbrook spinney and quite near to her home. The villainous driver, Butler, was lying on the ground a little way from the carriage and groaning horribly, but at least he seemed incapable of any further attacks on her. Alfred Westbury was still unconscious and the anxious Perkins, in spite of his own shock and distress, was intent on helping him out of the carriage. She was determined to slip away from the scene and escape to safety.

'I shall go to get help for you, Mr Perkins,' she promised, and before he could ask any questions, she sped off along the path which led to Felbrook Manor. She hoped she was not too dishevelled after her ordeal, and automatically put her hands up to her head and smoothed a few strands of hair under her prim Sunday bonnet as she ran.

Hugo had also been on his way to church. After his conversation with Sir Benjamin and the distressing revelations of the last few days, he had deliberately turned his thoughts to more pleasant things. The morning was misty, but he knew that it

173

held the promise of a fine early autumn day, with enough warm sunshine to raise even the lowest spirits. Not that he needed his spirits raising, he reflected, because today he was going to be in the company of two people who were becoming increasingly dear to him. He already loved Charlotte Grayson and as for Lucy Baker, in spite of his utter ignorance and total inexperience of small girls, she was the most charming little scrap of humanity he had ever met. Her bright energy and pretty little face were absolutely captivating and her natural intelligence and enthusiasm were equally appealing. What a dear little creature, to be sure. With a wife like Charlotte, he dared hope that Sir Benjamin's desire for him to have a family of his own should surely result in a lovely child such as Lucy Baker. . . .

Lost in thought and smiling to himself rather foolishly in his pleasurable anticipation of meeting Charlotte, he completely forgot about his declared intention of being vigilant. He was not even aware of a group of rough types lurking in the trees which bordered the road to Felbrook village. This time, he'd had no sixth sense of danger, but as he afterwards admitted to himself, that was because his mind had been distracted and he well knew what that distraction was.

'Right. Get him, lads!'

Hugo's daydreaming had not prepared him for this surprise and his fury at the threat caused him to react in a way that was foreign to his usual cool confidence in the avoidance of trouble. He dismounted from Gypsy and as the three ruffians approached, proudly met and held the eye of the man who had spoken.

'Get him, I say!'

The thug was brandishing a particularly evil-looking knife and his words were accompanied by a powerful lunge which carried him away from his tough friends and in close proximity to Hugo Westbury.

'It's time you was silenced, yer poke nose. You'll soon see no one wants yer meddlin' and muck rakin'.'

This verbal assault took Hugo completely unawares. It was so unexpected, he didn't at first connect it in any way to his enquiries into his grandfather's death, and those few vital seconds of hesitation might have made a difference. As it was, the gang watched approvingly as their leader swung his long-bladed knife like an avenging axe and quick though he was, Hugo's twisting evading action was too late. The razor-sharp weapon sliced into his left side.

He felt the thump of the blow, but there was no pain and quickly summoning all his strength, he dealt a punch to the man's chin with his clenched fist. He realized that although there was no immediate pain, he had been badly injured, and this was his one chance to hit back before his wound got the better of him.

Hugo had always been a sportsman, practising boxing regularly and invariably choosing the strongest of sparring partners. The ruffian with the knife went down like a sack of potatoes and his friends didn't even pause to help him up, let alone 'get' Hugo, but fled into the bushes. It was all over so quickly, he could hardly believe it had happened, until he tried to walk towards his horse.

Hugo staggered weakly to Gypsy and stood leaning against the horse's flanks with his head bowed. He wasn't even out of breath, but he had to keep an elbow pressed tightly against the cut in his side and so was unable to prevent the man on the ground from gathering himself together and lumbering off after his companions. He wondered fleetingly why the rogue hadn't paused long enough to finish him off, but no doubt he'd considered him as good as dead, he thought cynically.

Hugo knew that he hadn't the strength to mount his horse and could only cling on to Gypsy's reins. He could feel the warm trickle of blood under his clothes and as he stumbled on some uneven ground, the trickle became a sudden hot gush and in spite of the support of his horse, he staggered and nearly fell. The wound was beginning to hurt him now and the pain increased with every step he took. As he paused for a moment to let his head clear, he thought suddenly that he was nearer to Felbrook Manor than he was to St Paul's Church. He might be better to try to make his way there and seek assistance.

He turned Gypsy's head in the direction of the Graysons' home and although he hadn't the strength to guide the horse along the footpath, Gypsy seemed to know his intention and walked slowly in the right direction. The pain in Hugo's side was even more insistent and he bit his lip in an effort not to groan. He closed his eyes as his head began to swim.

'Mr Westbury?'

He forced himself to open his eyes. She was standing before him, the soft glow of the sunlight making a halo of her shining hair. She was so dashed beautiful, she almost dazzled him. He felt suddenly dizzy and needed to lie down. At the same time, he had an insane impulse to keep the knowledge of his injury from her. If she knew about the attack, she'd feel vindicated in her criticism of his foolhardy actions, he thought. Then the swirling blackness which he had fought for the last few minutes overcame him and he clung even more fiercely to Gypsy as his legs buckled and he tried not to swoon.

'Mr Westbury, what is it? You are hurt?' Her voice quivered and she stepped forward anxiously. 'May I help you?' she began again and he straightened up from his position against Gypsy and pressed his elbow even harder into the painfully burning wound in his side.

Summoning up all his strength, he took another step, staggered and was about to fall, when suddenly, miraculously, she was beside him, supporting him with her slim body.

'You are hurt,' she said softly, but there was no accusation or reproach in her beautiful low voice as she lifted his good arm and draped it round her shoulders. Looking into his ashen face, she made a swift decision to take him back to her mama. He was obviously badly hurt and she would need someone to help her.

Speechless and dizzy, he allowed her to guide him slowly and painfully along the footpath to Felbrook Manor.

It was less than five minutes later when they were met by the Felbrook party who were on their way to morning service. Almost weeping with relief, Charlotte relinquished Hugo to the strong support of Robert and Phoebe while Kitty led Gypsy back along the path to Felbrook.

Seeing Charlotte's white face and stricken expression, Mrs Grayson thought at first that it was the shock of Hugo Westbury's injuries and put a comforting arm around her daughter's shoulders. Only then, in the safe haven of her mama's love, was Charlotte able to gasp out the story of Alfred Westbury's attack on her. She sobbed as she described the horror of the accident and her determination to run away.

'And then . . . and then, Mama . . . Oh, Mr Westbury is also hurt . . . and oh . . . my head hurts. . . . What is happening to us?'

'Hush, my darling. See, we are home now. You are safe. Alfred Westbury is wicked and evil, but he will be dealt with by Sir Benjamin. Let us first attend to Mr Westbury and then we may deal with your own wounds in a little while.'

Once home, they summoned the help of the groom to carry Hugo upstairs to Mrs Grayson's own bedchamber. 'For it is already aired and made up and he may be comfortable until the doctor has seen him,' she said airily. She and Robert eased him on to the bed and then Jane Grayson directed Kitty to send up Phoebe with some hot water and she despatched the groom to the church to interrupt the doctor at his Sunday worship and to inform Sir Benjamin Westbury of Hugo's whereabouts.

'Now, if you are feeling a little better, give me a hand with Mr Westbury's jacket, my dear,' she said to Charlotte, but her mother's busy hands were suddenly stilled at what was revealed when the jacket was removed. Jane Grayson had seen many distressing and unfortunate sights in her life as a parson's wife among the rural poor, but even she gave a shocked gasp at the amount of blood which was still oozing from the cruel wound in his side. Nevertheless, only the trembling of her fingers revealed the extent of her horror and anxiety. She merely said calmly, 'Now, slip downstairs and tell Phoebe to bring up some bandage strips from the linen press, my love. If your shoulder is not too painful, you can carry the water for her and then we will make Mr Westbury comfortable.'

Charlotte, as shocked and horrified as her mother, forgot her own injuries and hastened to do her bidding, as Hugo sank gratefully into the softness of the double bed.

Charlotte picked up the discarded jacket and looked on anxiously as Jane Grayson placed a folded pad of dressing on the dreadful wound and with Phoebe's help, bound it in place.

Hugo winced and groaned, but before subsiding into unconsciousness he became aware that he desperately wanted to tell her something. As he tried ineffectually to cling on to sentient thought, he wondered wildly whether he would ever get that opportunity. Now, as he drifted off, his eyes were heavy and beginning to close, but he opened them as widely as he could, in order to try to remember what it was he wanted to say to her before it was too late. Yes. That was it! He must tell Charlotte Grayson that he loved her . . . truly . . . madly . . . passionately. . . . He must insist . . . insist . . . that she should love him in return. . . .

He awoke very painfully with the sting of Doctor Armstrong's needle, as the good doctor proceeded to clean up the wound and put in the stitches that would enable it to heal. Charlotte and her mother seemed to have been banished from the room, for which he was profoundly thankful. He clenched his jaw at the pain of his side and then used a strategy which had always seemed to work when he was but a lad at Eton and had dealt with the agony of a caning. It consisted of resolutely thinking of something else. At that time, he had thought only of his mother. Of her soft gentleness. Her perfume as she used to bend over him and kiss him good-night. The feel of her caressing hand as she smoothed the hair back from his face before pressing her lips to his cheek and her low American drawl, as she whispered a final endearment before leaving him to settle into a contented sleep.

Now, instead of the memory of his mama, he allowed thoughts of Charlotte to invade his senses. The smoothness of her skin as her arm had brushed across his cheek when she was untangling the Bakers' kitten. The pink, ripe softness of her lips whenever she spoke, be it sweetly, angrily, calmly. In whatever mood she was in, her lips were always voluptuously beautiful. He remembered particularly the moment when he had opened his eyes to see her mouth so near his own. He had wanted so desperately to kiss her. . . .

Through the miasma of his pain, he was aware that she had come back into the room and with a supreme effort he overcame the acute discomfort, and even the effect of the morphine draught administered by Doctor Armstrong, so that he could open his eyes again and look at her. As though she felt the intensity of his gaze, Charlotte looked directly back at him and smiled and only then did he let his eyes close once more.

'Lie still,' she said softly. She touched his hand as it lay on the coverlet. 'Close your eyes. Doctor Armstrong says that your wound will be easier in the morning.'

He nodded as he obediently allowed his eyelids to close, and his hand momentarily tightened over hers. She was afraid that he would slip into unconsciousness, but it was obvious by his restless movements that he was not unconscious, or even asleep, and she continued softly, 'What happened to you?'

When Mama had taken off his jacket, there had been so much blood. She glanced down at the dried stains on the pristine whiteness of Mama's bed linen and she was afraid. She

179

bent her head closer to him, to hear what he would say.

'A few ruffians with a knife. . . .'

He lapsed into silence and appeared to be dozing. His grasp on her hand loosened and his breathing became more even and relaxed. It seemed that he was not going to reveal any more for the time being, at least.

Doctor Armstrong was stowing away the various instruments and medicines into his case and her mama bustled in with a tray containing water and a glass for the invalid. Charlotte moved her hand away from his and went to sit in a chair by the window. For the first time in her life, she felt most terribly frightened. She wished more than anything that Doctor Armstrong would stay, that he would continue to minister to Hugo's needs, that he would heal the dreadful wound in his side. But the doctor was calm and merely said, 'I hear you met with an accident of your own, Miss Grayson. A collision with Squire Perkins' gig, was it not?'

What had Mama told him? She wondered what he would think of her if he knew how stupid she had been in her encouragement of the evil Alfred Westbury and her foolishness in not taking Phoebe with her on her walk. Not that Phoebe would have been any protection against Jim Butler and Alfred, she thought. In spite of Mama's special salve on her bruised head and shoulder, she was still painfully aware of her own folly in taking such risks. Her mind was buzzing with the turmoil of her thoughts. She liked and respected Doctor Armstrong and was tempted to confide in him and ask him if he thought the two incidents were connected.

Instead, she answered rather tremulously, 'Yes, sir. After the accident, I . . . I was going to get help for him when I met with Mr Westbury and . . . and. . . .'

'Never fear, my dear,' he said gently. 'Squire Perkins was able to summon his farmhands and neither he nor Mr Alfred Westbury seem any the worse for their adventure. But while I am here, I will take a look at your own cuts and bruises.'

Afterwards, the doctor took his leave of them very quietly,

as though there was no danger, no emergency, and yet Charlotte still wanted to scream at him to stay. She felt as though Hugo were about to die and that she was powerless to do anything about it.

As he was shown out by Phoebe, Doctor Armstrong smiled reassuringly at her mother and said, 'As I thought. Miss Charlotte has only minor bruising which will soon disappear.'

Her mother gave Charlotte a searching look, but said merely, 'Doctor Armstrong will call again tomorrow and Sir Benjamin has been informed of the attack on Mr Westbury. I expect he may wish to visit.'

Charlotte was left feeling that not only was she powerless to help the wounded Hugo Westbury, but also that nothing was going to be revealed to her about his investigations into the death of his grandfather. In fact, Hugo might not even survive the night, given the grievous injury that he had sustained. She clasped her arms around herself as tightly as she could and took a deep breath. She knew that she desperately wanted him to live.

With the help of Doctor Armstrong's sleeping draught, Hugo slept all through the rest of Sunday and well into Monday. Sir Benjamin visited early on Sunday afternoon and suggested to Harry Bunfield that notices could be given out at evensong in St Paul's requesting information as to the whereabouts of Butler and Alfred Westbury. Bunfield replied cautiously that he had already instigated a search for Hugo's attackers and a substantial reward had been offered among the criminal underworld of Norwich and King's Lynn for any relevant information.

'It might be best to keep low at the moment, sir,' he said simply. 'Sometimes it's the best way to flush 'em out.'

Sir Benjamin bowed to his superior judgement. He was assured by Doctor Armstrong that Hugo was stable and was holding his own, even though there was a chance he might develop a fever. Charlotte and Kitty were taking turns with Jane Grayson at sitting by him, although Jane had insisted that she should be the one to sit up with him at night, as long as Phoebe was on hand to help with changing the dressing on his wound. Sir Benjamin was suitably comforted by the standard of care that Hugo was receiving and came every day to see his beloved great-nephew.

But Mrs Grayson's care of Hugo ended abruptly on the third evening when she herself was laid low with a violent headache and was forced to seek rest in one of the guest bedrooms. Even through her own pain, Jane Grayson was adamant that if Charlotte were worried or unsure, she must send Phoebe to fetch her.

Charlotte sat in a chair near the bed, reading by the light of a single candle, but she was totally unable to concentrate. Phoebe dozed quietly on the day bed, but Hugo seemed restless and unable to settle. As fast as Charlotte covered him up, he threw the covers back, muttering unintelligibly all the while. She tried in vain to bathe his temples with the lavender water set there by her mama. It was useless. He pushed her hand away with surprising force, and she bit her lip and looked across at the still-sleeping Phoebe. No help there. Poor Phoebe deserved her rest after all the work she'd put in. She felt hopeless. She'd never done any nursing before and had certainly never looked after a helpless man. Even during Papa's fatal illness, it was always Mama and a woman from the village who sat up with him.

Hugo's head was tossing about wildly on the pillow, which was now burning hot. She tried to moisten his lips with a little water, but he refused even a trickle into his mouth. Finally, in desperation, she reached both of her arms across the bed, trying to hold down the covers at each side of him and make him be still. But she wasn't strong enough. With one forceful lunge, he dragged her down on top of him, pinioning her arms so that she couldn't escape and all the time muttering incoherently, but louder now. And as he pulled her even closer to him, she could make out broken, disjointed sentences which at first seemed to have no meaning.

Then, quite out of the blue, he declared very clearly, 'I love you, Charlotte.'

She gasped and tried to draw away from him, but he held her tighter still and she couldn't move. All of a sudden, he put his good arm on the back of her neck and drew her lips to his in a long and sensual kiss.

Horrified, she made another desperate effort to pull away but she knew she wasn't strong enough to fight him off and part of her didn't want to. She was enjoying his kiss too much. But this would not do. At any moment, Phoebe might wake up and in any case she needed Robert to help her to hold him still. There was quiet in the bedroom now, and suddenly his head fell back and his grip loosened as though he slept. She was desperately worried that his exertions would pull out the stitches in his side.

Very gently, she disengaged herself and stood up guiltily, smoothing down her dress with trembling hands. Phoebe still seemed to be sleeping peacefully. It would be hours before morning and she knew she would be unable to sleep. Her feelings were so tumultuous that she felt as though she herself were the feverish patient and not Hugo Westbury. She took a sip of his water and moved back to her chair by the side of the bed, trying to make sense of what had just happened to her, but she found it impossible. Impossible also to make head or tail of her feelings. She was confused and unable to sort out her thoughts, and in spite of feeling terribly tired, her emotions were still in turmoil. At least Phoebe would soon be awake and ready to take her turn at caring for Hugo. She sighed and leaned back against her chair, trying to get comfortable. The house was very silent now. Phoebe snored softly and Charlotte took another sip of water in order to ease the pain of her parched throat. Then she closed her eyes again, trying to calm herself, and managed to doze off.

But even the longest night must have a dawn and it seemed that she'd only just fallen asleep at last when Phoebe brought in some hot chocolate and toast. She managed to eat and drink a little and then, after bathing Hugo's still-sleeping face, she went to her own room to wash and change her clothes.

She and Phoebe said very little to each other. Although it was daylight, the household was barely awake and when Charlotte at last reached her room, she drew the heavy curtains and stretched herself out on her bed and closed her eyes. In spite of her body being bone-weary, her brain would not let her rest. She went over again and again her meeting with Hugo, when she'd found him so badly injured and, as she had thought, likely to die. Yet Doctor Armstrong had been quite positive that he was strong and would recover. Unless he died of a fever, that is.

Tears began to run down her face in the dimness of the bedroom, but even as they flowed, she was reliving the soft, sensuous feel of his mouth as it had moved so seductively over her own. She pressed the back of her hand to her lips in an effort not to cry and whispered, 'Oh, Hugo, darling Hugo, I love you. I love you. . . .'

Finally, her exhausted body was unable to keep going any longer and she slept fitfully, to be awakened by the arrival of her sister Kitty. Mrs Grayson was still confined to her room, but Kitty knocked gently on her door and came to tell her that Doctor Armstrong had arrived.

Somehow, as though she had managed to shut off reality for a few minutes, she hastily washed and dressed and quickly tidied her hair before going to join her sister in Mama's bedroom. Her eyes immediately sought the restless figure on the bed. His own eyes were still tightly closed, his hands clutching the edge of the blankets as he tossed first one way, then the other.

Noticing her glance and the heavy pallor of her face, Doctor Armstrong said sympathetically, 'I am so sorry your mama is still indisposed, Miss Grayson, but at least our invalid seems to have turned the corner.'

'T . . . turned the corner?' she said in a bemused voice.

'Well, almost,' he said. 'Mr Westbury is still restless and a little feverish, but wounds that are inflicted by knives often look very much worse than they are. The stitches are mending nicely and will probably be removed by the end of the week. God willing, by then, he should be on the mend. I think when Sir Benjamin visits tomorrow, he will find him much improved.'

CHAPTER THIRTEEN

The next day, her mama was also much improved and, in spite of her sleepless nights and the pain of her migraine, seemed back to her usual energetic self. Under her watchful gaze, Charlotte and Kitty continued to help with Hugo's care and although he was not allowed to get dressed, Robert was on hand to shave him and help him with his more intimate needs. After Dr Armstrong had departed, Charlotte was sent to the parlour to have a rest and some refreshment. She left reluctantly and sat alone at the small dining table. The other women were busy at their various tasks and Robert was engaged in holding Hugo up while Mrs Grayson put a clean bandage on to his wound.

Charlotte managed to eat a little and drank thirstily before going up to her room. She removed her dress and washed herself, but instead of changing her clothes, she lay down on the bed, all sorts of thoughts whirling through her head, making it impossible to sleep. She closed her eyes and behind her lids saw again Hugo's handsome face and firm mouth. He was not allowed even to leave his bed, but he could sit up, with assistance from Robert. What would she say to him when she had at last to meet his eyes? He had kissed her in a moment of fever or delirium and she had thoroughly enjoyed it. She hoped fervently that perhaps he would never be able to recall that moment when she had been both unable and unwilling to resist his kiss. She blinked back sudden tears of shame. There was some excuse for such behaviour from a wounded patient, in a fevered moment, when delirium had overset his self-control, but for the well-brought-up daughter of a clergyman, none whatsoever. She hoped fervently that it would not be too long before he was able to go back to Westbury Hall.

As she lay agonizing with her thoughts and tormenting herself with feelings of regret and shame, Phoebe tapped on the door to say that Mrs Grayson requested her presence in Mr Hugo's bedroom. Sir Benjamin and Mr Bunfield had arrived.

She dressed hastily and rinsed her eyes with cold water. As she looked in the mirror to tidy her hair, she deliberately raised her head and forced her drooping lips to try out a cool smile. That was better. A little powder would lessen the redness of her eyes and a few pinches to her cheeks would lend her pale face a little more colour.

When she walked into the bedroom, she was more composed, but was still unable to meet the gaze of Hugo Westbury, who was sitting up in Mama's bed, supported by three plump pillows and wearing a nightshirt which had once belonged to her papa. Her mother was sitting by the window, her hands quietly folded on her lap, her eyes downcast. It was obvious that she was not a player in the Runner's investigation, but was merely observing the proprieties.

Mrs Grayson's bedroom was a large one and Robert had brought in extra chairs to accommodate the guests. Both gentlemen stood as Charlotte entered the room and bade her 'Good afternoon', to which she responded with a formal curtsy. Still she didn't glance at the quiet figure on the bed, but sat as far away from him as possible, and looked attentively at Mr Bunfield.

He opened the proceedings by saying gravely, 'Well, Sir Benjamin, ladies and gentlemen, we all know what our business is here, this afternoon. Both Miss Grayson and Mr Westbury have suffered violence at the hands of local criminals. I intend to bring them to justice and set them before the magistrate and already my scouts and I are on their trail. You need not fear. They will be forced to address the crimes they have committed.'

He bowed in Sir Benjamin's direction and then, more softly, he spoke directly to Charlotte. 'Miss Grayson, I trust you are somewhat recovered from your ordeal now and able to answer a few questions about the attack which was made on you and the circumstances of your meeting with Mr Westbury.'

'Yes, I am, sir,' she said in a low voice.

'Did you recognize either of the two men who took part in this attack?'

'Only one of them.'

'And he was?'

'Mr Alfred Westbury.'

She glanced across at Sir Benjamin and saw his shoulders sag a little, but almost immediately he straightened up.

'And you say you did not know the other fellow. Would you recognize him, if you saw him again?'

Charlotte felt a tremor of fear go through her body at the thought of that rough grip and the vile, animal smell of him. Nevertheless, she raised her head and answered bravely, 'Yes, indeed, Mr Bunfield. And I heard Mr Alfred Westbury call him "Butler", as he told him to drive on.'

'And do you have any idea of the motive for the attack on you? Was there any indication as to why?'

Charlotte thought quickly. She didn't wish to suggest any emotional involvement with Hugo Westbury, and yet she wanted these criminals to be punished, not just for the attack on herself but for what they'd done to her darling Hugo. Dear Papa had always said that it was just as sinful to tell the truth with intent to deceive, as it was to tell an outright lie. With a silent prayer to his revered memory, she answered, 'Alfred Westbury intimated that I might be the bait to entrap Mr Hugo Westbury.'

'Do you remember his exact words?'

She did, but was definitely not going to mention the word 'sweetheart'. With a deep breath, she said, 'Alfred Westbury suggested that if they captured me, Mr . . . Hugo . . . Mr Hugo . . . Westbury would try . . . try to rescue me and they . . . would k . . . kill him and let me go.'

'Tell me how you managed to escape, Miss Grayson.'

'As I was driven towards Felbrook village, there was a collision with Squire Perkins, who was travelling to church in his gig. Alfred Westbury was stunned and the other man was . . . was . . . injured. I went to get help.'

'And that was when you encountered Mr Hugo Westbury?'

'Yes.'

Now, she did glance at Hugo. He looked both pale and tired, and yet . . . and yet . . . there was such a lively gleam in his eye as he looked at her, that she was obliged to look away and clench her hands tightly together in her lap. If he remembered the shameless way she had responded to his fevered kiss, she would sink with mortification.

'Thank you, Miss Grayson. Now Mr Westbury, sir, prior to your meeting with Miss Grayson, where were you, sir, and what were you doing?'

Hugo sat a little straighter on his pillows. 'I also was on my way to church, Mr Bunfield. I was just passing Felbrook spinney when the three men attacked me. I was stabbed by the ringleader. When I fought him off, they all ran away.'

'One more question, Mr Westbury. You were not in your carriage, sir. Were you not out a little early for morning service?'

'It was a beautiful morning, perfect for riding. I knew Sir Benjamin would be driving to church later and we would return to Westbury Hall together. One of the grooms would take my horse back to the Hall.'

'Did you recognize any of the men involved?'

'No, but I have only recently returned to Norfolk after a number of years abroad.'

'Thank you, sir. I hope this hasn't been too much of an

ordeal for you, on top of the dreadful injury that was inflicted on you.'

'Not at all,' said Hugo politely. Although his face was drawn and he rubbed his forehead wearily, he did not seem inclined to lie down, or close his eyes.

Sir Benjamin now spoke for the first time. 'Jim Butler has disappeared but one of Hugo's assailants was apprehended at Wells. He is to be brought before me for questioning and we will be able to find out if any other local men were involved, apart from Alfred Westbury,' he said almost to himself 'Miss Grayson. Are you sure that Alfred Westbury was unconscious when you got out of the carriage?'

'Yes, Sir Benjamin.'

'Then it is obvious that he recovered in time to make good his escape and so did his accomplice. Mr Perkins had no idea that anything was suspicious. He assumed you and Alfred were on your way to church, as he was himself. However, he recognized the driver as Jim Butler and the local watch have been alerted to look for him and apprehend him when he is found.'

Everyone was silent for a while and then Harry Bunfield spoke slowly. 'For the moment, it would be well to let the villains think that they have got away with it and that they've managed to leave Mr Hugo Westbury for dead. If you agree, Sir Benjamin, I think we should keep very quiet about Mr Alfred Westbury's involvement in the attempted abduction of Miss Grayson and the attack on Mr Hugo Westbury. Obviously, Squire Perkins may talk of the collision, but seemingly he was a little . . . ahem . . . worse for wear, so perhaps he will not be so eager to gab to his neighbours about it. His farmhands and Sir Benjamin's groom dealt with the unfortunate horses involved and my constables have rescued the wrecked carriage belonging to Mr Alfred Westbury. There is absolutely no evidence of any accident now. The most important task at the moment is to ascertain Alfred Westbury's whereabouts and I hope you will entrust that to me, Sir Benjamin.'

'Of course,' Sir Benjamin agreed.

Once again, his thin shoulders sagged and Charlotte thought how unutterably weary he looked.

There was more general talk now, about Hugo's return to Westbury Hall and Doctor Armstrong's opinion was that Hugo might be well enough in a couple of days.

Half of Charlotte was singing with delight at his recovery, but the other half was unaccountably cast into gloom by the prospect of his departure from Felbrook Manor. She was conscious all the time of the tension between them. Every contact with him was heightened by the memory of that kiss. He'd been so dependent on her help and that of Mama and Kitty, and she couldn't help being more in love with him than ever.

But inevitably, the day dawned when the good doctor pronounced him fit to make the short journey up to the Hall and the coach with two stalwart footmen was despatched by Sir Benjamin to assist Hugo on his way. Although he looked pale, Hugo was still able to smile and wave as he was driven away.

Jane Grayson and her daughters were on hand to wish him farewell. They were silent now. It was early evening and the golden ball of the sun had all but disappeared, giving a slight chill to the atmosphere, and the house seemed a little emptier as they went indoors.

'Well, my dears,' Jane Grayson said as they entered the drawing-room, 'even now, Phoebe is changing the bed linen and tonight I shall be in my own bedchamber again. What a strange happening, to be sure, that Mr Westbury should have been attacked like that. Let us pray that he is able to make a complete recovery and that the rogues who did it will be apprehended.'

'Amen to that,' said a familiar voice and they turned to see Matthew King appear suddenly and unannounced. 'Forgive the intrusion, ma'am,' he said with his usual gentle smile, 'I was intrigued at the gossip in the village about Mr Westbury's mysterious accident and I felt I had to find out how he does.'

'Dear Matthew, come in. We are about to have supper. You young people entertain yourselves for a while, and I shall consult with cook.'

So saying, Jane Grayson sped away to the kitchen to make sure that an extra place would be laid for their guest.

After the initial greetings, Charlotte also excused herself and went up to her own room. She needed to get away from everyone and be on her own for a while. Without calling on Phoebe, she extracted a suitable evening dress and sat in front of her mirror, taking down her hair and brushing it out slowly, lulled by the comforting feeling of the regular strokes through her long hair.

Her thoughts turned once more to Hugo Westbury. She was puzzled by the attack on him, but also in the way that it had somehow been influenced by herself. Who could possibly know how much she had become attracted to Hugo Westbury and how much he had come to mean to her? Alfred? But how did he know her feelings? She was not close to him. She was never in his company. Had someone been observing Hugo and herself? Spying on them? As she changed into her evening dress, she gave a sudden shiver. No one knew where Alfred Westbury was. He was still at large and perhaps would be able to threaten her again. Thank goodness Kitty seemed to be in no danger from all this. She hoped Matthew would always look after her younger sister and wondered what was happening downstairs.

Left alone with Kitty, Matthew was at first constrained and shy, but as they had so much to talk about both of them became more natural, and when Kitty said artlessly how devoted her sister had been in nursing Mr Hugo Westbury, Matthew did not reply, but put his hands on her shoulders and turned her to face him.

She gazed up at him, tremulously, her full, sensuous lips soft and gentle and her grey eyes suddenly darker and more intense.

'Kitty, I have to talk to you,' he said, and then suddenly, he was at a loss as to what it was he was about to say.

'Yes, Matthew?'

Her grey eyes now seemed wider than ever.

'I have to talk to you,' he said again, but then he couldn't help himself, and he bent his head and kissed her.

As his lips met hers, Kitty realized how much she'd been wanting this and gave herself up to the pleasure of the moment, filled with longing for him. She reached up to kiss his lips again, shyly but lovingly, and Matthew caught her close and kissed her brow, her cheeks, her throat, and Kitty stroked his glossy hair, smoothing it under her hands as she felt such a glow of happiness that she could hardly stand still.

But she pushed him away, smiling at him. 'So, what did you have to talk to me about?'

'Never mind talking just for the moment,' Matthew said, and he drew her back into his arms. 'I just want to kiss you again.'

Kitty surrendered herself to the magic of his kisses once more and they were silent for a while, but at last Matthew released her and stood looking down at her. Her grey eyes were almost silver now, shining and full of stars.

'I love you, Kitty,' he whispered. 'I love you more than anything else in the world.'

They were both silent again and then he said softly, 'Kitty, do you think you could forget that I . . . that I . . that Charlotte and I . . . ?'

'Yes, Matthew.'

'It is all over between Charlotte and me, Kitty. Could you . . would you . . . marry me?'

There was no hint of refusal in her clear honest eyes as she raised a loving hand to caress his cheek. 'Yes,' she whispered simply, and then once again she was in his arms, unable to breathe because of his strong embrace, but glad all the same for his nearness and the security of his love.

By the time Kitty's mother and sister returned to the room,

it was obvious to Mrs Grayson that her younger daughter and Matthew King were sharing some happy secret, but she made no reference to it, merely serving supper and afterwards setting up the table so that they could play at cards. Matthew was given all the details of Charlotte's adventure and vowed to call at Westbury Hall to see how Hugo did.

For the sake of decorum and formality, Jane Grayson said that she and her daughters would visit Westbury Hall only once during the next week and this they did. Jane was delighted that it would be a splendid opportunity to ride in her fashionable new barouche. They would have it open to the air, she decided, and take their prettiest parasols to shield their complexions from the sun, which was still strong for September. Robert was only too pleased to drive them and, feeling smart in a dashing livery with deep blue braid, he brought the coach round at precisely eleven o'clock. Jane took some oat cakes, baked by the redoubtable Mrs Palmer and Kitty and Charlotte left some pretty, sweet-smelling flowers for Sir Benjamin's patient. Charlotte also left a copy of *Sense and Sensibility*, a book by Jane Austen, which she had discussed with Hugo and which he had professed himself interested in reading.

Hugo was still confined to his bed, but Sir Benjamin greeted them very graciously, offering wine and refreshments and reporting that Hugo was much improved and gaining in strength every day. Although Sir Benjamin was, as always, immaculately turned out and was an impeccable host, Charlotte thought that he looked more frail than usual and his thin shoulders were even more stooped, as though they carried a great weight. Still, he treated the women politely, accepting their gifts on behalf of his great-nephew and promising that Doctor Armstrong had declared that Hugo would be allowed to get up the next day and come downstairs. Jane Grayson was punctilious about not staying longer than the customary twenty minutes and the girls rose obediently as soon as she announced that it was time to go.

'We shall look forward to a visit from you on Sunday, ladies, by which time Hugo will be downstairs and able to sustain a social call,' he said graciously.

Jane Grayson said all that was polite as they left and they entered their newly acquired carriage and set off for home. Charlotte was silent and preoccupied on the brief journey to Felbrook Manor. Hugo's recovery after such a vicious attack struck her as little short of miraculous and she felt a sudden rush of happiness at the thought of Hugo restored to his former health and strength, but even more pleasure was to come. That evening, Matthew and his Aunt Lavinia called and he and Kitty revealed their love and shyly begged Jane Grayson's blessing.

Kitty's mother wasn't unobservant and had marked all the signs that her younger daughter was very smitten with the young lawyer. She feigned surprise, but this was merely to gauge Kitty's reaction and to confirm her belief that the two were genuinely determined to be wed.

'But, Kitty, my dear,' she said rather archly. 'You have never given any indication that you could hold Matthew in such high regard.'

Kitty blushed and protested, but Charlotte kissed Kitty and hugged Matthew and then held him at arm's length for a few moments.

'This is wonderful news,' she told him and then said, extravagantly, 'Congratulations to the two people most amiable in the world. And you are to be married! We should forgo the tea, Mama, and drink only wine. Our family will be a little bigger, but a lot better now that you are to be my brother, Matthew!'

Matthew experienced again the joy and happiness that he'd felt when Charlotte had first understood his attraction to Kitty and had set him free from their own understanding. Their quarrel was forgotten now and he was delighted that Charlotte wasn't unhappy about his love for Kitty. They would always be fond of each other, he thought, but as in-laws and friends, not as lovers. He drew a deep breath. He was now free to love Kitty unconditionally. He felt exultant, sure of Kitty's love, sure of his position in the law firm and sure of his acceptance by Jane Grayson.

In spite of the serious events of the last few days, everyone was in excellent spirits as Jane rang for Robert to bring in wine and set glasses on the table.

Mrs Palmer bustled in to set out an enormous supper, her red face beaming with pride at Kitty's news, for as she remarked to all those in the kitchen who were prepared to listen, 'Miss Kitty deserves some happiness. She's never been a leader like Miss Charlotte, being quieter, like, but Mary Palmer wishes her happy and you can't say fairer than that.'

Nor could they.

CHAPTER FOURTEEN

The next Sunday dawned with an unusually thick early morning mist as Alfred Westbury and his manservant, Josiah Bennett, met furtively at the entrance to the secret tunnel. In spite of their swift glances to right and left, Alfred was confident that they were quite alone and totally unobserved. The extensive grounds of Westbury Hall, shrouded in low cloud and the quiet stillness of the landscape all around, would make anyone feel that he was the only person in the world. Like Adam and Eve, thought Bennett bitterly, except that he was alone with his malevolent employer, a cruel bully, who Bennett knew would destroy him.

Alfred was, as usual, quietly, vindictively threatening, as he said softly, 'So, Bennett, the attack on cousin Hugo has proved a failure and the kidnap of Miss Grayson has been unsuccessful, due to that clod Perkins and his accursed gig. This is your final throw of the dice, Bennett. This time, you will use the insipid little Lucy Baker as the bait to kidnap Charlotte Grayson and so lure dear Hugo to his death.'

Bennett quailed. Though forced to obey Alfred's orders, he drew the line at murder. His face was a sickly white and his voice trembled somewhat as he said, 'Death, Mr Alfred?'

'Do not be afraid,' Alfred sneered. 'I am quite capable of doing my own dirty work. You need only obey orders. Position yourself near the Bakers' cottage and make sure you follow the child and nab Miss Grayson. I shall do the rest.

And under no circumstances should you try to get in touch with me, Bennett. When the lovely Miss Grayson has had time to cool down, I shall pen a ransom note to her handsome friend and once I have ensnared him, Miss Grayson will be released.'

'Very good, Mr Alfred, sir.' Josiah Bennett's face was now ashen, his palms sweating. He had no stomach for murder. He'd been with Alfred Westbury for years, first as a young footman and then, later, as his personal servant. There was nothing he didn't know about his master; there were no secrets between a gentleman and his valet. He knew how over the years Alfred's resentment at not inheriting the Westbury wealth had grown and festered inside him until he was consumed with hatred for Hugo. He knew of all the ploys Alfred used to extort money from young fools who gambled, from foolish old women who could be flattered into parting with their jewels and from wealthy parents anxious for a daughter's virtue. He knew that his master was not above stealing small valuable items or cheating at cards when he was a guest in some country house. He also knew that Alfred Westbury would stop at nothing to get rid of Hugo and inherit Sir Benjamin's fortune. Knowing all this had come at a price. He'd been an accomplice in various of Alfred's crimes, including eloping with a silly young heiress. The family had paid Alfred a small fortune for her safe return. He knew that if ever Alfred revealed the extent of his own complicity, he would surely hang. It seemed that he would never escape. And yet ... and yet ... he must try to break away. He had saved most of his earnings and might be able to make a bid for freedom. ...

No. Alfred Westbury would be sure to catch up with him and he had networks of bully boys to administer his own brand of punishment. No, he would never be free. Unless ... unless he could seize an opportunity when Alfred was too distracted to hold him back.

Aloud, he said in his usual servile voice, 'Very good, sir, I shall do as you ask.'

Gradually, the early morning mist began to clear and it was another perfect autumn morning. The air was still cool, but the sunshine was warm and Lucy Baker was fairly dancing along the path which led from her cottage to the church. Billy was not very well and Ma was staying at home to keep an eye on him. Pa was busy taking up vegetables to store in sand for the winter. Lucy was excited. She had on the dress that Miss Grayson had made for her and a new little shawl, knitted by Mrs Palmer up at Felbrook Manor. Her innocent happiness showed in every movement of her bobbing golden curls and in every joyous step she took towards St Paul's and her beloved Sunday school teacher, Miss Grayson.

Meanwhile, Josiah Bennett had made a desperate and half-baked plan to run away. Dressed for a journey and carrying a businesslike valise, he crept along the lane after her. As soon as his mission was accomplished, he would disappear.

He had friends in London and money for the stagecoach. What Alfred Westbury chose to do with Miss Grayson was none of his concern. He would await his opportunity and then steal away.

He would be free of Alfred Westbury for ever.

His every nerve ending was stretched in painful awareness of his surroundings and when Lucy Baker stopped for a moment, to pick some wild flowers, he stopped also, not knowing what to do. He froze, unable to control the panic which leapt up into his throat, almost choking him. He dodged behind a tree and waited.

When at last he glanced furtively in Lucy's direction, he was surprised to see a diminutive little face turned towards him and gazing up innocently at him.

He let out a deep breath and gasped, 'Oh . . . you are Lucy Baker. And what are you doing here, little girl?'

'I am on my way to meet Miss Grayson, my Sunday school teacher, I am.'

'Well, then, you may walk along with me, Lucy Baker.'

'No, sir. Thank you kindly, but Ma don't let me walk with strange genn'elmen.'

He decided he must keep her quiet and said persuasively, 'But I am not strange, my dear. I am a friend of Miss Grayson's and I have a penny for you.'

'A penny?'

'Yes.'

'And you says as how you are a friend of Miss Grayson's?'

'Yes. Come along now.'

'I be comin', sir.'

With that, Lucy scuttled hurriedly along the path, but still kept her distance.

'But not so far off, Lucy. You must walk beside me or you shall not get the penny.'

Lucy approached him very warily, taking care to stay out of his reach. Her normal ebullient skipping movements were now reduced to a slow, dragging walk.

'Well, Lucy, my dear, I think you *are* afraid of me.'

'No, I ain't afraid, not me.'

'Then why do you walk so far away?'

' 'Cos my ma says as I shouldn't talk to strangers and I ain't got the penny yet anyways.'

They were approaching a narrow part of the path and suddenly the sun seemed to go behind a cloud, leaving everything dark and bleak. Bennett held out the penny enticingly. 'Lucy, my dear little girl, I really *do* believe you are frightened of me.'

She snatched the penny and darted away from him. 'No, I ain't, but I thinks you looks nicer than you is.'

'But you know I would never hurt you, don't you, my dear?'

'No, I don't and, any case, my pa would hurt you no end if an' you did.'

By this time, they were in a very shadowy part of the lane and a little further along the road before them, Lucy recognized Miss Grayson, walking without her maid, and immediately she began to feel more brave.

'There's Miss Grayson,' she said boldly. 'There's my Sunday school teacher.'

'Quietly, my dear,' said Bennett as he halted and moved further into the shadows.

'No, she won't hear me unless I calls her,' Lucy said artlessly and she put her cupped hands to her mouth and drew a deep breath.

Bennett let his valise fall to the ground and sprang towards her, desperate to stop her calling out and drawing attention to himself. He grabbed her with merciless hands and dragged her deeper into the woods. Lucy let out a shrill scream which was swiftly lost as his choking hands clutched her slender, childish throat, trying to stifle her cries.

'Stop that, sir! Stop that at once, I say! Loose the little girl now, Bennett, or it will be the worse for you.'

It was Charlotte Grayson, surprisingly near, although Bennett had not heard her swift approach. Startled, he released his little victim and turned to find Miss Grayson gazing sternly at him, her grey-green eyes as hard as steel. She moved to stand between him and Lucy, her arms outstretched to shield the child.

'Quickly, Lucy! Run home to your mama,' she cried, and Lucy needed no second bidding.

While Bennett stood looking helplessly at Lucy's formidable defender, Alfred Westbury stepped forward with two tough bullies who seized Charlotte and stifled her cries immediately, before dragging her off along the path to Westbury Hall.

Lucy ran crying and distressed for home, to tell of the two bad men who had made off with her dear Miss Grayson, and Josiah Bennett slouched away into the bushes.

It had happened too swiftly for Charlotte to do anything about it. She bitterly regretted not taking Hugo's advice about not going out alone, but it was no use repining now. Her cries were stifled and her struggles were useless. Charlotte was blindfolded very efficiently and gagged and bound with her

hands tied behind her. Absolutely helpless, she acknowledged to herself. But in spite of this, she used the senses
remaining to her to guess what was happening. Her shoes
were scraping along every hump and hollow of the path as
she was dragged roughly along for several yards. Then, even
behind the blindfold, she could tell that there was a dimming
of the bright sunlight. Perhaps they were in a tunnel. Then she
was pushed unceremoniously into what seemed like a dark
cupboard. It was Alfred Westbury himself who pushed her
and forced her shoulders down until she sat on the floor. She
recognized the scent of his gentleman's cologne and hair
pomade.

Her legs were stretched out in front of her. She was on a
cold stone floor by the feel of it and already, in spite of the
warm sunshine outside, Charlotte shivered as she realized
that she was confined in some sort of dungeon.

She heard the sound of a well-oiled panel being slid across
and as it closed to, Alfred Westbury's hateful voice saying,
'There, my lads, no one will find her until I decide to give
dear Hugo a hint as to the whereabouts of his rebellious
sweetheart, by which time she will have lost the strength to
struggle.'

Then silence. She strained her ears for the slightest sound,
tried desperately to wriggle out of her blindfold, struggled to
try to remove her bonds, but it was to no avail. They were tied
too tightly and instead, tears of frustration and rage ran down
her cheeks, underneath the oppressive cloth tied round her
eyes.

She stifled them almost immediately and thought seriously
as to where she was and what might be her fate now that she
was obviously in the power of the evil Alfred Westbury. She
guessed that as the first attack on Hugo's life had failed, she
was now to be the bait which would lead to his capture and
certain death. Cautiously, she tried stretching out her bound
feet, to try to gauge the dimensions of her prison cell.

It was quite small, she decided. Swivelling sideways, she

stretched her legs once more and as if visited by a stroke of sudden lightning, realized that she was, in fact, confined in the secret priests' hidy-hole behind the panelling in the library of Westbury Hall. She began to tremble and shiver uncontrollably. She had the macabre feeling that she might be lying on the same patch of stone floor as the unfortunate Charles Westbury. She wondered wildly if she were lying on that dreadful dark stain that Adam had said was dried blood. Would she, like Hugo's grandfather, die alone in this place and not be found for years?

Swiftly, she pulled herself together. Who would be in the house at this time? Sir Benjamin? Hugo? Servants? It would do no harm to try to attract attention. She began to thump with her feet on the wooden panelling and shouted for help, until she was quite hoarse and her legs were absolutely exhausted with the effort. There was no response. Her light summer slippers were too soft to make any significant noise and her toes were already sore because of being dragged across the ground. Shouting was useless. The panelling was too thick to allow her voice to be heard. She wondered desperately where Mama and Kitty were. It must be long past the time for church. She thought wildly of what would happen if she were to die in this place. What would they think when they found her mouldering remains? Surely Mama must soon wonder where she was. But would she visit Westbury Hall to see how Hugo was getting on, or would she decide just to go straight home from church?

Would Lucy Baker have raised the alarm? Would anyone be looking for her?

In fact, Charlotte's mama was very put out by the apparent disappearance of her eldest daughter. When Charlotte didn't appear at morning service, she confided in her brother-in-law, Bertram, that it was very remiss of dear Charlotte and hoped at least that she would be at Sunday school. Bertram tutted in disapproval, but as Aurelia Casterton appeared at that moment, he bowed jauntily to her and offered to escort her home. No one recollected seeing Charlotte that morning, except for Phoebe, who reported that Miss Charlotte was going out to collect foliage for the flower arrangements. Later, when Jane discovered that Charlotte in fact had not attended Sunday school, she became alarmed, but her first emotion was anger and disappointment at what she thought was Charlotte's inconsiderate behaviour. She sent Robert and the groom to look for her, but Charlotte was nowhere to be found. As for Lucy Baker's garbled version of events, her report of a 'nasty man who had given her a penny and then frightened her by taking Miss Grayson away' was not at first given much attention. Billy was hot and feverish and Lucy's pa was late home for dinner. No one had much time to listen, but at last she was taken seriously and a message was sent to Felbrook Manor to Miss Grayson's mama, who was chagrined because just when she needed Bertram to help in the search, he was out paying court to Aurelia Casterton.

Miss Casterton's mama had graciously condescended to allow Aurelia to go for a pleasant stroll with Mr Bertram Grayson, with Aurelia's abigail in attendance, of course, and they set out on a very decorous walk, Miss Casterton holding Bertram's proffered arm and the maid trailing a little way behind. Bertram was in fine fettle. Aurelia, as became a well-brought-up young lady, responded consistently to his over-tures with modesty and reserve. Nevertheless, he was experi-enced enough to know that his little captive bird needed very little coaxing now, before she gave him her heart, utterly and completely. Even the hawk-nosed Augusta, he knew, had finally come round to the view that Mr Bertram Grayson was personable, in possession of a modest but adequate fortune, had a town house in London and another in Norwich and was well connected in Norfolk society. Not only that, but Aurelia, her pride and joy, her one and only little darling, was obviously head over heels in love with him. What mama could possibly deny her dear offspring the opportunity of connubial bliss? Certainly not Mrs Casterton. After all, Aurelia had a very considerable fortune in her own right and Mr Grayson, although not a youth, was just the right age for matrimony and just the right partner for her dearest Aurelia. She was more than willing for the two of them to get to know each other better on a gentle leisurely country stroll and hoped that perhaps today Mr Grayson would finally declare himself and offer for Aurelia.

She was gracious in her best wishes to Aurelia and Bertram for a refreshing and healthy walk. After all, thought Augusta, a trifle cynically, a bird in the hand and all that. And Hugo Westbury had proved more than disappointing, not only not coming up to snuff, but also sustaining a mysterious and violent attack which had confined him to his bed. . . .

Hugo, in fact, was not confined to bed. He was in a comfortable chair, reading Miss Austen's novel and concentrating well, in spite of his distracting thoughts about the adorable Charlotte, while Latimer hovered in the dressing-room, putting away some of Hugo's clothes and keeping a watchful eye on his beloved master.

Sir Benjamin had informed Hugo that Miss Charlotte Grayson had not attended divine service this morning. Only Miss Kitty and her mama and uncle had been in the family pew. 'But they asked after you, dear boy, and hope to visit later,' he said, before going to the library for a brandy and a snooze before lunch.

Latimer entered the bedroom and put out clean linen. He asked Hugo if he could get him anything, but Hugo smiled and said, 'No, nothing. Unless you could arrange a new pair of eyes for me. Mine feel strangely tired.'

'Perhaps the print is a trifle small,' Latimer said soothingly and went back to his duties.

Neither of them noticed Bennett's departure or knew anything about a note which had been delivered for the personal attention of Mr Hugo Westbury. The butler had refused the request of the rough type who'd delivered it to 'make it snappy' and instead had closed the door and placed it on his silver tray for later, telling him that there was no reply and that he could clear off.

Quite by chance, Bertram and Amelia strolled along the self-same path taken by Josiah Bennett and Lucy Baker, which led them past the imposing gates of Westbury Hall. Bertram noticed Alfred Westbury's servant, Bennett, creeping slyly through the trees in a decidedly furtive manner and wondered what the man was doing. Surely he should be indoors, attending to his master's needs? He decided to follow him, but Bennett seemed to have disappeared. In the presence of the maidservant, Bertram had to confine his wooing to ardent glances, gallant remarks and the occasional meaningful pressure of his large hand on the diminutive fingers in their lace mittens, but Miss Casterton was shyly responsive and returned his touch demurely. The scene was an idyllic one, the verdant grass and fine trees of the Westbury estate, the singing of the birds, the wild flowers, all contributing to lend a romantic atmosphere to Bertram's skil-ful courtship.

Suddenly, there appeared the dishevelled figure of Josiah Bennett, running away from Westbury Hall and closely followed by the Bow Street Runner. In her fear and nervous-ness, Miss Casterton clung to Bertram most deliciously and he felt compelled to put a protective arm around her. As they watched the dramatic scene enacted before them, it became obvious that Josiah Bennett was well and truly caught. Bunfield tripped him expertly and then held him by the simple expedient of sitting on him.

Panting a little, the portly Bunfield warned him, 'Josiah Bennett, you are wanted to answer some questions and I think you know why and wherefore, but if you want me to tell you. . . .'

Bunfield blew three short blasts on his whistle and two of

his scouts appeared, as if by magic.

Desperately, Bennett managed to escape from beneath him and leapt up again, in a last bid for freedom, but he had reckoned without Bunfield's toughness and strength. He was overpowered and Bunfield soon had him lying on the grass again, dazed and winded while his men proceeded to tie his hands behind his back.

Bertram was behind Bunfield and looking along the expanse of the dark green tunnel of foliage, which led to Westbury Hall, he had an idea. Perhaps this was the so-called secret entrance to Westbury Hall, the entrance that led to the hidy-hole where Charles Westbury's body had been, found.

Taking Aurelia firmly by the hand, he sauntered casually along the green leafy tunnel, which led to a small wooden doorway. Aurelia didn't seem too concerned when Bertram tried the door, and finding it locked, put his broad shoulder against it. He had no qualms about involving an innocent young miss in the crime of breaking and entering and as far as Aurelia was concerned, he guessed she would view this as an adventure on a par with some of the romantic novels that she devoured so avidly. They would explore the secret room and he would impress her with his bravery. . . .

But even Bertram was unprepared for what they found.

Charlotte was still lying on the floor, now too weak and hoarse to shout and kick any longer. Aurelia, overcome with compassion for poor Miss Grayson and all her former antagonism forgotten, gave a little cry and swooped down to kneel on the stone floor beside her. Swiftly, she untied the blindfold and Bertram released Charlotte's hands from their cruel bonds and helped her to her feet.

'Uncle Bertram. Miss Casterton,' she said faintly. 'How delighted I am to see you both. But how did you know. . . ?'

'By following that wretch Bennett,' Bertram said grimly, and as they led her out into the sunlight, Charlotte blinked back her tears of relief, for there was Lucy holding her father's hand, come to look for her dear Miss Grayson.

Forgetting all her own troubles, Charlotte immediately swooped on her precious little Lucy and picked the child up in her arms.

'Did that wicked man hurt you, Lucy, dear?'

'No, miss. Only my froat,' Lucy said bravely, although her blue eyes were bright with tears at the memory of the cruel Bennett.

'You poor little darling,' she said, kissing her cheek. 'Your papa will take you home to your mama and give you something nice to make you better.'

And so a few minutes later, with Bennett bound securely and being escorted back to Westbury Hall by Mr Bunfield and his men, Bertram and Aurelia escorted Charlotte home to Felbrook Manor to her mama and Kitty.

When Mr Bunfield's men reached the quiet stable yard at Westbury Hall, Josiah Bennett was made to await questioning by Mr Bunfield. He sat huddled against the door of Gypsy's spacious stall, his shoulders hunched, glaring down at his shackled hands, his discarded valise lying at his side.

Mr Bunfield's man sat on an upturned feed bucket nearby and puffed calmly on his pipe. The church bells had long since finished their peal to call the congregation to Sunday prayers. Nothing seemed to be stirring at the Hall and Mr Bunfield's scout stared straight ahead at the idyllic scene before him.

Then he sat up with a jerk and removed his pipe for he heard his boss's footsteps and a deep sigh as Mr Bunfield came to stand beside him. 'No luck, my lad,' Bunfield said. 'I thought I might 'a got the felons as did for Mr Westbury, but they seem to have got clean away, apart from one, that is, and for 'im, it's too late.'

'Dead, is he, Harry?'

'Ar! Jim Butler. Dead as a doornail, Sam. But 'ow about me laddo 'ere? He's looking a bit worse for wear.'

'Resisted arrest, Harry, and tried to run away, sir.'

'Did he, Sam? The nasty lad. Can he talk?'

'Dunno. He groaned a bit back, but hasn't said nothing yet.'

Harry Bunfield walked over to the wretched prisoner and peered down at him. 'Josiah Bennett, can you hear me?'

The miserable heap, huddled near to the stable door, remained silent and motionless and Mr Bunfield poked at him with the toe of his boot. 'Are you listening to me, Bennett?'

The prisoner nodded slightly.

'Good. Now, Josiah Bennett, you are apprehended for planning the murderous attempt on Mr Hugo Westbury's life, by setting up villainous rogues to attack him, whereof he was left like to die and this against the peace of our sovereign lord the king and furthermore you are accused of luring away and attacking an innocent child, on purpose to aid the kidnap of Miss Charlotte Grayson. Have you aught to say?'

Bennett's head moved slowly from side to side and then fell on to his chest.

'No? Then listen again, Josiah Bennett. As sure as eggs is eggs, you shall be strung up on the gallers, Bennett. Hanged, Bennett. You are heading for the nubbing cheat, the Tyburn jig, caught in a noose, rope gargling, while you kick and jump your nasty life out. . . . Unless you turn's King's Evidence, that is. . . . Unless you names your evil accomplice. . . . The dastardly villain as aided and abetted you in all this and put you up to it. . . . You only has to name him to save your own bad and worthless life. . . .'

Bunfield paused to give Bennett time to speak but there was no reply. Bennett drew a deep shuddering breath, but remained silent.

'Nothing to say, Bennett? Well, let me tell you what's going to happen. You will be stood on a cart and dragged through the streets, for all to revile you and spit on you. Your arms will be bound and the hempen necklace will be put round your scraggy neck. When the cart's drove away from you, you'll be left to dangle and choke for long agonizing minutes, until all the evil life is squeezed out of you. Now, are you goin' to testify?'

Bennett squirmed and groaned.

'Very well, Bennett. After your long choking death, you will be cut down, stripped and coated in tar, to be hung at some crossroads gibbet as a warning to other felons. If you is lucky, you might be given to the surgeons, to be used for practice . . . to be sliced into pieces, Bennett, and your body parts given out to students . . . to cut up and examine, Bennett. For the last time, will you testify, and save your wicked life and miserable body?'

'Yes . . . yes . . .' Bennett groaned at last. 'Yes . . . I'll tell you everything you want . . . I'll speak . . I'll tell you how he drove me to it . . . how he tormented me night and day. . . .'

'Good man,' Bunfield said with satisfaction. 'Come on, Sam, help him up and let's take him to the house.'

CHAPTER FIFTEEN

In Westbury Hall, all was quiet. Hugo Westbury had dispensed with his valet and was engaged in trying to dress himself. He pulled on his clothes, wincing a little, because although his wound was healed it was still a little sore. Even putting on his shirt was very testing and he rested after getting one of his arms in the first sleeve, before groping behind him for the other. The twisting of his body set the scarred flesh at his side singing with pain, but he was determined to persist. This morning, he had ordered his valet to direct the small hand mirror from his dressing chest to his wounded side so that he might see the progress of his injury. He had been pleased and delighted at the sight. Doctor Armstrong had removed the stitches and there remained only a narrow red line to show where he had been injured. Armstrong had assured him that, unless he indulged in undue exertion, the flesh should now be completely knitted together.

'It will eventually fade into a fine silver line and no one will know of it but yourself, sir,' the good doctor had said.

In spite of the discomfort, Hugo smiled. Now he was ready to be up and about and the long tedium of bed rest and medication would be forgotten. Soon he would be back to overseeing the repair of the estate cottages, he would even be able to see Charlotte. . . . This thought made him pause even longer over his attempts to shape his starched cravat into an acceptable arrangement. He gazed into the mirror. His face was still pale with the sort of pallor which was induced by confinement indoors and he was looking somewhat gaunt because of lack of appetite. What he needed, he decided, was a gentle ride along the lane which led to Felbrook and if he should reach Felbrook Manor, why, he could call in and greet his friends, the Graysons. But the very effort of dressing and standing before the mirror was too much and he was obliged to sink into a chair and rest.

This was only a temporary defeat. Tomorrow, he would call for his groom and have him saddle up Gypsy and bring him round to the front door. He was determined to try to ride.

In the library, Sir Benjamin was sitting alone, gazing down at a letter he had just received from Harry Bunfield. He took his paper knife from the desk and slit open the envelope.

Sir Benjamin,
I have the actual criminal, viz. Josiah Bennett, as attempted to murder Mr. Hugo Westbury, and twice attempted the kidnap of Miss Charlotte Grayson, but his accomplice and the man who put him up to it, I cannot apprehend, for lack of proof, so I cannot name him, although you know him, being related, like. I beg leave to warn you that my informers say that this murderous villain is planning to call on you very shortly, so be on your guard sir.
Your obedient servant,
H. Bunfield

Having read the note twice, Sir Benjamin stood up stiffly and walked with some difficulty over to the great carved fireplace, which had been completely restored after the damage of the thunderstorm. He released the secret opening of the panelling which had recently been Charlotte Grayson's prison and set it wide open. Then he sat down at his desk and began to write.

My dear Hugo,

Tonight, I will surely die, either by my own hand or by that of your attempted murderer, so this seems a good opportunity to tell you, in a few words, how my brother, Charles, your grand-father, met his death.

Briefly then, I was seated alone in the library on the night of November 19th, fifty-nine years ago when the secret panel, which very few knew about, was dashed violently open and my brother, George, burst into the room. Behind him came a man called Tobias Todd who was later revealed to be William Ingram, and his companion, a common sailor named Rudkin. They were supporting my younger brother, Charles, who seemed desperately ill. They laid him on a sofa by the fire. He had been injured when the Golden Maiden *had capsized, but was given every attention by myself and my servants. The sailor, Ted Rudkin, was rewarded and despatched back to Cromer, but George and Todd stayed on.*

Later, when Charles was somewhat recovered, there was a massive argument which came to violence. Both my brothers had been in love with Lady Mary Spence and her decision to marry Charles had continued to rankle with George. On this particular night, George drew his sword and cried, 'Dastard and seducer draw your sword!' He bade Charles defend himself. Charles had no alternative but to obey. He snatched up a small sword from the wall and returned the attack. Deaf to my pleas, they fought furiously. Charles, being already weak, was soon wounded, quite grievously and turned away, but in that moment, George sprang towards him and stabbed him deeply between his shoulder blades and thus my unfortunate brother Charles died instantly and my other brother George was only slightly scratched.

Then I committed the most serious folly of my life. With the help of the evil Todd, I hid Charles in the priest hole and closed the panelling. To avoid all risk of scandal, I paid Todd and sent him on his way, but of course, I could not be rid of George so easily. This is why my hateful brother and I lived for years hiding the guilty secret of your grandfather's death not to be revealed to a living soul. But I know that George passed the information on to his equally hateful son. It is why Alfred has been so resentful of my decision to choose you as my heir. He is determined to get rid of you and I am equally determined that he shall not.

This night shall see the problem resolved and I shall sign myself for the last time,

Sir Benjamin Westbury

He sat for a few moments with bowed head, studying what he'd written, and then sanded and folded his letter as he heard a discreet tap on the door.

'Come in, Alfred,' he said expressionlessly.

As Alfred stood gazing at him silently, Sir Benjamin said, 'Yes, come in and close the door, if you please, and be seated. You are just the man I want to see.'

'Oh, really? Any particular reason, sir?'

'Only that Mr Bunfield informs me that your man, Josiah Bennett, has been arrested in connection with the vile attack on my heir, Mr Hugo Westbury, and I know that you have personally been involved in that and also in the attempted kidnap of Charlotte Grayson. I wish to hear all that you know of the matter.'

'I? What should I know?' He sat down in the chair opposite to Sir Benjamin and began to fiddle with an ornate Indian curio which was lying on the desk. It was a slim silver dagger from Benares, which Sir Benjamin used as a paper knife.

'What should I know?' Alfred repeated and began to stroke the silver knife between his fingers.

'You know why, how and wherefore you set those rogues on to your cousin Hugo and left him for dead,' Sir Benjamin said quietly, 'and why you kidnapped Charlotte Grayson and hid her behind the panelling there.'

'Oh no, Sir Benjamin, not I, you are mistaken.'

'No, I am not mistaken,' Sir Benjamin replied calmly. 'I

know you are as guilty as hell,' Sir Benjamin continued as though Alfred had not spoken, 'but I would like you to have this chance to make your final peace with Almighty God, before you die.'

'Before I die? What the devil do you mean?'

'I mean that I am going to kill you, Alfred.'

Alfred Westbury stiffened. His knuckles gleamed white as he grasped the knife in both hands and glared at Sir Benjamin.

Then he consciously relaxed and made to appear at his ease, lolling back in his chair and observing Sir Benjamin through viciously narrowed eyes. 'Why, what talk is this, sir? You speak as though your brain is disordered. I fear that you are out of your mind. . . .'

'Not so,' said Sir Benjamin softly. 'I was never more sound of mind and as for my body, it has not always been old and feeble. Once, I was as tall and strong as an oak, and can be again. Just as long as it suits my purpose, Alfred,' he said serenely.

To Alfred Westbury's horror, Sir Benjamin rose to his feet and straightened up to his full height. Suddenly, the years fell away from him, his shoulders expanded, his head was erect as though his strength was restored to him.

Alfred leapt to his feet and raised the only weapon he had near at hand, the glittering, enamelled knife. 'You must be insane. Stand back,' he snarled, 'or it will be the worse for you.'

'Oh no, Alfred.' Sir Benjamin's voice was quiet but deadly. 'On the contrary, it will be the worse for *you*.'

He stepped even closer to Alfred, as though he wished to clasp him in his long arms and Alfred, pale with fear, leapt at him with the knife, driving it into the old man in a vain attempt to halt his inexorable advance. Then with a scream of terror, Alfred turned and made for the priest's hidy-hole, with Sir Benjamin staggering after him, his hand now pressed to the wound which pulsed in his chest. Alfred sped along the secret tunnel, with Sir Benjamin staggering after him, to the place where it came out into the woods. There, Alfred turned, ready to strike again, but Sir Benjamin, with a final effort, wrested the weapon from his grasp. There was a terrible gurgling scream as with his last strength, he thrust it unerringly into Alfred's throat.

Then silence. Sir Benjamin collapsed on the floor and tried to drag himself back along the secret tunnel, but after a while, he sank on to his face, his silvery head laid on the ancient stone, and he was still.

It was Harry Bunfield who found him. Once Josiah Bennett had been safely bestowed in Lynn Gaol, he made his way up to Westbury Hall and once admitted by the butler, he presented his card and insisted on being shown into Sir Benjamin's library. The butler remained impassive as Bunfield followed the trail of blood and devastation to Sir Benjamin and Alfred Westbury, but as he told the housekeeper later, he had been all of a tremble at the sight of the open panel and all that gore.

He'd had to retire to the sanctuary of his pantry and seek a well-known alcoholic restorative to calm his jangled nerves. But when the full horror of the day's events had finally been revealed, all the servants were equally affected, Sir Benjamin being a loved and popular employer.

It only remained now to inform Mr Hugo Westbury of the deaths of his two relatives and here, Harry Bunfield uncharacteristically engaged the help of the good Doctor Armstrong in this mournful task.

Hugo was lounging on the day bed in his room, restless, bored and still listless with the enforced inactivity of the last few days. Sunday was always so confoundedly dull. Charlotte would be busy with her Sunday school and would not be visiting. Sir Benjamin would no doubt be at church and then would have his lunch and an afternoon nap during the long hours before dinner. He was allowed downstairs for meals, but the devil of it was, he never felt hungry. Tomorrow, with or without Armstrong's permission, he would take Gypsy out. He felt strong enough now and, with a groom in attendance, could manage a short, gentle ride in the grounds of the Hall. He might even meet Charlotte. This possibility occasioned such a pleasant reverie that he was surprised when the butler knocked on the door to announce Doctor Armstrong. There was no doubt in his mind that the good doctor was pleased with his progress. He could leave off the sleeping draught now there was no need to have the wound looked at. Even the slightest precautions against any over-exertion were unnecessary. And there was no objection to healthful exercise, provided he did nothing foolhardy, of course.

All this was a source of quiet satisfaction to Hugo, but then he was further surprised when at the end of his visit, the doctor walked to the door and invited Harry Bunfield to come in, before taking a seat at the side of him.

Both men were very grave and Bunfield said softly, 'I have something to report, sir, which is of a very serious nature, Mr Westbury.'

'Oh yes, and what can that be, I wonder?'

'Well, Mr Westbury, brace yourself for a shock, sir,' Harry Bunfield said. He paused for a long moment and then said, 'Today, Alfred Westbury's manservant was apprehended for being involved in and organizing the attack on yourself, Mr Westbury. The said Alfred Westbury returned to Westbury Hall this afternoon and he and your great uncle, Sir Benjamin Westbury, fought to the death. . . . Both are deceased, Mr Westbury.'

Hugo looked at him uncomprehendingly. 'Fought to the death? Deceased?' he asked in a wondering voice.

'Yes, I am afraid so, sir. I have arranged for both parties to be laid out on trestles in Sir Benjamin's library. The servants are forbidden to enter until they have your permission, sir.'

Doctor Armstrong clasped Hugo's hand and said gently, 'I

am so sorry about this, Mr Westbury, and I only hope this tragedy does not set your own recovery back.'

Hugo nodded slightly, totally bemused at the turn the interview had taken and unable to either take in the information or make any reply.

'It is a bad business,' Bunfield said, shaking his head, 'and if I had acted sooner, mayhap I could have prevented it. . . .' He gave a long sigh. 'But the best thing about it is that the mystery of the dead body is now solved. When I takes down the full statement of that villain, Bennett, all will be explained and I hopes as then you will be able to get on with your own life in peace, Mr Westbury.'

'Meanwhile,' interposed Doctor Armstrong, 'I shall arrange to have your great-uncle and your cousin taken away for a coroner's inquest.'

He looked more keenly at Hugo and said quietly, 'If I were you, I should forgo horse-riding for the time being. I shall give you something to calm your nerves and shall visit you again tomorrow.' Hugo nodded and leaned back against the sofa cushions, his brain unable to take in what Bunfield and Armstrong were saying to him. Only after they had departed and he was finally alone did his weary mind begin to process the information it had received.

That his hateful cousin Alfred had wished him dead, nay, even plotted his murder, was bad enough, but that Sir Benjamin Westbury, his benefactor and the one source of kindness and affection in his life, should also be no more, hurt him to his innermost core.

He let his head fall back and put a weary hand over his eyes. Yes, he would certainly follow the doctor's advice and forgo horse-riding for a while. He had hoped to give little Lucy Baker her long-awaited treat and perhaps see Charlotte and ride with her. Realistically, he knew it would not be more than that. He would not be able to do more than talk to her or perhaps hold her hand . . . would not be able to give way to his overwhelming desire to take her in his arms . . . hold her close . . . kiss her. . . . Even without a chaperon, he knew this would be impossible. He would have to be modestly satisfied with a word, a glance from those fine grey eyes. But even just to see her . . . to be with her. . . . He gave himself an impatient shake and rang the bell for the butler to get him some brandy.

And so, the rest of the day was spent in lonely misery.

The following days were no better. Hugo kept to his room, barely speaking to his servants and with only Doctor Armstrong to keep him in touch with the distressing reality of the inquest and the arrangements for the funeral. As the neighbourhood gradually found out about the death of Sir Benjamin and Alfred Westbury, condolence cards and floral tributes were left at Westbury Hall and Hugo was aware that friends, including the Graysons, had called to pay their respects, yet still he remained aloof from it all.

The *Lynn News*, had a large spread, headed:

ALFRED WESTBURY'S DARK DEED

Alfred Westbury caused Mr Hugo Westbury to be attacked and left for dead and when confronted by his great-uncle, Sir Benjamin Westbury, he stabbed and mortally wounded him. Sir Benjamin defended himself and both men were found dead yesterday in the grounds of Westbury Hall.

Sir Benjamin will be remembered as a good and fair landowner, liked and respected by his tenants and friends alike. He had recently returned from India, and is succeeded by his heir, Mr Hugo Westbury, who, it is reported, is now recovering from his injuries. Two suspects are being examined by the magistrate in Lynn.

After all the formalities were over, Sir Benjamin was interred in the family vault, at a quiet ceremony attended only by Hugo, the vicar, assisted by his curate, Reverend Andrew Preston, and Doctor Armstrong. Even Bunfield was not present. No mention was made of the disposal of his cousin's body and Hugo was utterly indifferent to Alfred's fate.

At church the following Sunday, Hugo and Charlotte merely exchanged polite bows and a quiet 'Good morning'. Even the servants did not intrude on his grief, only the irrepressible Bunfield, who visited doggedly and kept him abreast of the developments in his enquiries.

Hugo was still too sick at heart to care about the details of the case and it wasn't until Adam Brown requested an interview that he came out of his self-imposed silence to welcome him to Westbury Hall.

Adam was not on this occasion accompanied by Matthew, but by the vicar, Mr Swift. They were invited into the library and offered a glass of wine and Hugo was aware that both men were looking at him with some interest.

The three men were silent for a while and then Adam Brown said gently, 'I am so sorry at the way things have turned out, sir, and would like to extend my profound sympathy at the loss of your esteemed great-uncle.'

Hugo noted in passing that the lawyer did not say 'to you and your family'. Because he had no family, he thought bitterly. Some far-off relatives in America, perhaps, related to his long-dead mama and whom he had never seen, and that was all. He nodded without replying and waited for Adam Brown to continue.

'The reading of Sir Benjamin's will is just a formality, Mr Westbury. I have asked Mr Swift to be a witness, but as no one else is concerned in any bequests, there was no need to invite anyone else to the reading. Sir Benjamin left all his considerable fortune to yourself, sir. As well as this country estate, Sir Benjamin owned property and farms in Yorkshire and Leicestershire. He owned a substantial town house in Berkeley Square, which is at present leased to a relative of Lord Hampton and, of course, his business concerns in India, which were sold out and wound up earlier this year.'

Adam Brown coughed softly and continued, 'In all, Mr

Westbury, your inheritance is somewhat in excess of two hundred thousand pounds. Please peruse the document and ask any questions that you might have.'

As if in a dream, Hugo read through the legal document which was his great-uncle's last will and testament. The words 'I bequeath all these to my great-nephew, Hugo Westbury' were repeated after every itemised possession and bank account that Sir Benjamin had owned. There was no mention anywhere of Alfred Westbury or any other member of the family. Apart from a few minor bequests to old servants and a sum of money for the restoration of St Paul's bell tower, there was nothing more to mention and Hugo returned it to the lawyer without speaking.

After Mr Swift had departed, Adam remained, conversing in his quiet, gentlemanly way about his betrothal to Matthew's Aunt Lavinia and their forthcoming marriage, but Hugo was paying little attention to what he was saying and merely answered in monosyllables. At last, Adam also took his leave and Hugo was left completely alone.

After a solitary dinner, he sat for some time, still brooding on the events of the last few weeks and wondering, almost despairingly, why Charlotte was suddenly so unfriendly and aloof. Even Latimer dared not disturb him and Hugo's mood became blacker than ever. Finally, as the evening sun began to set in a spectacular red sky, Hugo squared his broad shoulders and made a sudden resolution. He would forget about going riding. Tomorrow, instead of brooding alone, he would walk to Felbrook Manor and insist on seeing Charlotte. He would refuse to leave until he had spoken to her.

Once this plan was firm in his mind, he rang the bell for Latimer and took himself off to bed.

The next morning, he set off immediately after breakfast, a most unfashionable time to go visiting, he reflected, with a half smile, but he was determined on it. He wore his country gentleman's nankeen jacket and breeches and a simple stock, rather than his usual elaborate cravat. The morning was cool, but with the promise of autumn sunshine still to come and in spite of his anguish at Sir Benjamin's death, his heart felt a little lighter, even though his thoughts were disjointed. He would see her today. They would be able to talk in private. He was determined to ask her to marry him. He would refuse to take no for an answer. He loved her. He was almost certain she loved him in return. If not, he would court her and make her love him.

His wound was not paining him at all now. It had completely healed and there was only a thin, jagged, pale line in the flesh of his side to show he had ever been injured. Not yet silver, as the doctor had promised, he thought grimly, but still, all healed up. He rejoiced that the evil Alfred's plan to remove him had not succeeded and wasted no time on hypocritical thoughts of sorrow for his cousin.

All these meandering thoughts sped away from him like a hare before the hounds when he saw her coming towards him. After the first shock of surprise and recognition, he noticed that she was not walking with her usual upright confident stride, but her head was bent and she walked slowly as though lost in thought. But what a delight she was to look at. Her high young bosom rising and falling with her breathing. Long slender legs, silhouetted faintly through the light fabric of her gown. Slim shapely hands whose touch he remembered so well, inflaming him when she had disentangled the Bakers' kitten and soothing him when he had been injured. Was any woman ever so bewitching ... and so tormenting?

His heart beat faster, but he managed to greet her coolly as he slowly advanced towards her. 'Good morning, Charlotte.'

'Good morning, Mr Westbury,' she said demurely. Then her natural curiosity overcame her and she asked, 'Why are you out so early when ... when you are so ... so badly wounded?'

'I thought that was obvious. I came in pursuit of you.'

Charlotte turned her head away and fidgeted with the satin ribbons of her pretty straw bonnet. 'Oh, indeed, Mr Westbury?' she said faintly.

'Yes,' he said, taking her hands firmly away from the ribbons and holding them in his own. 'And what is more, Charlotte, I love you and am determined to marry you.'

In her agitation, Charlotte pulled away from him and stepped backwards, but unfortunately, caught her heel on an inconvenient tuft of grass and fell backwards on to the dry springy turf. Regardless of his wound, Hugo immediately threw himself down beside her and pinioned her arms above her head.

'Now,' he said. 'The tables are turned. You were on top of me when I was ill, but it is I who am on top now.'

'You knew?' she gasped. 'Oh, it is so dishonourable of you to mention it. . . . Let me go, Mr Westbury . . . how can you be so . . . so ungentlemanly?'

'Very easily,' he said, smiling down on her wickedly. 'Especially when I have you in my power like this.'

'Please, Mr Westbury. This is most improper. Let me go. . . .'

'Not a chance,' he said in a whisper and then he lowered his lips to hers and kissed her, softly at first, but then he released her hands, to pull her body closer and kiss her more passionately.

Charlotte determined to lie passive and utterly still in his arms, in order to cool his ardour and bring him to some sense of the impropriety of his conduct. But her lips refused to act upon the message that her brain was giving them and seemed to have a will of their own as she found herself responding quite disgracefully to his lovemaking, her willing mouth softening under his.

Hugo rolled on top of her, pressing himself against her, and began to stroke her mouth with long, sensuous kisses until Charlotte's traitorous body arched upwards towards him and she returned his kiss with a passion to match his own.

As soon as he felt her response, Hugo freed her mouth and

whispered against her neck, 'So, you do love me, then?'

'You know I cannot think properly with you lying on top of me like this,' she complained breathlessly and then, immediately, she whispered softly, 'Yes. I love you.'

He rolled to one side and pulled her into his arms again. 'And you will marry me?'

'Yes.'

When she was finally able to raise her head, Charlotte realized that her bonnet had rolled across the grass and her hairpins had come loose, but she felt such a burst of happiness within her that she was inclined to forgive him.